DOUGLAS FORD

Let's Cut Up Dad!

(and Other Stories of Transgressive Madness)

First published by Vissaria County Dispatches 2025

First edition

ISBN (paperback): 979-8-9895731-4-1
ISBN (hardcover): 979-8-9895731-6-5

Cover art by Lynne Hansen

This book was professionally typeset on Reedsy.
Find out more at reedsy.com

Contents

Let's Cut Up Dad!

y now you've heard the stories from around here about people dying on their feet. "A Strange Phenomena," the headlines called it. Like Burl Malloy who died while standing in line at the post office. Not even falling over like you'd expect. Not even having the decency to close his eyes. The line behind him kept growing, everyone too polite to ask him to move up, so it took a moment to figure out that it was a dead man holding everyone up at the post office. Or Milton Crow, who died pretty much the same way in the produce aisle of the local supermarket, though I don't think he inconvenienced anyone quite the same way as Burl Malloy. Plus a few others, all within a few weeks of one another in a small area of the country. What you probably didn't hear about happened at my house.

By the time Dad died standing up, most of the other ones had already happened. No one knows why. Just natural causes, supposedly. People do die after all, and according to my biology teacher (he calls himself a scientist, but he just teaches, so judge for yourself), it happens: people can die on their feet without falling over. It happened one time in a mall in China or Hong Kong or somewhere like that. But more than one in such a short span of time? In such a small area? It makes you wonder about asbestos or a mad scientist poisoning the water supply.

I found Dad first and initially didn't notice anything wrong. I didn't even know what killed him. He just stood there at our kitchen counter, the side with the burned Formica, thanks to my sister Eunice putting a red-hot frying pan on top of it. She didn't know better on account of being just a kid, but Dad hauled off and smacked her anyway. When I got in his face, telling him not to do that because sisters stand up for each other, he picked up the frying pan and used it to hit me back. I still have a burn mark on my cheek from the hot side of that pan thanks to that. I didn't even cry, and I sure as hell didn't turn the other cheek.

Pretty much at that exact spot, and without any visible marks to explain how it happened, Dad died.

Seeing his eyes all open and glassy, I figured he was lost in thought.

But then I wondered how a man who never had a worthwhile thought in his life could suddenly find himself lost in one.

"Dad!" I snapped my fingers in his face. I clapped my hands. No reaction at all.

By this time I'd already heard about Burl Malloy and the others, so it took me a moment but I eventually deduced the situation I faced. I didn't even bother checking his pulse. Instead, I went to get Eunice out of Mom's room. Mom hardly ever left that room and slept there by herself.

I found Eunice doing what I expected to find her doing: rubbing Mom's bloated, purple ankles, trying to help her get some circulation going. Mom wanted Eunice to do this because Eunice, despite being younger than me, had big, meaty hands, and Mom claimed that only constant massaging would allow her any hope of eventually getting up and about on her own, perhaps one day becoming a productive member of society. Those bloated ankles, an unmistakable sign of terrible hypertension, meant that walking posed an imminent danger for Mom. Even thinking about walking could result in death by heart attack, so Mom stayed in bed all the time.

I told Eunice she needed to stop massaging and come with me. Mom grumbled when Eunice stopped rubbing, but I kissed her forehead and promised to bring her right back.

Eunice shook her wrists as she followed me down the hallway.

"What's wrong?" she asked.

I indicated her wrists. "I was going to ask you the same thing."

"Going numb," she said.

I said, "You won't believe this."

"It can be anything," said Eunice. "I literally don't care. I need a break. Mom's ankles aren't getting any better. No matter how hard I rub."

Eunice stopped complaining when I showed her Dad standing at the Formica counter. She knew at once he was dead. I find it kind of curious that she discerned the situation so quickly. It had taken me a moment to work it out, but Eunice began sobbing immediately. "No, no, no, no, no," she said, folding her hands under her chin, no longer caring one iota about her wrists. She made for the body like she intended to embrace it, but she also acted like the sight of it revolted her, so she kind of danced around it like she couldn't figure out what to do.

In truth, I almost wished she had hugged the body, just so I could see if this instant rigor mortis would hold up to Eunice pawing it. Would the body fall over? Or would the hand placed on the counter, right atop the burn mark, keep it anchored somehow?

"What do we do now?" Eunice said after she finally stopped dancing around.

People always expect big sisters to have all the answers. People expect us to take charge. I might make a mistake now and then, but I wouldn't let Eunice down. "I only know one thing," I said. "If we're not careful, we're fucked." I pointed to the stale crackers on the counter, the moldy bread, the open container of spreadable butter. Maybe Dad planned to make himself a sandwich before he kicked it. "Who's paying for food now?"

Eunice looked around the kitchen as if an answer would magically present itself. "Mom?"

"Mom can't work," I said. "Her ankles, remember? Her hypertension? Just the thought of leaving that bed would make her blood pressure skyrocket. With her gone, we'd be orphans. Me, I'd be fine. I'm almost done with school. I'll be out in no time. Then it's off to the F.B.I. Academy for me. Soon enough I'd have a job that earns me enough money so that I can fix this." I indicated the ugly burn mark on my face, practically a twin of that spot on the Formica. "But you? Just a kid, and not right in the head. They'll put you in the funny farm. You want to go to the funny farm?"

Eunice did not want to go to the funny farm.

By that point, Mom started yelling for Eunice to get back to her and her ankles.

"You better get back at it. I'll think of a plan. And quit that crying," I said. She made a poor attempt, but once she started massaging those big, purple ankles again, Mom wouldn't notice. If she did, I'd go in there with my ear buds and let Mom listen to the latest additions to my playlist, like some old songs by Iron Maiden I fell in love with recently, especially the songs on *Number of the Beast*. Mom would bob her head as she listened and not give Eunice's mewling any thought at all.

Meanwhile, I gave Dad's body another look. As a future F.B.I. agent, maybe I could use this situation to my advantage and gain some first-hand knowledge of what happens to a dead body. Last week, in biology class, I wanted to do a research paper on what happens to a dead body as it decomposes, but my teacher—a real stick in the mud—told me I needed to stick to his curriculum. He didn't even listen to my reasoning about how my project could turn into some useful career knowledge with the F.B.I. Now, I got to thinking about how one day I might get to investigate real life cases of people who died standing up, maybe eventually track down a mad scientist working for Russia or something.

A big carving knife sat near the moldy bread, giving me an idea.

I picked it up, feeling its weight. I tested its sharpness with the tip of my finger—just a little bit, a tiny prick, just enough to judge it plenty sharp. Unlike Eunice, I didn't like to cut myself. A tiny bead of blood told me all I needed to know.

Then I took the knife and slid the blade across the top of Dad's hand, the one he used to swing the frying pan at my face.

The blade opened up a slit in the hand, and dark red blood flowed for a moment, but not long.

Interesting.

It occurred to me that maybe I should write down the observations I made. I put down the knife and walked to the room I shared with Eunice, passing the open doorway to the one that Mom slept in by herself. I spied Eunice at the end of the bed, rubbing those ankles. She shot me a worried look.

To keep Mom from sensing anything wrong, I said, "Mom, you doing okay? Feeling better today?"

Mom said, "Your sister needs to rub harder."

"Eunice," I said, "rub harder."

Eunice glared at me but did as commanded. I got a notebook and a pencil from my stuff and went back to the kitchen. Then I noted the time and my observation about the slit in the hand and how long it bled. I also recorded how the blood began to coagulate—or at least I think that's the word for when it started to turn brown.

Then I got curious about another thing. What would happen if I cut off a finger? Would a knife like the one I just used also cut through bone? As a future F.B.I. agent, I ought to know such things.

I reached for a cutting board, but not a wooden one. You shouldn't use a wooden cutting board when you cut meat on account of contamination sinking into the fine grains of the wood. Always use plastic for meat.

Then I had another thought. If I moved the hand to the cutting board, that might cause the whole body to topple over. I didn't want that to happen. One of the things I wanted to learn was how long the body would keep standing on its own after death.

I decided to leave the hand where it lay. Besides, after Eunice's hot pan, no point in worrying about a little more damage to the Formica. Not like a little blood and some knife marks would make it look worse. I placed the blade of the knife against the index finger, but paused to consider something else. I ought to try the thumb instead. When Dad leaned against the counter, he had that particular digit splayed pretty good.

I pressed down on the thumb with all my might, and at first, it wouldn't go through the bone. I tried sawing, but that didn't do any good.

Very interesting.

Remember, I did all this so that I could become a world-class F.B.I. agent someday.

Then it hit me: a hammer! I left the knife embedded in the thumb and grabbed one from the toolbox in the garage. Then I used the hammer to give two good whacks to the dull end of the blade, and on the second whack, it went all the way through. The thumb popped off. It lay there on the Formica in a pool of dark red.

I watched to see if the missing thumb would throw the body off balance and cause it to fall over.

I didn't want that to happen. I really wanted to learn how long a dead body would stay on its feet. To my delight, it didn't even wobble. Dad's dilated eyes stared ahead, unblinking.

What a great paper I could write for biology if that bonehead teacher would just let me.

* * *

I started doing more things after that. What else did I have to do on a Sunday? Sit in my bedroom and act bored?

Eunice came into the kitchen, rubbing her wrists as usual, just in time to see me getting to work on cutting off the whole hand.

After my experience with just a stupid thumb, I got smart with this one. In the back of the knife drawer, I found a big bread knife with a toothy, serrated blade. Using plenty of elbow grease, I'd made it more than halfway through flesh and bone when Eunice saw what I'd done and started screaming.

I had to throw Dad's thumb at her to make her stop.

"You cut off his finger!" Eunice wailed.

"That's a thumb," I said.

More wailing.

"You need to hush," I said. "What's Mom going to think?"

"I'm going to show her what you did." But Eunice just stared at the thumb on the linoleum. I knew she wouldn't. She wouldn't even bring herself to pick it up.

"Remember," I said, "you'll go to the funny farm."

She kept staring at the thumb, so I went back to my sawing. Plenty of blood got on the counter. Later, I'd clean up what I could, but at this point, I didn't care about the mess.

When I finally cut through the hand, I felt an amazing sense of accomplishment. I pushed it away with the blade of the knife and stepped back to see what the body would do. I didn't even breathe, anxious to see if it would fall.

Once more, amazingly, it didn't even totter.

"Now that's very interesting," I said out loud.

Cautiously, Eunice stepped closer, curious in spite of herself to see what I found so fascinating. Her lips curled in disgust when she saw that I cut off the hand, but I'll hand it to Eunice (ha!): she didn't start wailing again.

"You see that? He's still standing up. I thought for sure that without the hand propping him up he'd topple over." Enjoying how Eunice looked over my shoulder, I wrote this observation in my notebook. Blotches of blood smeared the page, but I couldn't help it.

I turned toward her, tapping the eraser side of the pencil against my chin, imitating the thoughtful look my biology teacher would give me when I asked him to curve a grade.

"Eunice, do you know what rigor mortis is?"

She nodded, but I know she didn't.

"Everything stiffens when you die," I said. "Your whole body. I think rigor mortis might keep Dad standing forever."

Eunice nodded. I kept tapping the pencil as I spoke.

"Like, what would happen if I sawed off the whole arm? You'd think that might shift all the weight to the other side and then he'd fall over for sure. But then again…" I really wanted to try it, but I didn't know if I could pull it off with kitchen knives.

Then Eunice said something that made me want to hug and kiss her.

"Or his leg," she said. "He couldn't stand on just one, could he?"

Even a crazy head like her can say something profound once in a while.

"Indeed," I said. "Interesting."

Later, I stood outside the house smoking a cigarette, thinking. Eunice had to stay inside to do more ankle rubbing and, later on, fix Mom some dinner. Other than going to the bathroom, which she needed Eunice's help to do (and frankly, she did that in bed sometimes), Mom didn't really ever leave her bedroom. That gave me some alone time to do my thinking and to smoke the cigarette I got from Jace Armstrong in exchange for rubbing his thing behind the football stadium. I did that fairly regularly because I needed a smoke once in a while, and besides, I like seeing how the milk comes out of boys. Jace Armstrong sometimes asked me to let him put his thing somewhere other than my hand, but I'd always tell him no way. I just needed a couple of smokes. Jace wanted me to do it with my head turned to the side so he couldn't see the mark left by the frying pan, but I refused. If he wanted me to help him get the milk out, he'd have to see my whole face.

Smoking, I dreamed of the day that they'd call me in as an ace F.B.I. agent to figure out the mystery of why people died standing up. What I did now would help that day come true.

I thought about what Eunice said about the leg, and now I really wanted to try that. Ideas started forming.

Later, after some quality time with Mom where I let her listen to more Iron Maiden, Eunice and I went to bed. We shared a bedroom and sometimes talked before passing out, but tonight, we stayed pretty quiet.

The quiet broke when Eunice asked me a question.

"What killed Dad? Why'd he die?"

I thought about that already. "Well, he drank a lot. He put butter on everything. He put butter *on* his butter. You've seen him do that, haven't you? Probably a heart attack. Plus, he had a stressful job."

Saying that reminded me of something important.

"Eunice," I said, "you can't go to school tomorrow."

"Why not?" Eunice actually liked school.

"Because someone needs to be home if the people at the water treatment plant call up and asks why Dad isn't at work. You can't let Mom answer the phone and find out he's not there. She'll get wise to what's going on."

In the dark I could hear the gears turning in that crazy head of hers.

"How am I supposed to do that? I'll be rubbing ankles all day if I stay home. Please, Lou Ellen, I don't want to stay home."

"You can get up if the phone rings. It'll be for just a few days," I said.

"A few days? No!" That wailing started again.

I said, "I don't need to tell you about how what I'm doing will have consequences for the future. When I'm in the F.B.I., I can use this experience to solve crimes. Also, the money will pay for my plastic surgery. You don't want me to have this ugly mark forever, do you?"

I could have reminded her that I got it by standing up for her. I didn't need to. She thought about it quietly.

"Do you?" I said again.

"No."

More quiet, until: "Lou Ellen, would a stressful job make Dad do other things?"

I bit my tongue before answering. "What other things?"

She acted like she didn't want to say it. I had a feeling I knew what she meant. Dad liked to hit both of us, me especially, but he considered Eunice his favorite and sometimes touched her in different ways, especially after Mom got laid up with her ankle problems.

"Just other things," she said.

"God's bones, Eunice, I cannot fathom the ways of fathers. Or mothers for that matter." In truth, I didn't like to think about it. "Just go to sleep."

She must've tried because she got quiet, but after a bit I started to hear a rustling sound.

"Eunice, are you cutting yourself again?" When she didn't answer I knew she was, but after a while I fell asleep, and I assume that so did she.

* * *

Eunice kept grumbling about it, but I convinced her to fake some coughs the next morning, and it didn't take many to convince Mom that Eunice needed to stay home.

Meanwhile, I woke up refreshed and with a new plan.

When I saw Jace Armstrong in the morning, I said, sure, I'd meet him behind the stadium, but instead of a cigarette, he had to bring me something else: an electric tool I could use for cutting, something tough, like a saw I could hold in one hand. He looked at me like I'd gone crazy, but I threatened not to show up as usual, so he said he'd see what he could do, mentioning something about the equipment in the shop classroom. Sure enough, he came through. When the milk came out of him, it looked a little bit yellow, so I thought it my duty to advise him to see a doctor or something to have it checked out. I took the small bag he brought me and left him to figure that out on his own.

Eunice met me in the kitchen when I came home. She looked worried.

"Dad's alive, I think."

I looked at the body. It still stood as I'd left it, the eyes starting to turn the same color I milked out of Jace Armstrong not long ago. The surrounding skin looked brownish and had developed an oily sheen.

"That's impossible," I said, but I felt a lump of worry growing in my throat. "Why are you saying that?"

"He farted. Twice."

That made me breathe a sigh of relief. "Dead bodies do that," I said. "Gas moves around them. Things probably shifted a little, and he let one or two rip. That's all."

"It stank."

I sniffed the air. It still did, though some of the odor must've stemmed from the normal decomposition. I did detect a distinct odor in the air, something mixing with the fumes that clung to Dad from his job at the water treatment plant, a familiar farty smell, the kind that Dad's body used to let off after a big meal at KFC. Hopefully, I'd get to open up the stomach at some point. That oily sheen on his skin made me wonder what would happen if we put him into a giant fryer. Imagine the smells then.

"Besides," she said, still clinging to her illusions, "nothing shifted, right? He's still standing in the same place."

Good point. I needed to include the farting in my notes.

"You don't think," she said, "that he walked around last night, do you?"

Trying out my best F.B.I. impression, I said, "What evidence do you have?"

"Evidence?"

"You know, do you see any blood trailing down the hallway? A blotchy fingerprint anywhere?"

My sister stared at me. I did love her, I really did.

"Gadzooks, Eunice, you truly are destined for the funny farm. I'm trying to tell you that without evidence, we can conclude it didn't happen. The body's right where it's stood all along, which is truly a mystery unto itself.

And it's one that I'm developing methods of solving." I started to pull my new cutting tool from the bag when a thought hit me. "Eunice, pull down your shorts."

"No. Why?"

"I want to see the tops of your legs. You were cutting yourself last night, weren't you?"

"No. I swear."

"I mean it, Eunice. I know how you get."

Again, she swore that she'd done nothing of the kind, but something about the way she looked at the body gave away what she'd done instead. Leaning over the Formica, I saw what she did to the arm above the stump.

Several cuts, nine or ten of them. And she went deep, too, deeper than she went on herself.

I didn't know whether to yell at Eunice or to congratulate myself on deducing what happened so quickly. F.B.I. Academy, watch out!

Deep breaths allowed me to calm down and not yell. At least Eunice finally stopped cutting herself. Of course, now that she got a taste of what it felt like to cut someone else then maybe she'd now set off on the path to becoming a psycho killer, one that I'd have to hunt down someday. Imagine how that would play in the news: Star F.B.I. agent with a miraculously repaired face has to hunt down and capture her own sister who went psycho. For Eunice's sake, I sincerely hoped that wouldn't happen. No way could she ever elude me.

She watched as I set out the saw that Jace gave me. It came with a long cord. As I talked to Eunice, I plugged it in to the kitchen socket. "You've got to promise me that you'll never, ever touch this body again. Treat it like you would evidence at a crime scene."

She nodded and said something I couldn't hear because I pressed the saw's power button, letting out a shrill whine. That sound concerned me.

"What's Mom doing? Eating?" I asked.

Eunice shook her head. "Napping. I rubbed her ankles for hours."

"She might not sleep through this." Later, I decided; I'd use the saw later, when I could avoid waking Mom.

Inspiration for what to do in the meantime came from Eunice.

She said, "Cut off his legs so he can't walk down the hall and come into our room."

"He'd fall for sure if I did that, and what did I just tell you about evidence? He's deader than a doornail."

One look at Eunice's expression told me that I hadn't convinced her.

"I'll tell you what. There's something else I was thinking of trying. Let's say you're right and that Dad's really alive. Never mind the fact that I cut off his hand and he showed no reaction. Let's say he's just tricking us. He plans on waiting until we're asleep and then stalking us."

The look of fear on Eunice's face!

"I'm just saying 'what if.' He's not. But if he was, he'd need his eyes to see, right?"

Eunice looked a little more hopeful, but doubt still clouded her features. Nevertheless, she nodded.

"Well, I need to learn how hard it is to take out a human eye. What kind of tool a criminal might use. Mind you, I'm doing this to learn."

"For when you join the F.B.I."

"Exactly." I looked around the kitchen, not wanting to use a knife. For one thing, a knife might set a bad example for Eunice, and before I knew it, she'd go back to cutting the body the first moment I turned around. I picked up a spoon, but inspiration hit me when I saw a plastic bag with some left-over packets from KFC

I picked up a spork, that spoony instrument with sharp points.

"Perfect," I said to Eunice.

Next, I got a chair to stand on. Even though I stood just about as tall as Dad, I figured a little more height would help me do what I planned.

Eunice watched as I stood on the chair with the spork. If I had sleeves, I'd have rolled them up. Gently, at first, I started digging around the edges of the left eye, so foggy and unseeing now that Eunice really had nothing to worry about. Anyone could see he was dead. I needed to not only dig, but cut, digging through the spongy surface so that I could get behind the eye and pop it out in one piece.

It turned out that I didn't use a gentle enough touch. I punctured the eye and it broke apart. Out came a clear fluid (not at all like the yellow milk that came out of Jace Armstrong. I do hope he sees a doctor.)

"Goddammit," I said. But my mom didn't raise a quitter, so as Eunice continued to watch, I started again on the right eye.

I did a lot better that time. Out popped the eye, dangling by a veiny cord. The optic nerve, of course. "Fascinating," I said to Eunice as we both regarded my work. Surprisingly, she no longer fussed about the messes I made and which I'd need to clean up later. "See, Eunice, even though I messed up that one eye, it's still helpful for me to know what it looks like when you bust up an eye with a spork. And I can also know," here, I picked up the dangling eye and let it fall back against the body's chin like a pendulum, "what an optic nerve looks like. I wonder how hard it is to cut it."

If Eunice impressed me before by not gagging at all the goo that came out of the left eye or the bloody glob that dangled like rotten fruit from the other eye socket, she really showed me something by going into a kitchen drawer and pulling forth our best pair of shears. She held them out for me to see.

"Can I try?" she said.

"Absolutely not. You're just a kid, and I'm afraid you might decide you enjoy that kind of thing. You might decide to grow up and become a psycho killer, and then the F.B.I. will send me on a manhunt after you. You don't want that to happen, do you?"

"No?" She said it like she was asking a question.

"Then give me those shears."

It turned out not too hard to cut the optic nerve. Kind of like cutting a thick, wet string. The eye fell to the floor with a plop, but the impact didn't bust it. I decided to put it in the lunchbox I kept under my bed, where I'd already stored the hand and the thumb.

Before I could do that, Eunice started jumping and yelling. "He is alive, he is, he is!"

I about had a heart attack myself as I turned in time to see that the body did, in fact, seem to lurch and sway a bit.

"You need to kill him, Lou Ellen! Please, please, please."

"You need to shut up before Mom hears you," I said, but too late. Mom's voice came to us from the other room, asking what we'd gotten into and what exactly needed killing.

"Just a snake," I called back. "Crazy-head Eunice brought another snake into the house."

"You kill it right away, Lou Ellen. Cut off its head. Eunice! No more snakes in the house!"

Eunice started to shout that she'd done no such thing, but I gave her the stink-eye, and she closed her mouth real quick.

"He's not alive," I said to Eunice with my best indoor voice. "I just threw him off balance." Though I had to admit that it freaked me out just a bit to see the body move, but one of us needed to remain logical. The F.B.I. only wanted agents who could think logically.

Neither of us did so much as breathe as we watched to see if the body would finally topple. It looked likely to happen at any moment.

"I wonder if I could redistribute some weight on top," I said.

Of course, Eunice had no idea what I meant.

I said, "I'm thinking about cutting off the head. Or maybe just cut deep enough so that I can push it back down against his back. I still need to learn how long he can keep standing. For future investigations, of course."

Eunice said she understood, but I don't think she really did.

"Don't worry about what I'm going to do," I said. "You need to start rubbing Mom's ankles. Come with me."

On account of the noise I planned to make, I needed something to preoccupy Mom, so I led Eunice back to her room. As she gripped Mom's swollen ankles (which looked more and more like purple hams to me), I put my earbuds in Mom's ears. I'd gotten tired of Iron Maiden, but I still acted excited about a song called "Can I Play with Madness." I set it on repeat and watched Mom's big head move along with the melody.

"You do have such interesting taste in music, Lou Ellen," said Mom. Her eyes closed, and once I heard the moans and knew that Eunice had begun rubbing to her satisfaction, I went back to the kitchen to do what I *really* looked forward to doing: sawing into the body's neck.

No more reason to worry about the blare of the power saw. It fit perfectly in my hand, and even if I didn't have Eunice's iron grip (which would one day make her a formidable psycho killer), I could still handle it pretty well. Getting back up on the chair, I took some of Dad's sparse hair in my hand to hold him steady. Then I placed the blade against his throat, just above the Adam's apple, and then I hit the power button.

As I suspected, I didn't have to worry about blood. By now, the blood had settled down low in his legs.

But I didn't anticipate the other thing. The gyrating blade sent wet chunks of decaying flesh flying everywhere, including the floor, the Formica, and even my face. So much got into my eyes that I could hardly see. Tiny bits got into my mouth, too, and I accidentally swallowed them without thinking. They had the bitter taste of spoiled egg.

I kept at it, anyway, not even stopping when I got to the hard bits. In the end I had to hand it to Jace Armstrong (ha, there I go again)—he definitely came through and got me the right tool. Next time when I finished him up and he asked if he could kiss the good side of my face, I just might let him. Usually, I would tell him he'd have to kiss both sides, but I felt something warm for him now.

Thanks to Jace Armstrong, I now know how long it takes to saw nearly all the way through someone's neck—fifteen minutes exactly, and that involves using a mechanical tool. Plus, I could now record in my notebook how messy the process turned out. When I saw myself in the bathroom mirror, I looked quite the fright, covered with wet yellow and gray chunks of meat, some of it even stuck in my hair. I opened my eyes wide and made silent screaming faces at myself in the mirror. I wouldn't want to face myself as an F.B.I. agent.

I cleaned myself up a little before Eunice could see me. When I came out of the shower, I started a load of laundry in the garage. In the kitchen, I found Eunice already done massaging ankles. She stared at what I'd done with the body.

I didn't cut all the head off all the way, just enough where I could force it back so that if it still had eyes that worked, those eyes would see whatever stood behind it upside down. A chunk of windpipe stuck up from the neck. When I pushed the head back, I actually heard a sigh come up from it, along with whiff of an old KFC meal. I'd make sure to record that observation in my notebook.

Eunice seemed mesmerized by the body's appearance, which I admit looked weird, and she didn't say anything.

"Notice it's not wobbling at all," I said. "Pushing the head back like that definitely distributed the weight better. It has a small head to go with that small brain, and without eyes, I'm sure it weighs even less, but that certainly did the trick. It'd probably stand on its own for a long time.

"Dad."

"What?"

"You keep saying *it*, but it's Dad," she said.

"It was once," I said. "Not anymore. He can't see or walk down the hall anymore, Eunice. He can't come in our room the way he used to." For some reason, it hurt a little to say this out loud. She continued to stare at it, not even acknowledging what I just said.

"Eunice, I know you would always pretend to be asleep. I would, too. I'm sorry I never opened my eyes and did anything. I'm sorry the only time I ever did anything was that time with the frying pan."

Still not looking at me, she said, "I don't think this'll stop him. He doesn't even want to fall down."

"We should go to bed early," I said. "Maybe you can go to school tomorrow. I'll tell Mom I'm sick and stay home. You can say you feel better."

"I don't," she said. "I don't feel better at all."

"Wait and see how you feel tomorrow."

That night, I had such a weird dream. I dreamed that they finally took Eunice to the funny farm, but before she left, she had a pet snake, just a tiny one, and even though I hate snakes, I promised her that I'd take care of it in her absence. And I tried so hard to love that snake the way Eunice did, but every time I picked it up, it bit me. Even worse, no matter how gently I tried to hold it, it fought me and at one point, I accidentally broke the snake in half. In the dream I thought I killed it, but the second segment of the body grew a new head, so I wound up with two angry snakes to contend with.

What an awful dream.

I might have welcomed something wakening me up from it.

Just not what actually did wake me.

A whirring sound. The electric saw that Jace Armstrong gave me, blaring through the dark house.

I looked over at Eunice's empty bed and knew in an instant something awful was happening.

And I didn't have earbuds in Mom's ears. I took them out before going to bed. She would hear.

I rushed into the kitchen, and you won't believe what I saw.

Eunice had managed to unbuckle the body's trousers, and they lay with its boxers in a heap around its ankles. Its head still leaned way back, and the body showed no signs of falling over.

I could almost feel pride in Eunice for managing this feat, except for what I caught her doing.

She was using the saw to cut off the *thing* that the milk comes out of. I mean the balls and the pecker itself.

I came in just in time to see the last piece of rotten flesh give way and the whole package fall in a lump between Eunice's knees.

She looked at me with a face as horrid as the one I saw in the mirror, all covered in sticky flesh.

"Now he can't do anything," she said. The grin she flashed me signaled the emergence of a master criminal, a formidable psycho.

I almost smiled back.

Except Mom chose this moment to finally walk out of her room, to test the ankles that we all knew could never hold her up. She hadn't walked in so long, and she'd put on the kind of weight that those ankles just couldn't handle. But I guess all that massaging had finally paid off. A miracle, I suppose. "A strange phenomenon," one might say.

"What on earth are you girls doing?" she said, bracing herself against the wall as she rounded the corner in heavy, lumbering steps.

Seeing mad Eunice covered in ruined flesh must've done it. That along with the fact that I never did such a good job of cleaning up the kitchen. Not to mention the body's head pressed down against its back, gazing back at Mom upside down.

Mom died on the spot.

A heart attack most likely.

And here's the kicker: she died standing up, too, even with those terrible ankles.

The mystery continued, and I had a lot of work to do if I wanted to solve it.

Sacrifices

Because of what happened to the Air Force guy, Ian had to endure a babysitter. His parents announced that as the final decision, no more discussion necessary, and they warned him to not even try dividing them on this one, either.

And besides, look at what happened to the Air Force guy, that tough-guy pilot stationed a few miles away in Homestead. So mighty and indomitable that he didn't give a shit what neighborhood he went jogging in, until someone just snatched him off the street. Now he was lucky to even be alive, and Ian's mom couldn't stop talking about how all that military training saved him. Ian caught his dad rolling his eyes on the third iteration of the story—how the Air Force guy pulled himself out of that canal despite the ropes that bound his arms and legs. Tonight, Ian's parents planned to go to a church meeting about the growing presence of cults in their once-safe community, and Ian couldn't stay home alone like he wanted.

Which really sucked because of one fact: They had cable now.

The last goddamned house in the neighborhood as far as Ian knew, but they finally had it, and Ian could finally witness first-hand the glories of *Humanoids from the Deep*, a movie so depraved and uninhibited in naked, gory flesh that the kids lucky enough to have seen it struggled to even describe it.

With both parents out of the house, he'd have the perfect chance to watch it without their usual supervision. At the first sign of a single drop of blood or, God forbid, a nipple, they'd make him shut it off. This meeting of concerned parents sounded like the perfect opportunity, but nope, they had to find some babysitter. For a while it looked like they couldn't find anyone, but at the last minute someone came thanks to a friend-of-a-friend who had another friend-of-a-friend. By the time Ian checked the broadcast schedule and verified that *Humanoids* would show at the perfect time, his parents announced that they managed to find someone to come over to sit with him.

In the flesh, she looked not much older than Ian, two, maybe three years tops.

"How old are you?" the babysitter asked him. The inquiry made his parents pause in their last-minute preparations to leave. It had rained all day, so as they stood there with their rain-coats half buttoned, it looked as though even they didn't know the answer and wanted to know.

"Thirteen," said Ian.

The babysitter, who called herself Neti, a stupid name if Ian ever heard one, nodded impassively. Like she didn't really care and only asked to make him feel uncomfortable. Just like she didn't care when Ian's mom seemed to study her face one last time before departing. "You're about the age that Ian's sister would be today. Someone must've told you, I'm sure, about how someone grabbed her out of the backseat of our station wagon. Right in front of Ian. Her name was Ally."

This information didn't garner the usual outpouring of sympathy it usually drew from strangers. Just a blank, dead expression from Neti. Ian's dad put his hand on his wife's arm, trying to steer her toward the door. His eyes met Ian's briefly, a silent acknowledgment that he knew as well as Ian how these moments usually went—more monologue that would culminate in his mother weeping like the whole tragedy happened just yesterday, often with subtle blame directed toward Ian for doing nothing to prevent it, despite the fact that he wasn't even five years old yet. With a tight, humorless smile fixed on his lips, Ian's dad continued to nudge his wife toward the door.

But she insisted on continuing: "It was one of those backward facing rear seats—you know, where the trunk would be. Ally liked to sit back there with Ian so she could make faces at the other drivers on the road. What did I care? They didn't cause any harm."

More nudging from Ian's dad while the babysitter simply stared with dead eyes. *A regular humanoid*, thought Ian. She wore jeans and a raggedy Led Zeppelin t-shirt. Above her left eye, she sported a red scar shaped like a plus sign.

"I wasn't in the store for more than ten minutes," said Ian's mom, like she wanted to rehearse for tonight's meeting. "For ten minutes, fifteen at the most, I left them there with the back window lowered so it didn't get too hot. Just long enough for someone to pull her through the window and take her away from me. Nobody could tell me who did it, and nobody saw it. Except Ian."

Ian's mom looked at him like she expected a rebuttal. Soon enough, they'd all turned to look at him, as if he needed to finish the story.

"I don't remember any of it," he said.

"Naturally, you wouldn't," his father said. To Neti, he said, "Ian was only three."

"Four," his mother said. She studied his face for a moment as she always did when she reached this point in the story. "Exactly four," she said, a certain note in her voice that suggested that she didn't consider his age a good excuse for allowing it to happen, or maybe she simply harbored suspicion that even after all these years, he'd secretly remembered some of the details and kept them to himself.

Then with unnerving abruptness, she gave the babysitter her best fake smile, the one she used to hide tears, and along with Ian's father, she went off into the rain.

The clock read 7:30, and according to the listings, *Humanoids* would come on in thirty minutes.

Neti watched as the door shut behind them, blocking out the patter of rain.

"Real pillars of the community, I see," she said.

'What?"

"Your parents. You can tell they really give a shit. Want to clean things up."

"I guess."

Between Ian and the cable box stood this girl. Something interesting occurred to Ian just then. Even though Neti came in from the rain a few moments ago, she looked as dry as a bone. Ian didn't notice a raincoat or umbrella. Did someone else drive her here and walk her to the door with an umbrella before driving off? Of greater concern was the fact that she found his parents so upstanding. When it came time to turn on *Humanoids*, she might not want to accommodate his wishes out of fear that his parents wouldn't approve. Which they wouldn't. She'd probably make him watch *Happy Days* instead.

"They just want to hear the Air Force guy tell his story," he said. "He's a guest speaker or something."

Neti nodded like she knew already. She stood a half-foot taller than him and had dark blue eyes like his sister once had. "He probably has a lot to say. You know what happened to him, don't you?"

Ian knew the bones of the story. At least how it appeared in the newspaper, and while he normally just looked at the comics and the black-and-white ads for movies like *Humanoids from the Deep*, he'd found the article and read it. Maybe it had to do with the way her eyes peered into his, almost hypnotizing him, but he found himself using the word everyone else managed to avoid.

"Someone raped him," he said.

Somehow the newspaper managed to say this without actually *saying* it, but the whispered conversations around him confirmed it as a shameful fact. Unimaginable really for something like that to happen to a tough Air Force pilot. For Ian's part, he didn't understand the mechanics, and he felt ashamed for even wondering. Tentatively, he tried bringing up the subject with his biology teacher, whose relative youth made him more approachable than all his other teachers combined. Regarding the assault, his teacher had smirked and said, *Yeah, and I hear he actually complained about it.*

As he talked about it again with Neti, he almost repeated his teacher's joke, thinking it might ingratiate himself to her, even if he didn't actually consider it funny himself. Maybe she would laugh, and that could make her amenable to him watching *Humanoids from the Deep*.

But instead, she interjected something else. "Do you know what they actually did? Because you don't know the half of it. I'm sure they'd want to hide it from you."

She waited to see if he'd guess. Instead, he held his breath.

She said, "They grabbed him, put him into a van, and the reason he doesn't know where they took him is because they gave him something to make him groggy. They needed a receptive vessel for what they planned to do. Know where they took him?"

"They threw him into a canal," said Ian, who'd heard several times now how the Air Force Major fought against the ropes that bound him and worked his way to shore, where he called out for help. Someone walking his dog heard him and used a payphone to call the cops.

"Right, but what about before that?"

Beyond what the papers said, Ian didn't know.

Neti said, "They took him to an old cemetery. You know the one, I bet. It's the one that's had all the vandalism, graves getting opened up and stuff. Okay, well, they took him there, where they already had an altar set up, all decorated with bones and candles. Then, even with him drugged and tied up, it took three of them to drag him to the altar so they could use him in a ceremony. That ceremony needed someone just like him—a warrior. Hey, Ian? I'm getting tired of standing here. Mind if we sit down?"

Ian nodded, but he didn't want her to stop telling the story. Sure, he knew she probably made up most of it, but it captured his attention almost as well as he knew *Humanoids* would. He showed her the way into the TV den, where they sat down next to each other on his mom's favorite leather sofa.

Neti took in the furnishings, nodding appreciatively at what she saw. "They sure must've made a lot of sacrifices to afford all this stuff," she said. Then she pointed at the television and the new cable box sitting on top of it. "That what I think it is?"

Her question offered him a great way to bring up *Humanoids from the Deep*, but he hoped she'd finish the story first. Without waiting for permission, she picked up the controller and began flipping mindlessly through channels, occasionally pausing when something looked interesting.

Just when he thought she'd dropped the story altogether, she started talking again during a music video, "Whip It" by Devo.

"Once they got him to the altar, that's when they got down to business," she said. "They planned carefully, making sure they had the right kind of moon and the right kind of stars. Under those celestial lights they took off his clothes and used a special knife to carve symbols on his chest. Those symbols were actually the letters of a really old alphabet, and on his naked, sweaty flesh they spelled the name of the being they wanted to summon. They chanted the whole time and kept waiting for a sign that the right moment had arrived to get what they came for. I'll bet you know what I'm talking about. You know about the stuff that comes out of a guy when he has sex? Once he started to chant along with them, they recognized it as the sign they were waiting for, so they worked it out of him."

She made a hand motion to illustrate what she meant and waited for his reaction. On the TV, Devo sang about whips as one of them used a whip to cause a woman to lose one piece of clothing at a time. According to the clock, *Humanoids* would come in fifteen minutes.

"You don't understand what I mean, do you?" she said.

"Sure, I do," he said. He imitated her hand motion, but it seemed to only prove his lack of expertise. He chuckled in a way he hoped sounded worldly, but it failed to impress her.

"No, you obviously don't. Well, we have all these cable channels to help us out, don't we? Visual reference, right?" She pressed more buttons on the remote, quickly surfing through channels again, one after another so fast that Ian could barely process the images that flashed by.

She finally stopped when they arrived at a station with scrambled reception. The sound came through well enough though—gasps and heavy breathing.

"Looks like your folks, those pillars of the community, didn't pony up for this one. Fortunately, I know someone. A real wiz at this stuff. He can fix it for us. I just have to use your phone. Give me a few minutes to make a call, okay?"

She went into the kitchen where they kept the phone, leaving Ian in the den with the TV moaning as human bodies morphed into colorful rainbows dancing on the screen. He picked up the controller, though he couldn't quite bring himself to change the station. Turning down the volume, he could hear Neti say that his parents ought to be gone for at least a couple of hours and that whoever listened on the other end ought to come there pronto. The rest he couldn't make out, but she sounded used to bossing around the other person.

When Neti came back into the den, she sat a little closer to Ian.

"That thing about your sister. Tell me about how she got snatched in front of you."

After a sprinkle of information, people always wanted to know more. His mom never missed an opportunity to talk about the tragedy, and afterwards, like some macabre performance, whoever listened expected his testimony to follow, as if they couldn't just believe his mom. Usually, other kids at school wanted the whole scoop, not babysitters. "Well," he said, "it just happened." He looked at the clock again. Less than ten minutes until *Humanoids.*

"You really can't remember it though? Like, nothing?"

"Nothing. Not a thing."

In truth, he remembered it very well. Most things passed from his memory, but not that. He just didn't share it with anyone.

She studied his expression, as if she could detect his lie.

"I was only four," he said, hoping that would put it to rest.

"Yeah, I heard that. And she was what, like, six maybe?"

"Yeah, about."

"Your mom just left you guys in the station wagon like that. All alone. And we know what happens nowadays. All the time, practically. Kids disappear from a store or a mall, and later, they find a head buried in the woods. Parents go on TV, sobbing and crying, but you have to wonder how they let it happen in the first place. Whether they secretly wanted their kid to disappear. You'd think they'd have trouble hiding it when they're getting all that attention. The relief they feel. No more burden about how to afford food and school clothes. Paying for college. Raising a kid costs dough, and things like cable aren't cheap. You remember what she looked like?"

Ian remembered very well. "Just from pictures."

"You have one you can show me?" she asked.

The clock continued to tick, but the urgency to see *Humanoids* quickly diminished. For a brief instant, the image on the television resolved itself, and Ian saw the close-up of a breast with a strawberry-colored nipple. It didn't even look real, and it was gone a second later. He stood up and adjusted his pants to hide any arousal he felt from the scrambled images. Then he made his way to a table that his mother kept as a shrine to his sister where he retrieved a framed photograph. He offered it to Neti as if it represented the final proof that no one wanted Ally to disappear.

Neti studied it, almost seeming to smile at one point. "She doesn't look much like you. What do you think she looks like today?"

Ian shrugged, though the image of bones buried in a vacant field shot through his mind. That image came to him often, and he felt the familiar urge to scream. Good thing he knew how to hold it in, just as he knew he push aside his memory of the man who approached the open back window of the station wagon. The police asked him repeatedly to describe the person who took his sister, but at the time he struggled to do it, frustrating everyone. The face came back to him in dreams, though, and if someone forced him to do so today, he could easily describe the heavy brow, the dark hair cut almost flat, the eyebrows thick and black, almost like something painted on with a magic marker. When they sent a sketch artist to work with Ian, the resulting picture looked like the Frankenstein monster, so nobody took it seriously. But if Ian saw him again, he'd recognize him at once. He could picture the way he just reached into the car, as well as the way Ally lifted her arms and let him take her. He could still hear the way the man said, "You want to see her again, you say nothing. *Nothing.* Keep your mouth shut, and you keep the rest of your family safe. Then someday, she might come home."

He never conveyed this part to anyone, half out of fear, but also half-wondering if he made that part up all on his own. Some kind of wishful thinking that his silence would eventually serve a purpose.

Neti repeated her question: "You think you'd recognize her today?"

"Yeah. No. I mean, I don't know."

Neti said, "I don't think you would. They say that about Jesus, you know. Your parents, they look like church-going people. I'll bet they tell you Jesus is coming again, but no one really wants him to. Anyway, if he really and truly did, no one would recognize him. They expect him to show up wearing a white robe and sporting a halo, but he wouldn't, no more than the devil's son would show up with horns and a pitchfork. Your sister, too. You'd never recognize her."

She handed the framed picture to him and leaned back on the sofa. As Ian returned the picture to its precise place, Neti began rubbing her stomach.

"None of those things are true," Ian said when he returned to the sofa.

She didn't answer. Her eyes remained fixed on the television's scrambled images, as if they held hidden meanings she alone could decipher.

Ian said, "All those things you said about the graveyard, I'm not stupid. I know you're making it up. Everything. It's bullshit."

Not looking at him, she continued to rub her stomach.

"Just bad people who tried to kill him by throwing him into a canal. But he was too strong."

Now she looked at him and smiled, her hand still rubbing her belly, like she'd just eaten a big meal.

She said, "You like to think your warriors are so mighty and strong. Tougher than iron. But they're not. People like your Air Force Major will whine and beg for their lives when the chips are down. That's what he did: whine and beg so much that they wondered if their ritual would even work. What they hoped to summon wouldn't want the body of someone so weak and cowardly. Only a strong body can tempt it away from its kingdom in the Pit. The body of a warrior. Know what? When they finished with him and threw him in the canal, they hoped he wouldn't die. If he didn't die, that meant they chose correctly. That meant that the one they summoned still lingered inside his body. They knew it would bestow blessing with its seed." She sighed. "Never forget this kid: there's always something out there more powerful. Something we're all making sacrifices to."

Ian knew she made it all up to rattle him, so he tried to force his mind elsewhere. He'd forgotten all about *Humanoids* and found himself thinking about the meeting taking place right now. All those concerned moms and dads listening to the Air Force guy talking about the way he escaped a blood-thirsty cult who tried to make him a human sacrifice. His mom would probably stand up at some point and exclaim that, for all she knows, the same cult snatched her daughter. Then they'd start talking about all the different groups coming into the community, people unlike themselves who brought with them strange languages and practices, like Voodoo and Santeria, and how they worshipped blasphemous gods, even Lucifer himself.

Someone rang the doorbell, and Neti stopped rubbing her belly. "Finally," she said. She got up and began walking toward the front door, her gait kind of funny, as if that big meal made her feel too bloated to walk.

Ian followed and watched as she opened the door with the air of someone who lived there all her life.

"What kept you?" she said to the man who stood in the doorway, shaking off the rain. His hair hung long and damp, and when he looked at Ian, Ian saw eyebrows that looked so dark and long that appeared painted on with barely any space between them. Of course, lots of people have eyebrows like that. He didn't seem old, just a few years older than Neti, Ian guessed.

Though he looked at Ian, he talked to Neti. "Van needed gas."

"You bring your stuff?"

"This is a waste of time." But he held up a gray toolbox clutched in his left hand.

Neti said, "This is Ian."

"I know," the man said with the barest hint of a nod in Ian's direction. "We don't have time for this."

"Cable box is this way."

The man sighed and followed her into the den, where he opened his toolbox and took out a wad of tangled cords, along with a square box. He began untangling the cords as if it amounted to painstaking work. At one point, he did something that made the wad look even more jumbled and confused, causing him to swear in frustration. Neti gestured for Ian to sit next to her on the couch. With one hand placed on her stomach, she took Ian's hand in the other. The scrambled images continued to play on the screen, but Ian kept his focus on the man. He didn't squeeze back when Neti squeezed his hand.

"This is the Wizard I told you about," said Neti as the man began working from the other end of the wad.

"We'll see what kind of wizard I really am," he said, not looking up.

Neti rubbed her stomach and laughed. "Sure, we'll see."

A moment later, the Wizard made a sound that suggested he scored some kind of victory. He held up the untangled wire the same way Ian's dad did to a line holding a fish he caught in Biscayne Bay. With one end of the wire, the Wizard did something to the cable box. Then he did something to the gizmo he carried in with him. In an instant, the scrambled images on the television resolved themselves into the fleshy colors of writhing, pumping bodies. A lump formed in Ian's throat when he saw them in motion.

"Eureka!" said the Wizard.

"Shut up, Mr. Wizard." To Ian, she said, almost whispering, "This is the truth they always want to hide. The only truth that matters. Behind closed doors, where you can't see, they perform this act out of fear and shame. But it's the source of the greatest magic the world's ever known. They corrupt that magic with their greed and shame and bigotry, but it's a real and powerful thing." With the hand she used to hold Ian's, she placed the flat of his palm on her stomach. "That magic will bring real change. The new will destroy the old. There will be a complete re-set, where fear and shame will no longer exist and people can just be themselves. It'll be rough at first. The whole world will go through something horrible, a disaster that will kill millions of people. But someone will be there to lead those of us left to a glorious new world, where there won't be the need for any more sacrifices. Whoa, did you feel that?"

In fact, Ian did feel something under his hand, but he thought it was just gas moving around. Nevertheless, she acted like it amounted to something fantastic.

"You do, don't you?" she said. "That's not a fart."

"Ally used to say that," he said.

"What?"

He looked at her to avoid the stunningly clear images on the television. They made him feel both excited and ashamed. On the floor, the Wizard sat with his legs folded, entranced with the television and not paying any attention to their conversation.

Ian said, "Ally would say that whenever she farted. 'That wasn't a fart,' she'd say."

"Is that so? Well, she's gone, isn't she, and you tell everyone you can't remember anything about her. But that's okay. She'd forgive you. Everyone lies. Your teachers lie. Your parents lie. That Air Force guy definitely lies. Right now, they're trying to hold their world of lies together. But it'll all come crashing down soon enough, in one great fire. It might be a nuclear fire created by your Air Force guy when he's flying his plane, or maybe one he starts by pressing a button once he's president someday, I don't know. But whatever happens, the whole world will be remade."

"Year Zero," said the Wizard, still watching the TV.

"We're going to leave you for a few minutes," said Neti. "Me and the Wizard are going into your parents' room. We're going to leave them something. Call it a gift."

"Oh, yeah?" said the Wizard. He looked at his watch, the only time he took his eyes away from the television.

"Yeah. You can't watch that stuff without wanting to do it yourself, so we're going into their bedroom for a few minutes. And Ian? While we're in there, I want you to give some thought to something. If the man who took Ally reached out for you, too, would you have gone? Would you have reached out to him the same way Ally did? She went willingly. She was young, but she dreamed the whole thing before it happened, so she knew what to do when those arms reached for her. What about you? Do you ever dream the way she did? Because sometimes life has a way of preparing you for choices, and you have a choice to make tonight."

"I don't think we have time for this," said the Wizard.

"We have time. That meeting's still going strong. They're busy blaming all the wrong people, the Cubans, the Haitians. What's that bumper sticker on your dad's car, Ian? What does it say?"

Ian knew the one. "Will the last American leaving Miami please bring the flag," he quoted.

"Right. They love their flag. Well, *we're* going to leave before they get home, and we want you to come with us."

"I really think we should just grab him and go," the Wizard said. In his hand he held a bottle of clear liquid he'd taken out of his toolbox.

Neti ignored him. "We're going back to the bedroom now, and I want you to look for a sign that tells you what you should do. Look everywhere around you before you decide. You can say no, that's okay. We won't make you. But if you look around this room, you'll find a sign. I don't know what it is, but if you look hard, something will speak to you." She squeezed Ian's hand one more time and stood up. "Come on, Wizard, I need to do this."

The Wizard made a resigned sound and closed his toolbox. He followed her out of the den.

Ian sat alone in the den, the televised images of moaning flesh now monotonous and unstimulating. The phone in the kitchen beckoned him. But who would he call? What would he report her for, saying crazy things and finding creative ways to creep him out? Corrupting a minor? He recalled the joke his teacher made: *I hear he actually complained about it.* They'd say that about him next. Would he want that?

Plus, that ridiculous notion that the room contained a sign, a stupid joke played by a horny babysitter.

Still, what she said about Ally made him want to look. No lie, that got to him. Everything she said got to him.

He deeply missed Ally, even if the whole thing happened more than nine years ago, even if he spent his waking hours trying to pretend like none of those things happened and she never existed. Sometimes the weight of the guilt became so heavy that he wished he could just let everything go and float away. Hold up his arms and disappear the way she did. He could never share with anyone how often he thought about that day, how deep down he blamed his mother for letting it happen, for being so stupid as to let them sit there with the back window down. Now he hated her for talking about it the way she did, as if only she felt the pain, just as she talked about what happened to the Air Force major as if she experienced it herself. The way she obsessed over it, as if she actually *liked* discussing the details.

The urge to look once more upon the picture of Ally came over him.

He picked up the framed photograph.

What he saw made him disbelieve his own eyes.

Then he realized that he'd found that sign Neti told him he would find, the sign that made him believe everything she said.

* * *

Waiting in the living room, Ian watched Neti and the Wizard emerge from the hallway. A substantiative change came over the way he perceived them.

Neti saw the photograph he held and the recognition in his eyes. She smiled.

"You found the sign?"

Ian held out the photo for her to see. Where the picture once showed a smiling little girl, it now looked blank. The entire image had vanished, though the photo paper remained the same. All that remained were the name and date written in blue link in his mother's unmistakable hand: *Ally, June 1975.*

"How'd you do it?" Ian asked.

"We may call him the Wizard," said Neti, "but he's not the only one with magic. There's plenty to go around. Plenty to share. In fact, we left some on your parents' sheets."

"I need to get my stuff," said the Wizard as he straightened himself out. "Then we really need to leave."

"Leave it here," said Neti. "No one'll need cable in the new world."

"Year Zero could be quite a few years away," the Wizard said.

"Or just nine months," Neti said, rubbing her stomach.

Ian placed the picture frame on the coffee table his mother used to entertain guests. At first, he placed it face down, but he reconsidered his decision as Neti and the Wizard moved to the door. The Wizard moved his feet impatiently, but Neti watched Ian impassively.

She seemed to read his thoughts.

"Go ahead and turn it over," she said. "It'll be the first thing she sees. It'll tell her everything she needs to know." Before she stepped over the threshold, she tilted her head toward him, and for the second time he noted the cross-shaped scar over her eye.

Only, with that head-tilt, he saw it differently this time, in a way that helped him understand.

Not a cross, but more like an X.

Before following them out the door, he positioned the frame so that it would face whoever came inside the house. A merciful way of leaving a message, he thought, but not quite complete. He had other options, like filling the house with gas and lighting a match. Something to let them know that he'd finally crossed himself out, and the humanoids decided to arrive early, before Year Zero. No, to complete the message, he needed a picture of himself.

Just one in this room, taken a long time ago, capturing a look of hopeful anticipation on his face before he realized that sisters didn't return and that no one kept their promises.

His mom's blue pen did the trick.

Before stepping into the rain, he drew an X over the face in the photograph, the one that used to belong to him.

Ladders

Rusty found the old ladder buried in the earth after the work crew's departure. Tripped over it, in fact, nearly killing himself. Only the top rung showed above the dirt, and when it caught Rusty's foot, it almost sent him head-first into the remains of an old oak that had once housed a family of woodpeckers.

Rusty considered his own position one of solidarity with those woodpeckers. Like them, and the rabbits and the raccoons and the bobcats that had once lived on the lot, he too appeared destined to become homeless.

The foreclosure notices on his own house started arriving not long before the empty lot next door sold to developers, who quickly started clearing it to make way for the construction of a new home. The same thing happened everywhere else in his once heavily wooded neighborhood. Originally, the remoteness of the area attracted him, but eventually he fell in love with the trees and the wildlife. Now it all seemed poised to vanish. Like him.

"Motherfuckers," he said to himself between sips of beer. He walked over to the bulldozed clearing next to his house—the latest parcel of land to go. Across the street, a minivan pulled into the new house facing his, and an entire family poured forth. They all smiled and waved to Rusty.

Rusty returned the wave, but not the smile.

The driver of the van, a balding man who seemed to wear only polo shirts, stopped and called out to him. "We're getting a new neighbor, I see. Isn't it wonderful?"

Rusty didn't know the man's name. Like their houses, the neighbors all looked the same. He wondered where they kept coming from.

He raised his beer in a mock toast. "I'd say it's a fucking shame of epic proportion."

The neighbor's smile vanished briefly, replaced by an empty stare of confusion. No doubt he thought he had misheard. How could anyone object to progress, to development, to the rising value of real estate?

Rusty could. He had a file full of foreclosure notices for Exhibit A.

Bile rose in his throat as the neighbor's smile returned. Raising his hand in a farewell salute, the neighbor followed his family inside the air-conditioned interior of that new house which would, no doubt, look like the one about to take shape on the vacant lot.

When Rusty turned on his heel to look at the rest of the damage, he tripped over the ladder.

* * *

It made no sense. If someone in the work crew left behind a ladder, why would they bury it?

It didn't seem like a simple act of carelessness. Not that this would surprise Rusty. He expected no less from the callous idiots who didn't give a fuck about displaced woodpeckers. They did their damage, and why would they care if they left some hardware behind? But a buried ladder? Maybe he'd just found a small step ladder that some fat-ass stepped on, causing it to sink into the soft dirt.

But when he tried to pull the ladder free, it wouldn't budge.

It looked old, and its faded brown color caused it to blend in with the rest of the terrain. From a certain angle, it looked like a natural feature growing from the earth itself.

More curious now, Rusty went to his carport—a very modest structure compared to the giant garages attached to the newer homes—and returned with a pick and shovel, which he used to clear away the dirt around the ladder.

The day still had a good hour of light left, and the mindlessness of the work helped sober him and distract him from his own problems. But the more he cleared, the further he realized the ladder went.

Finally, he hit something solid with his shovel. Clearing more dirt away, he unearthed an irregularly shaped barrier made out of rough material. The ladder twisted at an angle, extending down into whatever the barrier covered. Sensing a kind of hatch, Rusty tried to pry it away with his fingers.

That didn't do the trick, so he tried the pickaxe, and the barrier broke away into pieces, falling into a crevasse that opened beneath it.

Rusty stared into the gaping blackness. The ladder twisted downward, like a root that had grown sideways to accommodate the barrier, but it maintained the form of a functioning ladder. It didn't look natural, but it didn't look manufactured either. A strange scent wafted from below—an earthy scent—with traces of what smelled like chemicals. Ammonia perhaps.

Maybe an old bomb shelter, he conjectured, or a hideaway used by bootleggers. Long ago, such renegades prospered in this region, way back before people paved over everything.

He needed to make a decision: go down and investigate, or try to cover up the hole with the remaining pieces of the hatch.

Rusty knew he should do the latter.

Start minimizing the amount of trouble he got into.

Nah.

Maybe he owed the impulse to the beer, or perhaps the fatalism that had come over him as of late.

First, he tested the ladder. If it originated during the Prohibition era, it might crumble beneath his feet. But its sturdiness surprised him. It supported his weight handily, though he couldn't quite determine the material. Something between wood and iron. He couldn't see what held it in place, but it seemed reliable, so down he went into the darkness.

Quite a distance, in fact.

The walls of the passageway narrowed around him. It now occurred to him that he'd found an old well, or God forbid—an abandoned septic tank. In the dark, he reached out and touched what felt like limestone. Someone cut this away a long time ago, he guessed.

Before descending further, he needed a flashlight, so he crawled back up into the fading sunlight. When he emerged, he once more saw the neighbor across the street, still wearing his polo shirt and now using a hose to water his hedges. Again, the neighbor waved to him, but Rusty pretended not to see him and returned to his carport to get what he needed. When he returned, he noticed the neighbor was watering his driveway, oblivious to where the water sprayed. In truth, the neighbor was observing him and trying not to make it obvious.

"You're wasting water," Rusty said.

"What?" the neighbor answered, but Rusty knew he heard him just fine because he now aimed the water at the bushes.

"Don't waste water," Rusty said. "It's a precious commodity."

The neighbor laughed, as if he'd just heard a funny joke.

Rusty pretended to laugh back before saying, "Fuck you." Instead of waiting for a reply, he stormed back to the ladder, now armed with a decent flashlight. It felt good to say that to his neighbor, so he returned with a hop in his step. Normally, his knees bothered him, the result of dislocating them too often, but curiosity made him forget about his pain.

All the way down, the ladder seemed to twist and vary in width, like something grown instead of installed. After about twenty feet, he came to a rounded-out cavern of rock and dirt. It proved just tall enough for him to stand, though the roots of long-dead trees dangled overhead. To see anything, he had to push them out of the way.

Definitely not a well or a septic tank. He thought again of the possibility that he'd found an old cache for liquor barrels. Yet the light from his flashlight revealed only roots and dirt.

Until he moved the beam to the northeast corner. There he saw it, the body of a naked man, encircled by the same twisting roots that hung overhead. It looked like someone had tied up a corpse and left it underground.

The sight caused Rusty to call out in alarm, the sound of his voice filling the enclosure. But the man didn't react to the sound. He continued to lie there motionless, eyes closed.

In his panic, Rusty revised his earlier conjecture: not a hideaway at all, but a tomb housing some sort of mummy.

Heart racing, he leaned closer.

The man's skin didn't look withered or decayed—it looked pink and healthy, like baby flesh. Not only that, the root system didn't seem to just grow *around* the body; at certain places, like the abdomen and groin, it seemed to grow *into* it, like a series of umbilical cords delivering nutrients to the slumbering form.

Besides the roots, there was something else.

Tiny gray worms.

At first, he made the mistake of thinking they were maggots feasting on the dead. But a closer look revealed that instead of consuming the body, the worms were secreting a fleshy paste of some kind. As if working in concert with the worms, the root's branches seemed to pulse, reminding him of a scorpion flexing venom into the body of its prey.

More fascinated than afraid, Rusty leaned closer. His light revealed two other bodies just beyond the man—a woman and a child, both naked and connected by the same series of roots, their bodies host to the strange worms.

A term for this discovery formed in his mind: a *nest*.

As he pondered, he heard a sound close by, something moving in the dirt.

He moved the light to find the source of the sound, catching a glimpse of the man's face. This time, he didn't just call out in astonishment.

He screamed.

Then he scrambled his way back to the ladder, dropping the flashlight in the process. He didn't bother going back for it, instead groping his way up the twisting ladder. His heart hammered as the climb seemed to take an eternity, but eventually he hoisted himself out of the hole and back onto the ground. Hurriedly, he threw the pieces of the broken hatch over the opening, along with handfuls of pinecones and mulch. Anything he could grab to place between him and what he found down there.

"Oh, my Jesus, oh, my Jesus," he said, over and over.

Down there, in the darkness, the man's eyes had opened.

Rusty sat on his haunches, staring at the rungs of the ladder sticking up out of the earth, and he didn't move until he felt certain nothing would follow him.

* * *

In the days that followed, Rusty did all he could to dismiss what he'd seen. He told himself that it was an illusion brought on by too much drink. Still, he avoided going back to the lot, and besides, the construction of the new house proceeded quickly, covering any traces of the ladder.

The only person he tried to tell was Charlotte, his ex-wife.

She called him two days after his experience, so he still felt shaken. Thus, he struggled to process what she wanted.

"The check is late," she said, apparently for the third time.

After what he'd seen, money hardly seemed to matter. He could barely remember to eat.

"You remember the lot next door?" he said. "It sold, and they're building another house…"

He couldn't finish the rest. He didn't know how to say it. Worse, he knew what she'd say. Something about his drinking. Even worse: she might have a point.

"Still carping about crimes against Mother Nature? Trust me, the squirrels and tortoises will find a new place to go. They always do. I'm so sick of all this doomsday shit you buy into."

"It's not that," he said, irritated now.

"I'm not done. You act like nature is some benevolent enterprise. But it's not. It's nasty. It's worms and blood and death. Remember the carcass we found that one time?"

"Jesus," he said. "Not this again. Animals have to eat."

Just before Charlotte had left him for good, she stepped outside to retrieve the mail and came face to face with a vulture pulling strings of flesh from an enormous, dead rattlesnake.

"Yeah, and it would eat you if it could," she said. "Nature's just a malicious machine that's biding its time before it can figure out how to do us in. Just remember this: everything in nature wants to kill us. Give me air conditioning and computers and microwaves and processed meals any day. I choose those things. You've chosen something else, and that's why we could never live together again."

Rusty closed his eyes and rubbed his temples with his free hand. "You weren't always like this. At one point, you wanted to buy the property next door. Just to keep it from development."

"That's rich," she said. "You want to talk about why we didn't? Where's that money you talked about saving? And oh, yeah—where's my check?"

"Bet money's not a problem anymore."

Charlotte lived with a real estate developer now. The cause or symptom of her current disease, Rusty couldn't tell. Now she couldn't look at a tree without imagining how to chop it down to build a new auto parts store. Because that's what the earth really wanted: more steel and plastic.

"It wouldn't be," she said, "if you got your priorities straight and started worrying about practical things.

"How does the saying go? The check's in the mail."

"I'll bet. Why don't you go chain yourself to a tree?"

"You'd like that. Just so you could bulldoze it, along with me."

"Would I ever," she said. Then she hung up.

To cool his rage, he took a long walk. Not like he had a job to go to. He walked briskly and without direction, covering areas of the neighborhood he'd not seen in a while.

Everywhere he looked, new houses were going up, and he passed several bulldozers sitting in ravaged lots, just like the one next to his home. Every new house looked the same. Even the people standing outside watering their grass looked the same—the men with friendly smiles and glistening white teeth, the women with faces packed full of makeup.

When he passed one of the recently bulldozed lots, a tall pine drew his attention, mighty in stature and at least a century old. He worried about the fate it would suffer with yet another new house going up.

He stopped and gazed on its magnificence, already feeling as though he should mourn it, when he noticed something else.

The rungs of a ladder sticking up from the earth.

A voice called out to him from the house across the street.

"It's sold already!"

Rusty turned to see the source of the voice: yet another perfect male specimen standing on a well-manicured lawn, water pointlessly flowing from the hose in his hand.

"What?" said Rusty.

"It's already sold." Then that smile that looked like all the other smiles Rusty saw on his walk that day. "It's a seller's market, you know. As soon as a lot goes up for sale, boom! It's gone that day. Best try your luck somewhere else."

Rusty returned his gaze to the rungs of the ladder, and a horrible notion arose in him. If he dug away at the earth around the ladder, he knew he'd find another *nest*. He shivered as that word came to him again. He wanted to believe that he'd dreamed the whole experience.

"I say," the smiling man with the hose said in a tone that suggested he wanted to sound forceful without making it obvious, "you'd best try somewhere else."

Rusty didn't answer. A vision formed in his mind—the man's face beneath the ground, entwined with roots and vines, his features formed from the defecations and regurgitations of a thousand worms.

Rusty turned and walked toward home, and he didn't stop until the front door was locked securely behind him.

* * *

In the days ahead, every time someone cleared one of the quickly vanishing lots to build an ugly new home, Rusty found himself scanning the area. More often than not, he spotted the rungs of a ladder sticking out from the mulch left behind by the machines.

No attempt to even hide them, he thought.

Then he reminded himself about how he had tripped over the first one, and how they blended in with the land's natural features. Somehow, they *were* natural features. Now that he knew what to look for, he couldn't help but see them.

Once, at night, after he turned off all his lights to save electricity, a flashlight beam came through his front window. Immediately, he remembered the flashlight he had dropped when he went down into the nest. He never went back for it. Even if he still tried to convince himself that he imagined the whole experience, he'd have to explain away the missing flashlight. So he laid there on his sofa, watching the beam of light move across his wall, telling himself that it probably came from one of the new house owners walking his dog in the dark and using a flashlight for safety.

Just not *his* flashlight. Not possible.

Completed in record time, the new house next door served to emphasize how dilapidated, how unkept, how out-of-date his own looked. Its manicured lawn stood in contrast to how Rusty let his grass grow wild and unfertilized. Kudzu vines and palm fronds sprung up from the weeds that dominated his yard. The day after he watched the flashlight beam move across his wall, he looked through the back window and saw something moving through those weeds, which had grown over three feet high.

A raccoon or a rabbit, he assumed at first, but when Rusty saw its head, he nearly gasped out loud.

A Florida panther. Ragged, with one ear missing, ribs showing through its emaciated frame. Regardless, it still somehow possessed the majesty of a once dominant animal, now reduced to a desperate, endangered existence.

The animal looked set to bound away, when Rusty heard the unmistakable report of gunfire. The panther thrashed in midair, as if caught in an invisible net, and for an instant, a storm of blood and fur surrounded its body. Then it fell back into the weeds, its shredded body hidden from view.

Rusty made for the back door, not sure exactly what he intended to do. As he stepped out, a man met him from the direction of the new house, an assault rifle slung over his shoulder.

Rusty, who had not yet met his new neighbor, stared at the man.

"Afternoon," the man said. "Don't believe we've had the pleasure." Without offering a hand to shake, he introduced himself as Sam Manila, the occupant of that brand new house.

The sight of the man sent a chill through Rusty. Not just because of the weapon he carried over his shoulder, but because of his familiar face. Sam Manila looked just like the man Rusty found buried beneath the earth. Only now he wore a white polo shirt and checkered shorts.

"Maybe now you'll clean up your property," the man continued. "Can't see what's hiding in all these weeds. Dangerous not to know what's out there."

Rusty didn't reply right away. Instead, he waded through the grass until he found the dead panther. The bullets had torn off one of its front legs and obliterated its head. One thing was for certain: Sam Manila knew how to aim his weapon.

At that moment, two others appeared behind Sam, apparently the rest of the Manila family—a woman along with a boy of about thirteen. Rusty recognized them as the two others he saw beneath the ground that day.

"You get him, Dad?" the boy said, a perfect imitation of a real person.

Because Rusty felt certain they weren't real—not in the same way he considered himself real. Somewhere in his chaotic thoughts, he heard the voice of Charlotte, telling him that people couldn't really exist in harmony with nature. Loving nature made no sense since it couldn't—and wouldn't— love you back. Given the chance, it would fight back and destroy you.

Would it do it this way? By birthing replicas of people? As replacements? For protection?

Sam Manila kept his eyes on Rusty as he answered the boy. "I got him good. That creature was a nuisance, not even designed for survival. Just useless skin and bones. I was reminding our neighbor here about how he needed to tidy up his property. Cut back some of these vines."

"Any form of nuisance could hide in there," said the woman. "Things like rats. Rats attract panthers."

"You don't want me to get attacked by a panther," asked the boy, "do you, mister?"

"He sure doesn't," said Sam Manila. "Do you, neighbor? You don't want any of us to get attacked by a wild animal. It's them or us. Isn't that right?"

Rusty didn't answer. His blood had gone cold, frozen in his veins. Sam Manila withdrew the rifle from his shoulder. Rusty shifted his weight, not sure what the man intended to do.

It turned out he only intended to hand the weapon over to his wife. She held it and watched Rusty thoughtfully as Sam Manila began working something else out of his pocket: the flashlight Rusty dropped when he'd disturbed their nest. He held it up for Rusty to see.

"They found this on our property. My guess is you dropped it there."

Rusty shook his head. "Not mine."

The man raised his eyebrows. "You sure?"

"Positive," said Rusty.

Sam Manila seemed to consider this. Then he used the flashlight to point at an old oak that grew wild and untrimmed on the edge of Rusty's yard.

"That needs to come down," said Sam Manila. "It drops leaves onto my backyard. I've got better things to do than to rake them up."

Mrs. Manila said, "He needs to play with his son and make love with me."

The barrel of the rifle inched close to Rusty as she spoke these words.

The boy nodded. "We like to play ball and eat hot dogs. You got a kid to play ball with, Mister?"

Rusty shook his head.

"That's a damn shame," said Sam Manila. He put the flashlight back into his pocket. "Do something about the tree. I have a good yard guy if you can't do it yourself. He'll dispose of that creature for you, too." Rusty assumed he meant the panther, but a glimmer of doubt broke through the surface of his consciousness. By *creature*, did he mean something else? As if sensing his question, Sam Manila finished by lifting his chin toward the carcass. "You ought to do it soon, before the worms get to it."

Without saying any more, he smiled neighborly. Then the three turned as one and returned to their house, where presumably, Sam Manila would make love to his wife and play ball with his son.

* * *

Later, after considering his lack of options, Rusty called the state's Wildlife Protection Office to report the murder of the panther. He kept his voice low, as if Sam Manila and his family sat crouched outside his front door, secretly listening.

After remaining on hold for over an hour, Rusty finally reached an exhausted-sounding person who simply said *hello* without introducing himself or announcing his department. When Rusty said he wanted to report that an endangered panther had been shot on his property, the beleaguered man asked him to repeat himself. After the second iteration of the event, the man said, "Let me get this straight. You're calling to confess that you shot a Florida Panther? They're endangered, you know."

Rusty breathed deeply and tried to conceal his exasperation. "Not me. My neighbor. He had what I think is an A.R. 15." Rusty didn't know guns, but he'd heard about this one on the news and thought it would grab his listener's attention. "He shot it in cold blood."

"Hold on," said the man. It sounded as though he set down the phone to talk to someone else. When he picked it up again, he said, "How do you know it's a panther?"

"I asked it and it told me. Jesus Christ, it's got four legs, tan fur, and big teeth." When he got no reply, he added, "Well, about the teeth, I'm speculating. My neighbor practically shot its head off. He's not..."

Rusty didn't know how to finish the sentence. He's not what? Real? Human? He could say *not natural*, but that didn't seem accurate. Not with what seemed like an increasingly inescapable conclusion: that nature had accomplished some kind of strange adaptation beyond his ability to fathom.

"He's not *right*," said Rusty, finally.

"What's your address?" said the person on the phone.

Rusty told him. Once more, the man put him on hold so he could talk to someone else. Standing near his back window, Rusty could see the place where the panther had died. A cloud of insects hovered over the area, feasting on blood and spoiled flesh. Overhead, he saw a dark speck. A vulture, he realized. Soon, more of them would appear. The cleanup crew.

And down in the dirt, Rusty knew, the worms had begun to eat. Raw material to use for later, probably.

The voice returned.

"We already have a note about that address. Are you the occupant?"

"I'm the current owner," said Rusty. "What does that matter?"

The man didn't excuse himself before speaking to someone else. Rusty tried to hear the muffled conversation, but they kept their voices too low. When the voice spoke again to Rusty, it said, "Do you have weapons in the house?"

"I don't even hunt. Look, I think you ought to know what's happening here. I keep seeing people who aren't natural. I know this sounds ridiculous, but you've got to believe it's the truth."

"They're perfectly natural," said the voice. "Am I to understand that you have no weapons? Not even, say, a large machete?"

A wild thought came to Rusty. "You're saying I should get something to defend myself. You're saying I'm in danger."

The voice went silent. Rusty held his breath, straining to hear any muffled conversation. Nothing, until the voice resumed, enunciating each word carefully. "Just stay where you are. Someone will be there shortly. I'd like your assurance that you won't be any trouble."

"Trouble?"

"There are notes in your file. Also, something about a foreclosure."

Rusty hung up the phone. He checked the number, verifying that he had dialed correctly. Then he went to the front door, making sure that he locked it securely with the deadbolt.

No sense in making it easy for them to get inside.

Through the front window, he saw his neighbor across the street, once more watering his driveway and staring blankly in his direction. If he could see the new house next door, he knew he would see them standing outside as well. Everywhere in the neighborhood, they knew about him. They knew that he knew.

He retreated to the back window and saw the vulture slouching toward the panther's carcass. "Go away," he shouted at the window. "Just get away!"

He couldn't explain the terrible anger he now felt for the vulture. It only did what nature created it to do.

Of course, the same could be said about the neighbors about to descend on his house.

If he couldn't prevent his own fate, maybe he could do something about the panther's. It now seemed incredibly important to do something. Anything.

Despite what he told the man on the phone, he did own a machete. With it in hand, he ran toward the vulture now sitting atop the dead panther, prepared to decapitate the horrible bird if necessary. But it bounded off before he could land a blow. From a distance, it glowered at him for interfering with its natural function.

Still, Rusty was determined that he wouldn't surrender the carcass to it. He would bury it instead.

Using the same pick and shovel he had once used to clear away the earth around the ladder, he now worked at digging a hole. He chose a spot near the tree that Sam Manila wanted him to cut down. The vulture maintained its distance, but now and then it tested Rusty by trying to get closer. Each time, Rusty picked up the machete and threatened it away.

With the thickness of the weeds and shrubbery, he struggled to make progress on the hole. Finally, he used the machete to clear some of it away.

His work revealed ladder rungs sticking up out of the earth.

There, where he lived.

He dropped the machete and stared.

Sensing a change in Rusty's attitude, the vulture grew bolder and came close enough to the panther's body.

Rusty didn't care anymore.

What had the voice said earlier?

Are you the new occupant?

Beneath his feet, something new waited to take over. A new *occupant* lying in a kind of slumber, nurtured by the tree's root system, its form and body shaped from the vomit of worms. This new *occupant* would dress like all the others and look like all the others and wave to all the others as it wasted the groundwater by spraying it all over the brand-new driveway that would appear overnight, once they moved Rusty out. It would use automatic weapons to shoot befuddled wildlife that wandered onto the property.

Or maybe it held an *occupant* a long, long time ago, and Rusty simply couldn't remember. But that seemed impossible, so Rusty dismissed that thought.

But still, nothing seemed clear anymore.

Except that nature would defend itself any way it could. Even by becoming the very thing that threatened it.

But not if Rusty could stop it.

He continued to clear away the brush that grew around the ladder. Just as he reached the hatch that would lead him down into the earth, he heard the sirens and the sound of cars pulling up outside.

This arrival made him act with haste. He did not know if those running in his direction came from the same place as Sam Manila and his family and if they would meet him with violence. He did not pause to consider if whatever grew in the nursery below would begin its climb and reach him first. He did not even consider if its occupant had already emerged and taken its place in a house like his own, perhaps so long ago it had forgotten where it came from.

With his machete in hand, he began his descent, prepared to do whatever he needed to do.

The Layover

I don't know how it happened, but at some point, I missed an announcement.

And that can happen in any airport, especially the big ones, with all their loud chatter and their constant, chaotic movement. Even then, someone always comes looking for you. Eventually they find you, gather you up, and get you where you need to go.

Not there, in the lonely, empty place where all this happened. No one came.

Well, not at first. Eventually, *someone* came. Just not who you'd expect. And they came out of the shadows.

Until then, I roamed the airport alone, Drew having vanished into the men's room, thanks to his illness.

It was this illness that led us to take the trip in the first place, as we went in search of yet another miracle cure, this time in Miami, where he was lured by the promise that magnets would forestall the effects of his disease and give him what he deserved—the full life he expected, death at an old age. All that.

But we never made it to Miami, not with the storms that rolled in suddenly that evening and all the electricity in the air. We managed to take off, leading to a turbulent flight on a small plane with just a few other passengers. As the plane dipped, fell, and shook, Drew looked at me from the seat across the aisle and actually said, "Maybe this is how it all ends. This way. Both of us, together."

Maybe I said something reassuring, or maybe I didn't. I don't remember. I only know I prayed my life wouldn't end in a plane crash. A better person would welcome the opportunity to join her dying husband in a fiery death rather than allow him to waste away. Not me. I genuinely prayed we wouldn't fall from the sky, and I breathed a sigh of relief when the pilot's voice came over the loudspeaker, announcing that in order to avoid an endless holding pattern in the sky, we needed to land in nearby Vissaria County.

Vissaria County? Where? All of us on the plane looked at each other to see if we had heard correctly. *What was that name?* No one had heard of it.

But it did have airport. An odd one at that. Mostly just an empty field, with a tower that looked more suited to steering ships away from dangerous harbors than for guiding planes. Its main area resembled a raised train station surrounded by vast areas of standing water. Much of that water covered parts of the runway, so as the plane touched down, it felt as if the plane might ski into the terminal. Having skirted disaster, we disembarked across a wobbly ramp into a dimly lit area, empty except for the passengers of our little plane—just a commuter with a nervous captain, so we hardly cared, so long as our feet touched solid ground.

Right away, Drew started looking for the restroom, giving me an apologetic look that indicated he would take a while. Even without the turbulence of a plane flight, he struggled to control his body's functions. I smiled, hoping to disguise my alarm with understanding. I still struggled to find the right response to this thing that invaded our lives, this disease he carried. I lived in fear of its inevitable end and of what would happen to me when it finally took him. He still didn't believe it would happen and that he would beat it. Instead of planning for a realistic future, we spent our time and money chasing miracles, no matter how far-fetched. How does one say when they can no longer believe in the impossible?

"Just go," I said, "I'll sit."

"Maybe you can get something to eat," he said. He gestured toward the sparse selection of vendors.

"Just for me?"

Again, that apologetic look, followed by my pained smile. We had the routine down. He went into the men's room door, leaving me in a state of self-loathing.

Briefly, I did consider the food. The sign over the vendor said only that: *Food!* Nothing more descriptive than that, and no attempt to inspire beyond the exclamation mark. Only *Food!* you served yourself on gray cafeteria trays. It was all self-service by the look of it. Not inspiring.

And what about something to read and make the time go faster while you enjoy your generic meal? Nothing fit that bill. Instead, I saw another sign that read, *Shoes.*

The flight having killed my appetite, I headed toward the shoes.

And what an odd assortment I found: hundreds of shoes crammed against the wall of the alcove, different styles and types in no clear arrangement, and stranger still, most pairs not even matching. I picked up a sneaker, wondering who arrives at an airport without shoes. As I touched the shoe's material, I smelled it, realizing then that besides being mismatched, none of the shoes were new. All were quite used evidently, judging by their look and smell, and even stranger, worn recently.

I placed the shoe back on the shelf, deciding to take my chance with the food vendor after all, when I noticed a third business across the way. Another simple sign, perhaps all of them designed by the same lazy craftsman. This sign read *Tarot and Palm Reading.* The walls of this alcove looked bare, with no shelves or displays to entice customers. Just a middle-aged man standing in the entrance, wearing the kind of button-down shirt you expect to see on a high school math teacher. Wisps of gray hair covered his head. He noticed me, too, and smiling, he waved for me to come over, as if he wanted to share a secret.

Still thinking of shoes, I looked down toward his feet and saw that he wore none. Only socks.

I smiled back at him, but instead of answering his summons, I sought out the other passengers. They'd all gathered by a window where they could see the shape of the plane through driving rain. Periodic lightning illuminated the scene. Further off stood the tower that looked more like a lighthouse, and I began to feel like a castaway stranded on a desert island.

A woman standing close by turned and faced me. It startled me to see what looked like blood smearing her lips. It took a moment to recognize my error: not blood, but lipstick. Maybe she tried to apply it in mid-flight, a quick freshening up just in case someone had to pull her out of burning wreckage.

"We could've died up there," she said, as if I didn't already know.

I take no pride in my reply. "Maybe we did, and we just don't know it yet." I did my best to look serious. Cue the *Twilight Zone* theme music.

But I wanted to take it back when I saw her reaction. She looked stunned, like she believed it.

"You're saying we're dead, and this is the Afterlife. The Afterlife." Sounding completely credulous, she looked at our surroundings as if seeing them for the first time—the sign for the food, the Tarot reader, the shoes. "Are those *shoes*?" she said, more to herself than to me. Turning on her heel, she went to peruse them, all existential fear apparently evaporated.

Still feeling guilty, I moved away from the others and studied the walls in order to avoid the window. Several rows of photographs lined one area, dozens of them: black-and-white portraits of serious looking men and women, none of them smiling. Their eyes seemed to judge me. Maybe my snarky comment to the woman contained some truth I needed to face, something pertaining to the truth I kept from Drew.

I didn't fear his inevitable death.

I feared the aftermath.

What would happen to me.

Being alone.

We made no plans for that, instead spending our energy fighting the inevitable. Determined to resist to the end, Drew took vitamins no one had ever heard of. He bought into every new quack theory, magnets only the latest. With no thought at all to the burden it would create, he changed his living will to stipulate that doctors should make every attempt to resuscitate him and keep him breathing if he could no longer make decisions for himself.

A flapping noise from overhead distracted my attention. Looking up, I saw the source of the sound—a group of crows hiding in the rafters.

"They've been there forever."

Behind me stood the man dressed like a math teacher. Naturally, he could approach quietly. No shoes on his feet, after all.

I thought he meant the birds, but he gestured to the portraits.

"Ask who they are, and depending on who you talk to, you get different answers. This airfield used to belong to the military before it was turned over for civilian use. Those pictures date back to that earlier time. No one has the heart to take them down. People will say that they memorialize the workers from that era, while others claim they belonged to a secret society. But I have another theory."

Smiling, he stepped closer so that our shoulders touched. "That one," he said, pointing to one of the pictures, "looks suspiciously like Ted Serios, especially around the eyes. Ever hear of him?" I shook my head, and he continued. "Serios could psychically project his own thoughts onto film. In other words, he could form a picture in his mind and have it come out on celluloid. What he was doing here is open to anyone's guess, and mine is that he was involved in some kind of covert military experiment. Involving psychic powers, of course."

Fascinated, I gestured toward the other portraits. "Then all these others . . ."

". . . are all psychics being used in some kind of military project? Your words, not mine." He smiled and held his index finger to his lips. Another flash of lightning from outside revealed shadows on his face I'd not noticed, and his eyes gleamed, but not in the amiable grandfather way I believe he wanted. Judging by his age, he might have been a young man when the photographs were taken. I looked over my shoulder at the Tarot and Palm Reading sign. His eyes followed mine.

He said, "I only get business when there are layovers like yours. I'll give you a great rate."

I laughed, and it sounded forced even to me. "If there's time, maybe later."

He pointed toward the window. Beyond the glass, the lightning revealed wide swathes of water, a virtual flood forming outside.

"There will be a later. Trust me." He started to turn, then paused as if just remembering something. "If they don't reboard your plane," he said in a whisper, "come to me."

Above his head, one of the crows squawked.

"I'm sure we'll reboard," I said.

He looked at me with pity. "Why not come now? Sit down, and I'll give you a hefty discount."

"I'm waiting for my husband. He's—" I gestured toward the men's room. "He's under the weather."

He looked at his watch as if it could verify what I'd said. Then, without another word, he went back to his alcove. He left me with the sense that he didn't really want my business. Then what did he want? A person to talk to? I thought of the woman who went to look at the shoes, wondering if she could offer him the conversation he wanted.

But when I looked to see where she'd gone, I no longer saw her. In fact, the number of other passengers had dwindled when I turned my back.

I knew then that I'd missed some sort of special announcement. Maybe the plane would take off shortly and people would begin returning to their seats. For all I knew, the plane had taken off again, leaving us behind. I returned to the window, seeing nothing but rain pummeling the glass. Then, illuminated by a palpitation of lightning, I saw the plane still sitting there, like a rabbit returned by a crafty magician.

I needed Drew to come out of the men's room, and someone did choose that moment to open the door and step forth. Not Drew, but the pilot, who walked in determined steps toward the boarding platform.

I met him halfway, sure now that I'd missed an announcement. Stepping into his path, I saw his glistening face, his clothes damp with water, as if he'd just stepped in from the outdoors. But I know I saw him come out of the restroom.

I asked him a salvo of questions at once—did he see Drew in there, would a break in the weather allow us to take off again soon, did I miss an announcement?

"Fucking airport," he said, though I had asked nothing about the airport. He wiped moisture from his brow. Not rain, I thought. He stood over the sink and splashed water on his face. One hears of alcoholic pilots who fly inebriated. Maybe we had ourselves one of those, I thought, and he wanted to sober himself up. But that didn't explain the water on his uniform.

"This fucking, fucking airport," he said, as if he thought he didn't have my attention before.

"There was an announcement," I began, "I couldn't hear it." Because I now knew for sure I'd heard one while looking at the photos.

"No announcement," he said. "Have a seat. Read a book."

"No, I heard one. Please, let us back onto the plane."

He looked puzzled, and it took me a second to realize I said *us*, not *me*. I explained that Drew still hadn't come out of the bathroom.

"I thought you were traveling alone," he said.

I blinked. Did a pilot keep track of those things? "He was in there with you," I said. "Maybe you could go back in and check on him for me?"

One of the crows flew over his head, and he swiped at it with his cap, though it never came that close to him. He looked at the cap in his hand, as if it had gone defective. I noticed then his wet, thinning hair, plastered to his scalp.

"Fucking airport," he said, resuming his trek back to the plane. I kept pace next to him, until he stopped and gestured for me to remain back. "No passengers allowed on the plane," he said, not looking back. "Can't you see the lightning? It isn't safe."

"But everyone else is there," I said, now imagining that Drew had returned to his seat.

He turned for one more look at me. "No one's on the plane. Keep listening for an announcement. Get some coffee. It'll be a long night." Then he went out the door, and I heard it lock behind him.

Maybe I needed to heed his advice. I started toward the sign marked *Food!*. At that moment, a short, mousy woman appeared from the back and began pulling down a set of metal shutters. Walking more briskly, I got close enough to speak just as she pulled them down all the way. "Wait, before you lock up—"

Something in her expression prevented me from finishing the sentence. I touched the bars and watched her back away from the shutters. She touched a light switch and receded into the shadows.

She'd locked herself inside. I stood there for several seconds, wondering if she intended to stay in the alcove all night.

"Please," I said to the shadows. "Just a cup of coffee."

"Sorry," said a high voice from the recess of darkness. "It's closing time."

Behind me came the sound of more shutters, this time closing the kiosk with the old shoes. Another woman, petite like the first one, pulled down the metal bars, once more with herself on the inside. One could almost take the two as twins, but this woman didn't look at me as she also vanished into a thick of darkness.

"Over here!"

I wanted the voice to belong to Drew, or even the pilot, but it was the man who tried to tell my fortune. He called to me from where he stood under the Tarot sign, one hand holding his metal gate halfway down. He wanted me to join him.

Something in his voice and attitude told me I needed to obey.

"Hurry!" he said, and I did. I hurried, and I barely stepped over the threshold before he pulled the gate all the way down and locked it. He adjusted a dimmer switch on the wall, bringing down the lights so that the only illumination came from outside the alcove. Patting his shirt pocket, he smiled in a self-deprecating way as he struggled to find what he hoped to locate.

"Matches," he said. "Do you have any?"

"Matches for what?"

From a shelf he took a candle. "The less light, the better. Oh, I remember where they are."

He reached into his pants pocket and produced a book of matches. At that moment, the lights in the concourse dimmed. A spark of light erupted as he lit the candle. The flame revealed his face and a smile of self-satisfaction.

"What's everyone hiding from?" I asked.

"Not hiding," he said. "Not exactly. The light's really just a courtesy. They're not used to bright lights. Not like we are."

"Who do you mean by *they*?"

He held a finger to his lips. "They're coming. We don't really need to whisper. It's not as if they're ears are as sensitive as their eyes, but it seems rude to talk about them. It's better to act as if you don't notice them at all."

From the rafters came the sound of birds, and once more I thought he meant the crows.

But then I saw *them*.

At first, just silhouettes. They came in different sizes, different shapes, slouching forth like sleepwalkers. Because my eyes hadn't yet adjusted to the darkness, I could make out no faces.

His features lit by candle flame, my host said, "They live in the surrounding woods. A great deal of untouched wilderness out there. Excellent for concealment if you don't want to be found, especially by those who once tried to exploit you. People here don't easily forget the wrongs once inflicted on them and their ancestors. I've tried to locate their hideaway—simple curiosity, mind you. I mean them no harm. But they're naturally mistrustful and know how to hide. They use underground bunkers, I believe, carved out of the land in secret decades ago. Remember what I told you about the military using this area. They left behind more than this airport. I would love to find where these people hide. Imagine the secrets they could have in their possession, old documents perhaps. A buried history. You know, I actually found a skeleton on one of my searches."

He waited for my reaction.

"A human skeleton?" I asked, not sure where this conversation would lead.

"Maybe. Its bones were crooked, not from some birth defect or natural deformity, but as if someone used his mind to bend them like a spoon." He gestured toward the shapes of moving people beyond the door. "Don't misunderstand me. I pity them. They have nowhere to go when it rains like this. That's why the authorities open the airport and allow them to come inside. It's a humanitarian action, you see. Beneath the earth, the water would get in and they would drown."

My eyes adjusted so that I could now see faces. Gaunt and pale, ages indistinct, I could believe they lived beneath the earth and away from the sun. I saw one the size of a child, but when the face turned to meet my gaze, I saw the features of an old woman. Next, a stooped, slow-moving man who looked quite young, if thin and hungry. They seemed to wander without a specific destination, though some stopped outside the food area and tried to lift the metal barrier. When it proved unmovable, they seemed to lose interest and moved on.

"I know what you're thinking," my companion said.

"I don't think you do."

"I do. You see this as cruel. If the airport will give them shelter, why not feed them, too?"

"That's not it at all," I said. In fact, I realized I'd forgotten all about Drew. Did he ever emerge from the men's room?

"You *are* thinking it, I'm certain," said the man. "You should admit it."

His insistence made me go cold.

"I can read palms, remember? I can see the future as it's written in cards. I'm quite perceptive. You should let me do your reading."

He seemed closer than I remembered. I could smell his musk, his cheap deodorant.

"I'll give you a good rate. You won't be sorry. I can see things before they happen. I don't even need the cards. I just need to hold your hand."

"I should go," I said. "My husband is out there."

"Your husband? Oh, he's not out there. No one is out there. I mean, no one but them."

At that moment, a clanging sound drew our attention. It came from one of the visitors throwing their body against the gate. I thought it was Drew, until I heard the voice.

"*Clovis. I know that's you. Let me in.*" The figure pressed its face into the bars, revealing the profile of a woman. Something about her head looked wrong, as if the front part of her skull had been removed. That, combined with a witch-like nose, created the impression of a human crow. "*Clovis!*"

I looked at my host and saw fear.

"She means you," I said. "You're Clovis."

He answered by extinguishing the candle. We stood like statues, not daring to breathe.

Finally, the figure peeled itself away from the bars and resumed its trek through the concourse.

He let the silence pass and said, "I know what you're thinking: you can't leave Drew out there. That he needs you."

I said nothing, trying to remember if I had said Drew's name. He didn't need confirmation of the truth.

"But he may already be gone," he continued. "Your plane already departed. If you go out there, you might find yourself caught up with them. There's no coming back from that."

"I need to go," I said. "Open the gate."

He hesitated. "If you insist on it, it's best that they not notice you. You see how they almost seem to float out there. Try to do the same and make no sound."

I shook my head. "That's impossible."

He pointed down. "Take off your shoes and leave them here."

He set the extinguished candle on the ground and began unlocking the gate, knowing already that I would comply. As I untied my shoes, he rolled up the gate only far enough for me to crawl underneath on my hands and knees.

"Go on. Leave."

He lowered the gate before I could even stand. Through the bars we exchanged gazes. In one hand, he held the candle, its wick burning again, though I'd seen him blow it out only moments ago. In the other hand, he held my shoes.

"One last thing," he said. "You won't tell anyone, will you?"

At first, I couldn't discern his meaning. Through the bars, he concentrated his gaze, the candleflame illuminating his face. And then I knew.

"I won't tell anyone your name," I said.

He exhaled his relief. "Thank you. I'll repay you someday. I promise." He blew out the candle and vanished into darkness.

I turned and saw the shadows wandering through the terminal, some together, most of them alone, some stopping, as if frozen in mid-movement, others seeming to glide. Intermittent lighting only made the wells of darkness thicker, allowing just glimpses of pale faces and disproportionate bodies. One bumped into me, and I felt dense, soaked fabric and cold, wet skin. I remembered Clovis' advice and said nothing, instead trying to locate the door to the plane, doing my best to step softly.

But the movement of bodies, along with the darkness, disoriented me. I lost my way. Instead of the door, I found myself near a back wall where stood the woman who spoke Clovis' name from the other side of the gate. Unlike the others, who took no notice of me, she fixed one dark eye on me. I tried to walk away from her, but somehow that only caused us to move closer together, even though she seemed to move not at all. She floated instead.

Now just inches away, I could see her features, including a concave skull. She seemed to possess only one eye, until she turned slightly and I saw a second one on the side of her face, the two orbs so misaligned that she could likely see in two directions at once. She said, "That was Clovis, wasn't it?"

I remembered my promise. Opting not to lie, I said nothing. Just behind her, hidden by her body, I saw the door I sought, the one leading to the plane. I tried to reach the handle by leaning forward. She didn't move. More lightning, and in that instant, her head appeared momentarily normal, proportionate, how she looked before whatever malevolence took place here robbed her of flesh and bone.

When the darkness returned, she said, "Don't believe Clovis. He releases no one. He'll steal everything from you, your very soul if he could. He does it with his voice, his eyes. Controls your feet. Burrows into your skull. Rearranges things. Absorbs everything you have."

My hand touched the doorknob, and I turned it. I tugged at it, but it wouldn't budge. It felt like someone held it from the other side. Somehow, the door's resistance came from her, though her arms remained at her side.

"Has he rearranged you, too?" she asked. "Perhaps only your insides?"

I kept twisting the knob, but it wouldn't open.

"Together, we're strong. Stay with us, you'll be strong, too. Eventually, we'll find him. We won't use the kind of mind tricks he likes when we do. No, we'll use our hands to break his bones. We'll use our teeth. He'll die from a thousand bites. You can have one of them."

Another tug, and the door opened, but not far enough for me to step through. I continued pulling as I heard her say: "Bring me. Take me with you."

Stupidly, I thought of the seat on the plane next to me.

"But Drew," I said, though she couldn't know who I meant. I would find him on the plane. Or so I told myself. Anything to excuse myself from looking.

"Come back for me. Promise." She regarded me with a black, bulging eye.

"Okay," I said, making yet another guarantee I couldn't fulfill.

"I'll wait right here," she said, and only then did the door open.

On the other side stood the pilot. He shut the door quickly behind me. Still wet and exhausted, he glared at me as he turned a key to lock it. "There you are. You've delayed us long enough. We almost left you. But your husband . . ."

"He's on board then."

"Everyone's on board," he said, "except you."

I followed the pilot to the open hatchway.

"Is it safe to fly?" I asked.

"*Is it safe*, the tardy lady wants to know. Yes, it's plenty safe." He slouched toward the cockpit, not looking at me. "Find your seat."

I surveyed the passenger area, seeing a person in every seat except for my own, the one across from Drew. Even the ones I knew were empty before. Every face except Drew's looked at me with reproach. None of them looked familiar. I looked for the woman I frightened earlier but couldn't find her.

Smiling, Drew watched me buckle my seatbelt. Immediately, the plane began taxiing.

"What happened to your shoes?" he asked.

I didn't know how to answer. I made up something about losing track of time. "I missed an announcement," I said as I studied the other faces, most still turned toward me. Bluish lightning illuminated their disdain as the rain hammered the wings of the plane, trying to break it apart.

"I don't know where you went," said Drew, "but I had an amazing experience while you were . . . well, wherever you were. I know it's crazy, but I don't think we need Miami anymore. Something happened back there. A miracle." He paused so that I could absorb that word. Then he said, "I think I'm cured."

I studied the relieved joy in his face, struggling to understand. Had I, without realizing it, traded something more than my shoes? He seemed to sense none of the ambivalence I felt. He didn't notice how I hesitated to reach across the aisle and hug him or even squeeze his hand. His face remained frozen in a smile that showed too many teeth. One of his eyes seemed bigger than the other and much too large for his face.

Clotlice

elba and Charlie wouldn't stay away from the trees, no matter what their mother said. And she had good reasons for this rule. Their new house sat on a lot of recently cleared woods, and though they did have a few neighbors, most of the surrounding area remained wild with untamed animals and trees where they could hide. All those undeveloped lots filled with nature made home builders salivate with desire, but no matter how fast they cleared the woods, so many trees remained. After just a week of living in their new house, the mother of Melba and Charlie saw a pair of bobcats walk across their front lawn. Charlie and Melba heard their mother gasp in awe from where she stood at the front window with her glass of wine, and even though they ran as fast as they could, they missed seeing the bobcats for themselves.

"They were huge," said their mother, "and hungry looking."

"We want to see them, too," said the children.

"Well, you can't now. They've gone away. Just as well. There's not much land for them to hunt on anymore."

Still, when Charlie and Melba played outside on the swing-set their father built only for them (such a nice thing for a father to do, especially one who worked all day during the week and had so little spare time), they often stopped to go stand where the lawn ended and the woods began, hoping to see the bobcats. Whenever their mother saw them doing that, she would yell at them through the window, usually as she cleaned her wine glass.

"Get away from there!" she'd say, and the children generally obeyed, but eventually one of them would forget and wander back over.

In this way, Melba saw the face for the first time, peering back at her from the thick brush.

The face frightened her at first, so she let out a scream, but she didn't run away. Her scream drew Charlie's curiosity. He stopped swinging and walked over to see what caused the commotion. It startled him, too, but he didn't scream.

The face that looked at them smiled widely, and its teeth looked big and white. Its eyes looked big, too, only they had yellow coloring. The head seemed too small for such great eyes and such large teeth, and it contained no hair at all, not even eyebrows.

Over her initial shock, Melba leaned in so that she could study the stark paleness of the thing. Because the eyes didn't blink, she mistook it for a Halloween mask some older kid might wear. She even started to reach for it.

"Boo!" the face said, barely moving the lips that formed its wide smile, the mouth open just wide enough for her to see the white teeth, so long and crowded together.

Both of them jumped back, but only Charlie ran. As the oldest by more than a year, Melba shook off her alarm and once more leaned in. Small things didn't scare her, not even the bugs that made her brother groan in disgust. She would even keep spiders and lizards as pets if her mother allowed her to do so. This strange face didn't belong to anything large. It didn't look capable of standing, appearing limited to crawling through the sticks and dirt like a snake. And snakes didn't scare Melba, not even when they had a face like this one.

She leaned in for a closer look, even as the face continued to leer and grin. As she did so, she sensed Charlie come up cautiously behind her so that he could watch over her shoulder.

"Are you a kid?" asked Melba, not sure if she heard it speak or not. She picked up a broken branch in case she needed to defend herself.

"Yes," said the face, its grin like something carved in rock.

"Where's your mom and dad?" Melba asked.

The face's eyes moved slightly, not quite in sync with one another, as if this strange thing didn't yet know how to use them properly. One eye seemed to track Charlie, who now stood next to Melba.

"They're gone," the face said. "They abandoned me. And I'm not even done growing."

A thicket of shrubs covered the area behind the body. Melba used the branch in her hand to move them aside in order to get a better look. Now she could see that the face belonged to a body resembling a trail of snot, the kind you blew out of your nose after a gigantic sneeze. Charlie peered at it, too, and his lip curled in disgust, but Melba found it interesting. Using great caution, she poked it gently with her stick, realizing that it wasn't a gob of snot at all. Instead, it seemed more like a clear plastic baggie filled with what looked like chicken grease. She pressed it harder, wondering if she might puncture the clear exterior. She only managed to move the greasy substance around.

The expression on the face didn't change a bit, though it made what sounded like a cry of pain.

"Don't hurt it," Charlie said. Though Charlie hated bugs and spiders, he also didn't like seeing them harmed in any way.

Even though Melba remained curious and didn't share Charlie's level of sympathy, she obeyed his command and stopped pressing with the stick. The thing's body returned to its former shape, though it still looked more liquid than solid.

"Hungry," it said. "Need food to grow."

Charlie couldn't listen to anyone so much as mention food without becoming hungry himself. He reached into the pocket of his shorts and withdrew a small bag of fruit snacks. He began eating them. Turning away from the face on the ground, Melba watched him eat for a moment before sticking out her hand. "Give me one," she said.

Charlie hesitated. He didn't like sharing his fruit snacks.

Once more, the face's lidless eyes shifted slightly, moving from Melba to Charlie then back to Melba. "Hungry," it said again, but more insistently this time.

That proved enough to make Charlie hand a single fruit snack to Melba. Growing braver, Melba reached out with the tips of her fingers and placed the fruit snack in front of the thing's mouth. Without losing the semblance of a grin, it opened its mouth just enough to show her all its teeth.

"Be careful," said Charlie.

But Melba didn't require a warning. She had no intention of losing a finger to this creature, though she had begun to pity it and wouldn't deny it a treat. Both children breathed a sigh of relief when it gently took the fruit snack from Melba's fingers and ate it.

"More!" it said when it finished.

Melba extended her hand to Charlie, who reluctantly surrendered another fruit snack. And so on, several more times, until Charlie ran out of snacks altogether.

"More!" it said again, its smile fixed and eternal, like its hunger.

"We don't have anymore," said Melba. "You ate them all. It's time for you to go home and for us to go inside."

Its eyes shifted back and forth between them again. Other than its eyes and mouth, it seemed incapable of going anywhere.

"You ought to go home," Melba said, despite growing certain it couldn't obey her command.

"No home," it said.

"No home?" Charlie asked, because in Charlie's world, everything and everyone had a home.

No reply from the creature. In the silence, its eyes roamed their faces.

"What's your name?" asked Melba.

"Bonemash," it said.

"Bonemash?" Melba repeated, having never heard such a name.

"Marrowslice," it said. Hardly giving them any time at all to react, it burst out with another name. "Bloodrazor." Then more rapidly, one name after another, "Tissuecrack, Slitgristle, Veintwist, Shitpipe." The children laughed at this last one, and it stopped with the ridiculous names long enough to gaze upon their reaction. Then, with solemnity, it said, "No. My name is

Clotlice."

"Your parents named you *Clotlice*," asked Melba, still laughing a bit from hearing it say *Shitpipe.*

It didn't answer, at least not directly. "Clotlice," said the strange creature.

The children regarded this being they would soon come to know as Clotlice, taking in its puzzling form and nearly fixed face.

Before they could exchange any more words with it, they heard their mother calling them. Charlie started to run ahead of her, but Melba stopped him. "Don't say anything about Clotlice," she said, holding on to his arm. Charlie looked at her with imploring eyes. How would he get more fruit snacks unless he told their mother how Clotlice ate them all? Sensing his hesitation, Melba repeated her command. "Not a word." Only when he nodded did she let go of his arm. Then, before following after Charlie, she covered Clotlice's face with a handful of leaves so no one else could find and steal their amazing discovery.

* * *

The next day it rained, so they couldn't go outside. Instead, they had to listen to their mother pace about the living room with the phone pressed to her ear. "Again?" their mother said to the phone, "you have to stay late again?" As their mother listened to the reply, she took a big gulp from the glass of wine she held.

That conversation ended without another word, but it rained again the next day, confining them to the indoors once again. Their mother drank more wine and had another angry phone conversation, one in which she demanded to know some woman's name. Finally, on the third day, the bad weather lifted, and their mother allowed them to go out into the yard while she remained in bed.

At first, Melba couldn't find Clotlice and worried that he'd gone away, or that someone had stolen him, or perhaps all the rain turned his flimsy body to goo. Then she realized that she had merely hid him too well. Clearing away some brush and a fallen branch, she found him in the exact spot where she left him.

Once more, she regarded his strange fixed smile and viscous, slug-like body with amazement, though she didn't poke him this time.

"Hungry," Clotlice said like before. He hardly looked at Melba at all. Instead, he seemed to focus on Charlie.

Charlie took out his fruit snacks, but Melba waved him off. Instead, she removed a plastic bag she'd hidden inside her pocket. "Do you like meat?" she asked Clotlice.

Clotlice's notable eyes seemed to grow wider as it gazed at what the bag held. It contained a piece of baked chicken that she'd stolen away the night before. Fortunately, they had extra since their father didn't make it home to eat dinner with them. For the past few nights they'd seen so little of their father, though they barely noticed, what with the excitement of having discovered Clotlice.

"Feed me," Clotlice said.

Melba paused to consider the forcefulness of this request. Finally, she reached into the bag and tore off a piece of meat. Then she knelt and held it out for Clotlice to take.

"In my mouth," he said.

So Melba reached further, and he took the meat from her fingers.

"More!" said Clotlice after he swallowed.

Melba tore off another piece, then another after that, handfeeding them one after the other to Clotlice, until none of it remained. On the final piece, he bit Melba's finger. She called out in pain and looked at the resulting gash as it began welling with blood. Although blood didn't frighten her, not even her own blood, Melba hated pain. She began sucking the blood from her fingers, and when the coppery taste made her gag, she spit it out. With her other hand, she picked up the stick she used the other day to poke Clotlice. She held it up and considered beating Clotlice to death with it.

"Is it bad?" asked Charlie. "Did he bite it off?"

During that tense moment, Clotlice regarded her with his frozen grin. "Thirsty," he said.

It took Melba a moment to realize what he meant: the blood from her finger. He wanted to lick it.

"You'll bite me again," she said.

"Can smell it. Need it to grow," Clotlice said.

"Grow?" asked Charlie. The way things grew interested him greatly, and he always had many questions about plants and animals and how they grew.

"Grow strong," said Clotlice. His eyes shifted to Charlie. "You."

"Me?" Charlie looked at Melba with disbelief.

Melba put down her stick and considered the situation. Though the bite had hurt, she'd become used to Clotlice's appearance, and even if she would never describe his demeanor as friendly, she now likened him to the cartoon characters that she and Charlie enjoyed as they waited for their mother to wake from one of her long naps.

She said, "Give me your hand, Charlie."

"What? No." Charlie hid his hands under his armpits.

"It doesn't really hurt." She felt a little guilty for the lie. Yet, as she reminded herself, the bite hurt much less now, so technically she told the truth.

"No," Charlie said again. He started to walk back toward the house, but Melba grabbed him by the wrist. Charlie called out in surprise. Melba never, or almost never, treated him severely. In fact, she often coddled him in ways their parents did not, and Charlie loved being coddled.

Before Charlie could add any more protest, she pulled his hand down to Clotlice's mouth.

"Gently," she ordered Clotlice as he opened wide.

But Clotlice wasn't gentle.

Charlie screamed.

"Let go, let go, let go!" cried Charlie over and over, his index finger caught between Clotlice's teeth.

For a moment, Melba didn't know what to do. She thought she heard the crack of bone, and it seemed all but certain that Clotlice would bite off Charlie's finger. Charlie thrashed and Melba considered grabbing him by the shoulders—but what would happen then? If she pulled him back, his finger would surely come off inside Clotlice's mouth. And Clotlice showed no signs of letting go.

But he finally did let go.

Wailing, Charlie fell back against her. With his weight upon her, Melba struggled to sit upright. When she finally did, Charlie moaned as she studied his finger.

Charlie proved most fortunate in that Clotlice didn't bite off his finger.

But two deep gashes now marked it and blood poured forth. Charlie himself looked very pale.

All these things made Melba angry. Never mind the fact that she forced Charlie to put his finger into Clotlice's mouth. She disregarded that important fact as she got to her feet and picked up her stick once more. Determined to use it to beat Clotlice to death, she marched over to him.

She paused when she saw him. Eventually, she lowered the stick and watched him in wonder.

Clotlice's delicate body pulsed as currents of red fluid now replaced the colorless snot-like substance that formerly comprised his insides. Melba wondered what it would feel like to have such a body, with everything visible to the naked eye. Clotlice grinned at her as she watched. Once, her father ran over a toad sitting in their driveway. All of its insides came out of its mouth when the front tire crushed its body, giving Melba the opportunity to study organs. Melba could even see its little heart, miraculously undamaged, sitting in a pool of twisted organs. Before anyone could stop her, she picked it up and it actually beat once in the palm of her hand.

Clotlice, on the other hand, seemed to have nothing that looked like a heart. No lungs either, or anything that looked like an organ of any kind. Just a sack of fluids that, by the look of it, now consisted mostly of Charlie's blood.

"Come see," said Melba to Charlie.

Charlie whimpered and held his bloody finger, but he obeyed. He stopped whimpering when the saw the amazing thing happening with Clotlice's body. Despite his disconcerting grin, he now looked beautiful, almost like the lava lamp they saw in their Uncle Benjamin's apartment one time, only less defined in shape. Charlie even stopped fretting about the gashes on his finger. Melba forgot all about them.

"Growing," said Clotlice.

* * *

And grow he did. For one thing, he began growing a rib cage consisting of tiny white bones that began covering his nearly liquid body. He still had no arms or legs, but tiny nubs began forming alongside the rib cage, eight of them in all, and Melba speculated that from them Clotlice might grow a pair of arms and a pair of legs.

The children observed these developments inside the house, where they'd smuggled Clotlice into the Melba's room. Charlie seemed wary about this at first, and he only agreed to keep it a secret after he received assurances that Clotlice would never, under any circumstances, come into his own room. He also refused to touch Clotlice's body, forcing Melba to lift the strange creature herself. "He feels like a bag of grapes," she said, "if you squooshed all the grapes into juice." All except his face, of course, which felt like a lump of clay molded with the edge of a sharp knife.

Clotlice allowed her to lift him and fortunately refrained from biting her fingers. He seemed to like the idea of going inside their house and not getting left outside anymore.

Of course, their mother eventually wanted to know what happened to their fingers. Not at first though. It took her a couple of days to notice. In that time, Melba had taken Charlie into the bathroom, where she poured peroxide on his bleeding finger. He squirmed and complained about it stinging while this happened, but she forced him to stand still. "Stop crying," she said. "This'll make it better."

Clinging to that promise, Charlie stopped crying, and Melba used to a band-aid to cover the gashes on his finger. Afterwards, she did the same for her own wound, pouring peroxide on it over the sink (it did sting indeed), likewise applying a band-aid to herself when she finished.

Their mother noticed the band-aids during a meal of macaroni and cheese.

Melba earned her attention by asking for a hot dog instead. She liked mac and cheese just fine, but she wanted a hot dog to feed Clotlice. He liked meat. And blood, of course, but Melba didn't feel like giving him any of her blood.

Their mother didn't answer the request at first. Lately, she looked tired, like she'd stayed up all night, and instead of a bowl of food, a glass of red wine sat on the table in front of her. Since she seemed to not hear Melba at first, staring off into space instead, Melba repeated her question.

At that, their mother seemed to notice Melba for the first time, gazing into her face like she'd just popped into existence. Instead of replying, she focused on Melba's bandaged finger. Then she looked at Charlie and his finger. Though Melba's band-aid looked fresh, Charlie's appeared red with fresh blood threatening to seep through from underneath.

"What happened to you two?" Though her voice slurred a bit, she did sound concerned.

"Nothing," Melba started to say, but Charlie spoke up too quickly.

"We got bit."

"*Bit?*" said their mother. "Bit by what?"

"Nothing," Melba said. "It was a squirrel, I think."

A *squirrel*," their mother said, as if she'd never even heard of squirrels. Then her eyes got wide. She tried to stand up from her chair, but the wine had made her clumsy and she fell back into her seat. "Charlie, come to me. A squirrel? Jesus. It could be rabid."

Charlie avoided Melba's poisonous glare as he left his half-eaten bowl to approach his mother. She held his hand and began unwrapping the band-aid. Her lip curled, and she groaned at what she saw.

"This looks infected."

Melba stood up and came over to see what she meant. The cut on Charlie's finger looked glistening and purple, with white pus coming out of it. "Jesus. You need to stay away from squirrels or rats or whatever it is that you're playing with. Melba, let me see yours."

But Melba had already taken off her own band-aid in order to assess her cut. Hers didn't look as bad, though it looked a little red. She remembered how when Clotlice bit her, she began sucking the wound immediately, whereas she made Charlie leave his finger in Clotlice's mouth. She couldn't remember if Charlie sucked on it afterwards.

"You're going to have to go to the doctor," said their mother. "But I can't take you now. I don't feel good. Melba, go get the band-aids and the peroxide. We need to clean you both up, pronto."

Melba obeyed. But when she returned, she found their mother asleep on the couch while Charlie sat at his dinner chair, no longer eating but staring at his finger with great concern.

"I think there's something wiggling around in the white stuff," Charlie said. "Is that the rabies?"

"You don't have rabies," said Melba, though she had no idea if Charlie did or even if she herself did for that matter. "Come with me."

Using the kitchen sink, she once more poured peroxide over Charlie's wound. This time, Charlie didn't complain. From the sofa they could hear their mother snoring and mumbling something in her sleep.

"Does that kill all the rabies?" Charlie asked when she finished. Once more, Melba told him he didn't have rabies. She sent him back to finish his meal with a freshly bandaged finger. As for Melba, she lost her appetite, something which never happened with Charlie, so she went in search of a hot dog or something other kind of meat to bring Clotlice. Even if Clotlice gave them some disease, she still felt responsible for him. She wondered if mothers felt such heavy responsibility. In a weird way, she thought of herself that way: a mother to Clotlice.

It turned out that they had very little food left in the fridge, just bottles of wine.

So Melba took her bowl of unfinished mac and cheese back to her bedroom. She sat on the floor and lifted the skirt to her bed and called Clotlice's name.

The tiny protrusions on the side of Clotlice's gelatinous body had grown more, and he could use them to walk quite easily now. He did so like a spider on eight nub-like legs. His grinning face appeared under the bed, almost glowing, proud of his new-found ability to walk.

She showed him the mac and cheese.

"Are you hungry?" she asked.

"Oh, yes."

She took a macaroni noodle and held it out, but he wouldn't take it.

"Smell something better," he said.

Melba looked around her room. What he could possibly smell, she had no idea. The pile of clothes over-flowing in her hamper needed washing, and everything smelled like damp earth.

"This is all I have," said Melba.

Clotlice made a noise, almost the sort that their mother used to make when Melba made up an excuse for why she didn't clean her room. Lately, she left her room messy, but their mother didn't seem to care anymore.

Clotlice cluttered further out from under the bed, his bony legs moving him about like some kind of beetle. His over-sized head titled slightly, and his eyes moved in different directions, as if he needed to focus on more than one thing at a time. In lighting kept dim the way Clotlice preferred, Melba could see how the rib cage had grown almost completely around the sac of his body, and through the gaps in bone, she could see something dark and purple, pulsing like a tiny heart.

Clotlice passed her and went through the doorway and into the hall. Never had he ventured out so far, so his hunger must have become considerable. His boldness made Melba nervous, but she reminded herself that her mother probably wouldn't wake up for some time.

She followed as Clotlice scuttled toward the master bedroom. It looked just as messy as Melba's room. Clotlice paid no attention to the clutter. Instead, he veered toward the bathroom.

"In here," he said.

"This is where people pee and take showers," Melba said.

"In here," he said again. She followed his eyes and saw that he'd fixed his gaze on a waste basket.

"That's garbage."

"*In here!*" he said, his tone insistent and impatient.

Melba sighed and looked in the waste basket, which contained nothing more than a big wad of toilet paper. She could sense Clotlice's fixed smile boring into her back. For the first time, she felt afraid of disappointing him, so she picked up the wad of toilet paper. At the same time, Clotlice tapped one of his legs in anticipation. Melba opened the paper and found a piece of rolled cotton covered in blood.

"Yes," Clotlice said.

Melba didn't like holding the thing. It smelled funny. Not exactly unpleasant, but dark and earthy.

She held it out to Clotlice and watched as his jaw opened. He took the bloody cotton between his teeth and slouched back to Melba's room.

Melba saw no choice but to follow.

* * *

For the next few days, Melba managed to feed Clotlice by finding these wands of bloody cotton in her mother's waste basket. Eventually, she felt less revulsion to bringing the toilet paper back to her room and unwrapping it for Clotlice, who licked and sucked away all the blood. Afterwards, Melba wrapped the remaining cotton back up in the toilet paper and returned it to the waste basket so that her mother wouldn't become suspicious.

Of course, her mother hardly ever emptied and basket anymore, but eventually, Melba stopped finding the wads of toilet paper.

Over the course of that time, Clotlice grew even more, each of his legs growing out further and his whole form becoming longer and fatter. The ribs now encased his delicate body like a hard shell.

The first time Melba failed to bring him any blood-saturated cotton, he began to shake in anger. The fit climaxed with Clotlice standing on two of his back legs, the other six extending out like six wiggly arms, slashing the air in fury. Nearby stood Charlie, and Melba gasped when she realized that in an upright position, Clotlice stood taller than her brother.

"Hungry," Clotlice said, his voice now lower, more sonorous. At the end of each of his bony arms grew razor-like claws.

"There isn't any more. There simply isn't," said Melba.

For a moment, Melba thought that he would accept this fact. After all, she'd mothered Clotlice, a good thing considering how his own parents (what they must've looked like, she wondered) abandoned him in the woods. She would never intentionally deprive him of a meal, even such a gross meal. She thought she'd proven herself to be a good surrogate mother to this strange creature, and, to a lesser degree, Charlie had played the role of father to it. Not that Charlie actually did much, though Melba didn't exactly know what fathers did in general, not having seen her own father in several days.

Charlie wobbled and watched the stand-off between Melba and Clotlice with half-lidded eyes. He looked so sleepy lately, even though he slept all the night through, and most of the morning, too. Just this morning she applied a new band-aid to the festering wound on his finger. Charlie no longer complained about how it hurt, nor about the tiny wiggling things that came out of it and dropped onto the floor. Melba's own finger had healed just fine.

"There's nothing to eat," she said authoritatively, "nothing for anyone. Go back under the bed, or I'll throw you outside in the woods!"

Face grinning, Clotlice fixed both eyes on her and said nothing.

"A bobcat'll eat you," she said, hoping the threat would elicit a response, any response. In truth, she didn't think the teeth of a wild bobcat could penetrate Clotlice's armor-like exterior.

Clotlice moved his gaze from her to Charlie. "Hungry," he said once more. As if in agreement, Charlie nodded, his eyes vacant and sleepy. Snot ran down his face, and he didn't bother wiping it away. Some of it dropped onto the floor. Melba looked down and saw what looked like tiny worms swimming in the mucous.

It happened in that moment of looking away.

Clotlice sprang upon Charlie. Charlie screamed.

Panicking, Melba began clawing at Clotlice, pulling at his multiple arms that now wrapped around Charlie, his face buried in the boy's neck. It took so much effort to peel away one arm that Melba didn't know how she could possibly do it to all eight of them. Charlie's screams became low groans, and Melba nearly surrendered to the terrible truth that she couldn't help her dear, sweet Charlie, when Clotlice looked up as if he suddenly sensed something else. They he quickly bounded away from Charlie, who lay on the floor, shivering the bleeding from his throat. Meanwhile, Clotlice scuttled away on all eight legs out her door.

Melba didn't know what to do. She pulled the blanket off her bed and wrapped it around Charlie, but he kept shivering, his eyes now wide, staring up at the ceiling. So much blood flowed out of his neck. Tears ran down his face, and in the glistening wetness Melba could see more wiggling bodies, like a million tiny Clotlices. Was this how he was born and came into being?

To help stop the blood, she took one of the dirty shirts from the floor and wrapped it tightly around Charlie's neck.

Once Charlie stopped shivering, Melba decided she needed to punish Clotlice. Mothers did that often, and if she was Clotlice's real mother, she would punish him good for hurting her baby brother. In her closet, she kept a set of kid-sized golf clubs. At one point, her father told her he'd teach her how to play, but they never got around to it. She took the biggest club and went looking for Clotlice.

She found him in the living room, at the foot of the couch where her mother still slept. He crawled up her legs and sniffed at the cleft between her legs. Melba's mother wore a pair of jeans, and much to Melba's relief, she didn't seem to notice Clotlice at all. She just went on snoring.

Melba couldn't explain it, but just seeing her mother like that, unable to wake, made her feel even more rage. She swung that stupid golf club and struck Clotlice square in the middle of his bony carapace. Despite how well it fortified him, he actually bleated as if the blow caused him pain. He fell to the side of the sofa, and even as he continued to grin, Melba detected a look of surprise in his expression. He laid on his side like a tired rat, his legs wiggling as if he wanted to run but couldn't.

Melba dropped the golf club and felt the tears coming on. She couldn't stop them, so she just cried. She crawled onto the sofa and tried to wrap herself in her mother's arms. But those arms wouldn't embrace her, and her mother went on snoring.

When Melba could stay like that no longer, she looked down to see what had become of Clotlice and if she'd killed him.

She discovered him gone.

* * *

Such a flurry of excitement when her mother did finally wake up.

"Where'd he go, Melba? You need to tell me. This is serious. I rely on you two to look after each other."

Except Melba couldn't tell her what she already knew. If she did, her mother would hold her responsible.

As her mother slept, Melba had gone back into bedroom to see if Charlie felt better. She had a terrible feeling as she walked down the hallway. Silently, she prayed she wouldn't find Charlie dead.

Instead, she found a bundle of dirty, torn linen, the remains of Charlie's clothes.

Clotlice had come back to finish the job, apparently. Either he'd dragged Charlie off somewhere to do so, or he devoured him whole right there, leaving not a drop of blood or scrap of flesh. Just the clothes. He ripped them apart, but couldn't eat them, apparently.

Now, Melba stood silently before her mother, looking at her feet.

"Look at me. Was *he* here?"

Melba lifted her head as commanded, and it took everything she had not to cry. Charlie, Charlie, gone forever.

"Was he?" her mother asked, shaking her now.

The strangest notion came over Melba. By *he* she meant Clotlice. What a relief if her mother knew about Clotlice all along. Melba wanted to say, *Yes, yes, I brought him in, it's all my fault, don't hate me.*

Before she could, her mother said, "Daddy. He came in, didn't he? He took Charlie right out from under my nose."

For the first time in so long, her mother looked clear-eyed, so Melba didn't answer. She let her mother continue.

"I know I've been . . . well, out of it. I know I've left so much up to you. I just, I just—" Her voice trailed off and her eyes closed as she began stroking Melba's hair. Melba leaned into her mother's hand, feeling the smooth caresses. "Things are going to change. Once I get Charlie back from that no-good father of yours. They really will. You'll see." Then her eyes got wide, almost as wide as Clotlice's. "Oh, god, your finger." She grabbed Melba's wrist and studied her hand. "We never did anything about your finger. We never did anything about *Charlie's*. Jesus, I'm such a fuck-up, Melba. If your daddy sees that infection on Charlie, he'll call Child Protective Services. It's just the sort of thing he'd do. Anything to make me look bad. Your finger looks okay, though."

"It doesn't hurt," Melba said. She pulled her hand away from her mother. Her mother held empty air before putting her own hand down. "It's all better."

"I see that. I do. But . . ." Her mother seemed to watch something far off in the distance. "I need to go somewhere. Don't worry, I'll be back soon. I promise baby. Your daddy's playing games, and that means I have to play them, too. He caught me by surprise, and now I'm doing the same to him. Just remember that I love you, Melba. And I love Charlie."

"I love Charlie, too," said Melba, trying not to cry.

She watched her mother leave, and then she went into her bedroom, where she stretched out on her bed and watched the ceiling.

* * *

She must have closed her eyes at some point. She found herself awakening from a dream in which she struggled to hold Charlie still in the bathtub while trying to scrub him clean. *They're coming out of me everywhere*, Charlie said in the dream, meaning the tiny white things that crawled from his nose, his ears, his mouth, even the tear ducts from his eyes. When seen up close, each one of those tiny creatures had a sac-like body and a grinning face, just like Clotlice.

It took her moment to realize what caused her to awaken: her father, leaning over the bed, shaking her.

"Where are they, Melba?" he asked her.

At first, she didn't know who he meant. Her father's face no longer looked clean-shaven. *Maybe he's trying to grow a beard*, she thought. He also smelled differently. Some kind of cologne, she guessed.

"Your mother. Charlie. They're not here. Your mother called me, saying some things that just didn't make sense. She said I took Charlie somewhere. But I didn't."

Melba had become so unused to seeing her father that she couldn't stop looking at him. So fixed on her father's appearance she became that she nearly missed seeing the movement in the shadows behind him. Her wore a brand-new coat dotted with rain drops. Apparently, it was raining when he came inside.

He went on: "She's not well, your mommy. I know it's hard to understand, but she's gotten sick. Not with sneezing or coughing. A sickness that adults get that makes them confused."

"She misses you," said Melba. "That's why she drinks too much wine." She started to say something about the shadows behind him, but he cut her off.

"I know. It's not her fault. It's mine. We just couldn't live with each other, but I didn't realize how . . . off she was. I know it's hard to understand, Melba," he said, not bothering to ask if she understood, which she did, "but that's why this place is such a disaster. She went after someone, a new friend of mine. Mommy confronted that new friend at the place where she works. She demanded to know where Charlie was. It was—"

He didn't get to finish.

Melba now realized why the shadows seemed to move behind him.

As large as an adult now, Clotlice could still move quietly, slinking around walls and corners and even cling to the ceiling itself, all without disturbing a single mote of dust.

That is, not until he fell upon Melba's father, wrapping six of his bony appendages around him. Melba's father looked about in confusion, not able to see what held him, not able to see the wide googly eyes as big as saucer plates, or the mouth that opened impossibly wide with razor-sharp teeth, so long and wide now that they could cut off all of Melba's fingers with one bite.

Just before those teeth embedded themselves into her father's neck, Melba ran. She ran tot eh back of the house, toward the door that led outside, trying not to hear her father call after her, begging for help.

* * *

Hidden behind a stand of shrubs, her hair matted down from the rain, Melba watched the house. The wind blew the swings on the playset back and forth. That same wind caused an empty packet of fruit snacks to tumble her way. When she saw it, Melba realized that she'd crouched in the same spot where she and Charlie once found Clotlice.

She remained there, afraid to move, losing track of time. She desperately wished her mother would come outside and find her. Her stomach rumbled, so she picked up the fruit snack package, just to verify that it didn't have anything left inside.

But it proved empty, just as she suspected. As she returned it to the wind, she saw the back door open, and her hopes surged as she saw a familiar figure step forth.

Her father.

It seemed impossible, given what she witnessed, but perhaps she dreamed the whole thing. He couldn't have survived, could he? She saw him from the back as he stood outside in his new coat, looking off in the other direction, his collar turned up to protect him from the wind and rain.

Then he turned, and Melba realized her mistake.

Not her father at all.

Clotlice. So tall. So grown. Standing upright, so her father's coat fit him perfectly.

As he turned, Clotlice saw her and walked toward her, taking his time. He knew she wouldn't run, just as she knew she couldn't out-run him. Especially not if he decided to use all his legs, no, not at all. But for now, he kept the other legs folded around his torso, making him look larger and more muscular. He'd put his two upper legs through the sleeves of the coat and used them like arms. If you could disregard the white, bony head with the huge grinning mouth and wide staring eyes, he would almost look like a normal person. So weird considering how he started as something so small.

When he reached her, he bent down to her level so that they could study each other.

Clotlice spoke first. "Hungry?"

Melba at first heard the word as a demand, so used to his insatiable desires and need to eat. She almost failed to register the word as a question.

"Yes," she said. "I'm so hungry." She didn't know why she bothered answering. What could Clotlice do about that, especially after he'd taken everything away from her.

But he did something surprised Melba. With one bony claw, he reached into her father's coat and pulled out a packet of peanuts, the kind her father liked to snack upon. He held it out to her.

And Melba accepted.

He watched as she tore it open and ate them all quickly. When she finished, she looked at him. He stood now but kept a respectful distance.

"More?" he asked.

"Yes, I want more."

With that, he unfolded the four appendages under the coat and spread form the ones he used as arms. With the salty taste of the peanuts in her mouth, Melba regarded the weird, fixed grin on Clotlice's face, the unblinking eyes. It took her a moment to realize what he meant for her to do.

After a moment's hesitation, she did what he wanted.

No.

What *she* wanted.

She stood and wrapped her arms around his bony body and felt his six arms gently wrap around her at once. He didn't have the warmth she craved. In fact, he felt quite cold. But it would do, it would suffice.

They stood like so for several moments.

Clotlice was the first to let go. Then Melba.

Together, they went back inside.

Sounds to Make You Shiver

Call me a haunter of haunts.

I attend every so-called haunted attraction within reach, from the carefully orchestrated ones that occur every fall in theme parks, to the more disreputable ones that spring up in fair grounds and decaying strip malls. It doesn't matter if they reflect the careful craftsmanship of professionals, with sophisticated animatronics and special effects, or the slipshod work of cynical hucksters out to make a buck. I find them all.

And I always go alone, mingling with jovial, good-natured crowds of people eager for a good fright. They treat me like a ghost, giving me a wide berth, perhaps sensing I've come for something else, not the thrills and frights they hope to experience. I don't set out to dampen the mood around me. My simple presence does it. A certain demeanor about me, I suppose, one that doesn't belong on the midways decorated with pumpkins and orange lights. Busy night, slow night, it doesn't matter. I still show up.

Lately, I see more and more amateurs trying to make a name for themselves in the industry, their handicap usually less about money and resources than about artistry, or the lack of. They overcompensate with gallons of fake blood, inane screaming, and loud chainsaws, their mazes oversaturated with clamor and chaos, revealing a vital misunderstanding of the most important principles of the haunt—that it often comes down to what you don't show and what your audience *hears* rather than sees.

Not that I show up for the haunts themselves. Instead I come out of some vain hope I'll find someone inside. I want to find *her*.

I even go the haunts where they insist on signed waivers, the type run anonymously from some abandoned building or unmarked warehouse. They involve the same standard procedure: I show up alone and meet some towering goon with a shaved head, his bulk and muscle squeezed into a blazer at least a size too small.

Like the one I meet now.

He regards me with his hands folded at his waist, his stance wide, positions meant to create an imposing image before I even enter the building. He doesn't greet me as I approach. Instead, he asks me for identification before he pats me down. Once he verifies that I'm carrying no weapons, he opens the warehouse door and indicates that I should precede him inside.

I find myself in an office with bare furnishings, where a smartly dressed woman sits at a desk. She smiles in a business-like way, but she doesn't shake my hand. Instead, she places a four-page document in front of me and points to the places where I need to initial and sign.

She doesn't expect me to read the document, but I do, the whole thing, taking my time, even though it appears identical to the other ones like it that I've signed. I read every word, acting oblivious to the woman's irritation. She tries to disguise her impatience with a smile that doesn't quite reach her eyes.

Once I've signed and initialed every spot on the form, thereby guaranteeing that, in the event of injury, mental or physical, I won't take any legal action against the proprietors, she asks me for a credit card. I smile as I hand it to her. She taps her finger while waiting for authorization, all the while avoiding eye contact.

When everything clears, she thanks me and nods at the goon standing near the door.

He moves quickly, leaving me little time to react as the pillowcase comes down over my head. I expected it, but I still panic, hyperventilating as his arms bind me from behind. I hear the sound of a door and the clamor of feet. I cannot tell how many people have entered the room, nor precisely how many hands grasp me as I'm lifted into the air. Reflexively, I kick, and my foot finds its mark, resulting in a *woof* sound. I may have paid for this handling, but I still feel some level of satisfaction knowing I've caused someone at least some minor discomfort.

Though not a stranger to such handling, I still find the disorientation jarring. Not knowing how far from the ground they hold me, I worry about what would happen if they decided to let me fall. Someone might find a modicum of pleasure in this sense of floating, this primitive experience of someone else carrying you. If not for the roughness, it might kindle childhood memories. To some degree, I've come looking for precisely that. I force myself to give up struggling. What's the point?

Eventually they do drop me onto a cold concrete surface. Hands grip me again as someone removes my shoes, then my trousers. They leave my shirt in place and force me to my knees.

Then the verbal abuse begins.

A rough male voice accuses me of eating excrement. Then he asks why I enjoy sodomizing my own mother.

That he should ask me a question about my mother interests me greatly. Did this question spawn randomly in my interrogator's imagination—insults about one's mother are common enough—or does this question reflect a more studied calculus, some information they learned about me? I hearken back that feeling of being carried. Coincidence, I wonder, or everything part of the same design?

When I don't answer, I feel my hair pulled back, and they empty a bucket of water onto me, soaking the fabric covering my face.

I knew to expect it, but I feel genuine panic. I struggle to break away, my body acting on its own to escape the feeling of drowning. For several seconds, I wonder if I might actually die.

Then, something unexpected happens. From an electronic speaker somewhere in the room comes the pre-recorded sound of screaming and groaning chains.

Instantly, I recognize the source of these sounds. They come from a record I owned as a youth, *Sounds to Make You Shiver*. To this accompaniment, my interrogator once more accuses me of unsavory sexual practices with my mother. I might answer, denying this accusation, of course, but I become fixated on the record. I used to play it constantly in my room, imagining the scene it painted—a crumbling mansion that hosted scores of reanimated corpses, vampires, and werewolves. It seems almost quaint to hear it played here, a relic from a more innocent era.

Then comes the monologue, spoken by the record's narrator in an ominous voice: *"So, you would like to visit a haunted house, hmmm? I think I have one that should suit you. That is, if you dare follow me. You will? Fine. Shall we go then? Ah, here we are at the door. Happy haunting."*

Evil laughter follows, along with wind rattling in old rafters and the growls of monsters. But more than anything I notice the pops, hisses, and scratches that accompany these sounds. Somewhere, they have an actual record player and an actual record—an old one at that. Just like the one that used to belong to me.

"Did you?" my interrogator asks. *"Did you fuck your mother in the ass? I'm talking to you."*

Before I can answer, they pour another bucket of water on my face, and once again I struggle. Within my consciousness, a memory awakens. Finding that old record in a thrift shop and showing to my mother, a short time before the mania overtook her. On that day, she appeased me and bought the record, though she warned me it might not play properly. "It's probably scratched up pretty badly," she said, but I still wanted to bring it home. To my relief and pleasure, it played well enough, and I listened to it over and over, the needle of my old record player deepening its grooves and adding new scratches, until it began to skip and jump in places.

"Did you?" my interrogator asks again.

The record continues to play, and I notice it skipping in the same places as the one I owned. My brain begins to spin, and not because of the water that soaks me once more. Rather, because those skips and scratches sound the same. As I kid, I knew them as well as my own heartbeat, and I recognize them now.

Without warning, the hands grasping me let go, and I fall forward. Someone pulls off the pillowcase, but I can't see my surroundings yet. Just a faint light illuminates this place. My interrogator leaves, along with the buckets and his accomplices. They do so with such deftness and grace that I can only admire the choreography. All part of what I paid for. A new scene in this "haunted house" will now take place, but my attention remains focused on the recording.

With each passing second, I feel increasingly certain that the record I'm hearing now is the same used copy I found in the thrift shop.

It seems improbable, but deep in the rattling bones of my own skeleton, I know it.

That means I've finally found the right place.

Not that I knew precisely what sign to watch for during all my prior visits to theme parks, fairgrounds, and shopping malls.

I thought I'd come close once on a farm in Lexington. That haunt started with a wagon ride through a rural landscape full of pumpkins and leering scarecrows, and it culminated with a corn maze. There, the wagon's driver stopped and told his passengers that they would need to navigate the confusing rows of corn on our own. *See if you can find your way out*, he said in a sinister voice. Six other people participated with me, and as usual they sensed something wrong about my presence. I seemed out-of-place. As we entered the maze, I let them widen the distance between us. I wanted a solitary experience anyway, just so nothing could distract me from noticing even the most subtle signs around me. Anything might contain the information I sought—patterns in the hay, the garb used to dress a scarecrow, the carving of a pumpkin. Anything.

I quickly became lost and disoriented, but there, in the maze, I thought I saw her. Just a glimpse at first, but I recognized her auburn hair, so I stopped worrying about the maze and just followed her. I could never quite close the distance. As I rounded each corner, I expected to see her, but she remained far enough ahead that I eventually lost her completely, finally coming to a dead end, where a broken animatronic witch with green skin and a warty nose stood over a cauldron, its face a mocking stare.

Now, I find myself drenched in water inside this "extreme" haunted house, vomiting on the cold concrete floor. The record continues with a further round of screaming, followed by the rending of a pine coffin in a secret graveyard. That morphs into the voice of a witch, hissing at a menacing animal. *"Scat, you cat!"* After that, more familiar pops and skips.

No question at all. I'm hearing the same scratchy vinyl I once owned and later had taken away from me.

Without the pillowcase, my eyes continue to adjust to the dim lighting. I now see rows of bedsheets suspended from the ceiling, creating the illusion of a hallway that breaks off into different "rooms." If I inspected these fabrics more closely, would I find familiar stains, midnight ejaculations that never quite washed away, or worse, the blood that flowed when my mother punished me for touching myself?

I remember the threats I heard about how I would go to hell if I continued to defile myself in such a manner. She changed so much in a short time, her warmth becoming something else when the words of a charismatic preacher awakened something else buried in her soul. She began visiting that preacher often, in secrecy.

I recall how she first told me her secret—that she would soon leave my father and take me with her.

"This life we're leading here," she said to me while sitting next to me in bed, "we're bound for hell. I know that now. He's revealed the truth I've failed to see all these years. Your father never made me happy, and I finally know why. He doesn't know what love is. He doesn't love me. He doesn't love you."

She finished by whispering goodnight to me, and I laid there in bed, stunned. I had no idea my father didn't love me. Maybe he seemed distant sometimes, but he acted like everyone's else's father. And she used to seem like everyone's mother. She even indulged me by buying me monster toys and staying up with me for late-night horror movies, black-and-white fantasies of far-away places where distorted bodies lived in crumbling castles.

Like the one depicted on the cover of the record.

But all that changed as if overnight. Those things became forbidden as she appeared in my room with updates about her plans with the preacher.

"I'm going to leave soon and take you with me. We'll leave together. Your father, he's a monster, you know. Like one of these."

She picked up the record and pointed at one of the ghouls on the cover illustration, the one to the right of an over-sized Frankenstein monster, a fanged creature covered with hair that lurched forward, claws extended.

"Just like him," she said, and once more, she kissed me goodnight and left the room.

Did my father suspect anything? I couldn't tell. I waited for the day she promised, though I also dreaded it. I spent more and more time listening to my record, imagining a stone-walled tower filled with monsters and ghosts, wondering if it could protect me from the things I feared. Strangely enough, I knew I wouldn't feel like a prisoner inside.

Then the day finally arrived. Just not the one we anticipated.

This time, when she came to my room, tears streamed down her face.

"He's called it off. The whole thing."

I didn't understand, but I felt relief. I wanted us to stay where we were. I wanted things to remain unchanged.

Maybe she saw those feelings register on my face because she suddenly pinched me. She used her nails and actually broke the skin.

"Don't be happy," she said. "This is your fault."

I cried out, but she continued to pinch, and I bled onto the sheets.

"You're to blame. You're the reason," she said, and with that, she left the room.

But she appeared on subsequent nights, her visits involving more pinching, usually opening that first wound. Sometimes she did other things to make me bleed. She warned me not to say anything to my father. "If you do, he'll hate me worse. He'll hate you worse."

One night, she seemed normal again. She looked happy. "He's coming back to me," she said. "Things are going to be better, but we have to improve ourselves for him. You know what month it is, right?"

I did. October.

"Would you like to go to a haunted house with me?" she asked.

I certainly did.

"Well, then. Tomorrow night."

That evening she took me to a church, not for a worship service, but for a special event instead. The youth group needed to raise funds for a mission trip, so they'd decorated the fellowship hall into a haunted house. Over the entrance they'd hung spooky lights, and a hand-painted sign spelled out in blood-red letters, *WELCOME TO THE HOUSE OF SIN.*

I couldn't wait to go inside, and I thought doing so with my mother would help things get back to normal. Already, she seemed more like her old self.

Instead, she kissed me on the cheek and said, "I've got to get ready. I'm in the show." Then she pressed something into my hand. A ticket.

"When it's time," she said, "give it to him."

She pointed toward a man with a ministerial appearance near the door. He smiled at me and greeted me by name, even though I'd never met him. He winked as we'd known each other for years.

Then she left.

After some time, the door opened to allow me inside along with a group of giggling teenagers. I handed my ticket to the man, who once more used my name and said, "Pay attention in there." Once again, he winked.

I said I would and followed the others into a cloud of dry ice and strobe light effects. They sectioned the main room into different areas with wobbly partitions, and a guide met us inside, a girl wearing a white choir robe and a halo made of gold tinsel.

She gave us a lengthy introduction filled with Bible verses about the horrors we would encounter, but I only paid half attention. I wondered where I'd see my mother.

Then the angel led us to one scene after another, starting with a boy in a strait jacket. Hypodermic needles littered the floor around him, and he lunged toward us with a foaming mouth. "Drug abuse," the angel said. In the next scene she showed us a girl weeping while sitting in a rocker, her belly distended. "Premarital sex," said the angel.

Around that time, I noticed the sounds in the background. *Sounds to Make You Shiver.* Somewhere, it was playing. *My* record. I scarcely noticed the other scenes and the sins they depicted, wondering now if my mother had removed the record and brought it here to play. Perhaps she hid behind one of these partitions, watching my reaction to these small dramatizations, waiting for me to recognize these sounds. I thought for sure they served as a special message to me.

But to tell me what, I didn't know.

I found myself listening to the record rather than observing the scenes in the other areas, and I paid less and less attention to the moral lessons they imparted.

Until we came to the last area.

I didn't notice my mother at first, my attention drawn to the blood-stained sheets covering the bed. Next to it, a card-board box crudely decorated to look like a monitor. A hospital scene apparently.

In the corner huddled a woman with wild hair, her back turned to us.

I should have recognized her by the auburn hair. I simply didn't expect to see her there like that.

But then she stood, turned around, and staggered toward us.

Everyone screamed. Including me.

In her arms she held what looked like a very real fetus, its skin coated with a milky film

"The final sin," the angel said. "Abortion."

"Do you want to kiss him?" my mother asked us, holding out the abomination in her arms. She directed her next words to me. "Do you?"

Like everyone else, I lurched backward.

From behind her appeared another figure. Somehow, they hid him from our sight, though to this day, I don't know how. He seemed to materialize from the shadows, a special effect well beyond the scope of everything else there. A figure the same size and with the same features as the ministerial man who took my ticket, but with a face now painted red and horns extending from his forehead.

The Devil.

His arms enfolded my mother and glistening bundle in her arms, and he pulled her back into the shadows from where he came, both of them vanishing.

I never saw her again after that. How I reached the end of that nightmarish spectacle, I can't recall. I only remember the police afterwards. Their cars appeared around the church with flashing lights. Apparently, whoever acquired the fetus did so through some illegal means.

No one could find my mother, nor the minister and the thing my mother held in a bundle. Someone must have called my father, who arrived perplexed, having no idea about anything taking place there. The police questioned him for some time, and he managed to satisfy them.

Bits and pieces came to light as the years passed. My father had no knowledge of my mother's affair, and they never officially divorced. She simply ran away, maybe to avoid prosecution, though I don't know what role she played in acquiring the fetus.

Sometimes, during my more irrational moments, I think of it as a brother or sister that she preferred over me.

In any case, she managed to take my record in her hurry to escape, and hearing it now tells me I may have finally found her, and I can ask her why.

Why she didn't take me with her like she said she would. Why she took that abomination instead.

Now, the sound of the recorded wind fills the warehouse, resulting in a disorienting effect because the sheets hang still. No air moves through this huge chamber.

At the far end of the corridor of sheets, I see the pulse of a strobe light.

As I set off in that direction, I expect someone to lurch out at me from behind one of the sheets, a red-faced devil perhaps, who will drag me to the ground, spitting or evening urinating on me. I know what I've signed up for, but I also know the strobe light is there to beckon me. My vision remains blurry after the waterboarding, but soon I can make out a bed, with a table next to it. On the table sits a container with yellow liquid, and inside it I see something unspeakable with a face. On the other side, I see a small desk with a record player.

It looks like my old bedroom.

Someone stands by the record player, a woman with auburn hair, now with streaks of gray. She lifts the needle, creating a momentary silence before she sets it down again, letting it play from the beginning.

"So you want to visit a haunted house, hmm?"

I have found mine. I have come home.

She sits on the bed and extends her arms to me.

"I think I have one that should suit you. That is, if you dare follow me."

I follow her to the bed and feel her arms enfold me. Together we listen to the record as I await her pinch, the first touch of her nails.

The Widow's Tower

She drew the Tower card. Again.

Each time the Romany woman turned over the cards in order to interpret their message, they witnessed the return of that one particular image—lightning striking the tower, bodies falling to the earth below, the whole edifice splitting and crumbling.

The widow, as she called herself, might have suspected a trick if not for the way this recurrence clearly troubled the woman reading her fortune.

"It shouldn't happen this way," said the fortune-teller as she re-shuffled the deck. "Not with such frequency. If I deal the cards again and we see it once more, it will surely foretell terrible things."

Once more she dealt three cards, and again the Tower appeared. The two other cards mattered little at this point. They changed with each shuffle, but always the Tower appeared, a sure sign of impending destruction.

Even so, the widow smiled. "Do it again," she said, sounding much like a child who wanted to see a magic trick repeated.

Instead, the fortune-teller began to pack up her things. "We shouldn't tempt fate. You were good to let us set camp here. We've imposed on you." Outside the wagon, her kinsman continued to unpack their wares. These people spent their lives traveling, having no real permanent home. The widow sensed a kindred spirit in the fortune teller, the matriarch of the group, so she agreed to let them come to a rest on the grounds surrounding the ruins where she lived.

"Don't be daft," said the widow. She recently learned that word—*daft*—and liked its sound. "It grows late, and the weather threatens to turn violent. I've seen lightning in the distance. Tell your men to make the fires while they still can so they can prepare your meals. You're welcome here." The widow liked fires and relished the thought of looking out her window and seeing pockets of orange flame as strangers huddled in the gloam.

The fortune teller sighed and nodded, but she did not deal the cards again.

"You live up there alone?" the fortune teller asked as she stood upon unsteady legs. Though a small woman, she had to stoop to stand upright in the wagon. A woman with the widow's height would suffer terrible back pains if she tried to match the effort.

"Well, my children are there as well," said the widow.

"You have many children?" The fortune teller looked uneasy.

Outside, the ruins of the real tower overlooked dilapidated grounds, now filled with rickety wagons, still showing signs of the damage caused by an overload to the machines that brought the widow to life. Over time, gradually, pieces of the rubble disappeared, finding a place back in the structure. Almost never in the original place, however, so even if the tower became whole again, it would look as insane and misshapen as the creatures who rebuilt it.

"Yes, many," said the widow.

As the hour grew late, the wagon became darker. The fortune teller struck a march to light a cigarette. Then she held the match to the wick of an oil lamp. She didn't offer the widow a cigarette. If she did, the widow would have accepted. She really should try smoking one of these days, knowing that Pretorius enjoyed the habit. By the lamplight, the fortune teller seemed to study the widow's features—the sunken cheeks, the black lips, the wild hair that wouldn't surrender to brush or comb. And the scars, so many scars.

"No husband?"

"He died," said the widow. "Out there, in fact."

"The ruins," said the fortune teller. "They look uninhabitable. And lonely."

"They're under reconstruction. My children will see that my home is returned to its previous glory."

The fortune teller blew forth a plume of smoke and regarded the widow. The widow pointed at the cards. "Once more?"

The fortune teller made a dismissive sound, but she picked up the cards and for the last time dealt out three. And for one last time, they saw the Tower. The widow smiled and paid her.

* * *

Later in the evening, as she sat to watch the approaching storm and the dwindling campfires, the widow found the Tower card sitting on a window ledge. At first, she entertained the fanciful impression that the card decided to follow her, but movement in the shadows caught her eye, explaining the theft of the card. "Napoleon, this is your work, I take it?" As soon as she spoke the name, the form in the shadows withdrew. When they lived inside glass jars, Pretorius liked to grant his pygmy creations the names of rulers: Poseidon, Henry the VIII, Catherine the Great, and of course Napoleon. Napoleon had grown the least of all, but what he lacked in size he made up for in stealth and skills in theft, and the widow owed the small amount of money she possessed to this one. Apparently, he found his way into the wagon with her and the fortune teller and also took a liking to this card.

The widow lifted the card and kissed it with her black lips. "Thank you," she said to the room, not sure if she still shared it with Napoleon. In all likelihood, he'd moved on to the night's next endeavor, presumably to help the others move more of the rubble back in place and bring their tower closer to completion.

Be careful, my dear, the little ones weren't meant to leave their enclosures.

Pretorius' voice. She heard it inside her head more and more frequently, warning her of her of his earlier creations.

I not only gave them the names of rulers. I instilled them with something imperious. They each plan to rule the tower when it reaches completion. What will you do then?

That word—*imperious*—sounded bright and new to her, and she made a mental note to put it to use herself at the first opportunity. Something in her memory, the vestiges of a past, more delicate life clicked, and she intuited the meaning of the word. Instead of dwelling on Pretorius' message, she followed the wake of shadows left behind by Napoleon, moving deeper into the tower's recesses. In her hand she held the fortune teller's missing card. She intended to return it, of course. But then again, she might not.

She came to the tower's spiraling staircase, thinking it might clear her thoughts if she could go to its top-most portion—still unfinished and jagged—in order to watch the approach of the incoming storm. As with fire, lightning didn't scare her. She welcomed it.

On the next landing, she saw a different form hulking in the shadows.

"Why, who could that be?" she said, of course knowing the answer but hoping some light, affectionate teasing would encourage him to show himself. "Is that King Henry the Eighth?"

The form responded to her voice by shifting uneasily. Though the gaps left by the uneven stones came a flash of lightning without the sound of thunder, the storm moving slowly and still a good distance away. The brief light allowed her to see the bulbous head, once so handsome but now fat and gray and out of proportion with the rest of its naked, rotund body, squatting on its haunches. So hard to imagine, thought the widow, that he was once fit inside a tiny jar, where he sat on a little throne wearing a doll-size robe and crown. Now look at him. From its expansive jaws hung shreds of what looked like meat, but the shadows overtook it once more, and she couldn't ascertain the origin of its meal.

"Eating so soon? You think of nothing but eating. And what have you found for yourself? That looks much too large to be a mere rat."

The formed moved slightly but didn't answer. None of them could speak. Instead, she heard the sound of crunching bone. The leg of a deer perhaps.

"I'm told you're imperious," she said. "I can be imperious, too, you know. Or so I like to believe. Shall we be imperious together, or will your queen become jealous?"

The reply came in the form of more crunching and what sounded like a grunt. She knew this one liked to eat and move its bowels at the same time. Then ensuing stench confirmed that it had done so.

"I'll leave you to it, then. For now, you can be imperious for the both of us."

With that she moved on, passing others as she came closer to where the tower plateaued. To each she offered a greeting, asking them in what way they sought to demonstrate their imperious nature. Most appeared too busy with moving stones into place to heed her presence, but it turned out that only Henry took this time to eat a meal. Of all of them, he showed the greatest tendency to forsake his work to indulge in the pleasures of eating and shitting. The only one she didn't see was his queen. But the widow suspected she knew where to find her if the need arose. Instead, she went to an alcove that contained the pallet she slept upon.

Next to the pallet lay what little remained of Dr. Pretorius, stitched haphazardly together by his creations. They'd done a bad job of preserving him, and he consisted of nothing more than a head and torso, along with one leg stitched to where he once bore an arm before the explosion ripped him apart. The widow felt glad they practiced on him before going about her own reconstruction. No telling what she might have looked like when they finished. She took pride in her appearance. Even with the stitches and the unruly hair with streaks the color of lightning, she knew she looked beautiful.

Before gathering her blanket so she could take it to the summit of the tower, she kissed him where he once had lips, feeling the sharp edges of broken teeth instead. She tried to smooth his shock of white hair, as wild as her own.

"I can be imperious, too, my husband," she said, and then she resumed her walk up the tower's steps, the blanket in her arms. When she arrived at what, for now, constituted the tower's summit, open to the weather, she spread out her blanked so that she could fall asleep while gazing at the lightning. On such nights, when she slept at the apex of the tower, she dreamt of the wind lifting her and flying into the dark clouds, like the kites once affixed to the top, intended to draw lightning. No string held her down in these dreams, however—she just flew and flew. Next to her, she placed the tarot card, intent on dreaming again of that other stormy evening, when the tower remained whole and she felt Pretorius' touch for the first time.

* * *

Something shook her awake. She found herself drenched, her hair a mess, the rain having finally arrived after she feel asleep. She realized that she missed the full show of the lightning, and not dreaming disappointed her deeply.

She assumed the hands that awoke her belonged to one of Pretorius' mad creatures—most likely Lear, who maintained an inconsolable fear of bad weather and often sought her comfort during storms—but when her eyes cleared, she saw the fortune teller.

"You've stolen my card," said the woman, soaked to the bone. "And my people are vanishing. What kind of black magic are you practicing here?"

The widow shook her head to clear the cobwebs and smiled up at the woman. She held the smile even when she saw the knife pressed against her throat. A knife used to threaten her? How daft.

"I assure you," said the widow, "I may be imperious, but I don't practice witchcraft. And I have your card. I intended to return it."

But when she looked next to her, she saw that the card had vanished. What sort of fate would *that* foretell?

"Well, I *did* have it," she said. "I believe it's Napoleon again. Up to his old tricks."

"Napoleon?" said the fortune teller.

"One of my children. Come. I'll find him for you."

"There's something evil in this place," said the fortune teller. "The people left in my camp keep seeing things in the shadows. Something has made off with some of the men, as well as children."

The widow thought of Henry and the meal he enjoyed.

"Perhaps," she said, "the storm frightened them and they've gone into hiding."

"Storms don't frighten these men. Nor me, or our children for that matter. Someone has taken them. I know they're here. You'll take me to them," the fortune teller said, pressing the knife hard enough to draw blood, "and return to me my card."

"Of course, I'll return your card." The widow ignored the blood and got to her feet. She hovered over this tiny fortune teller. She thought of tossing her over the edge of the tower, a feat that would require little of her strength, and letting her fall to her death, just like the fool depicted on the card. But in truth, she liked this woman's fierceness. No wonder she served as the group's leader. "As for your missing kinsman, if they're here, I don't know anything about that."

Then she thought about how she hadn't seen Henry's queen that night. A thought occurred to her.

"You say children have gone missing, too?"

"Three of them," the fortune teller said, still brandishing the knife.

The widow thought of how Henry's queen loved children.

"I know where to look," said the widow. "Follow me."

The widow led the fortune teller through the slanting tower, down the winding steps. Pieces of the stairs gave way under the fortune teller's feet, and at one point, she cried out and steadied herself against the wall. The widow smiled and waited for her to find the confidence to move again. When the fortune teller took the next step, she waved her knife. "Don't try any foolishness," she said. "I've heard the stories people tell about this place."

It surprised the widow to hear this information. "Oh? People talk about my tower? You led me to believe you knew little about it."

"It once housed a monster," said the fortune teller, "made from the bodies of the dead."

Pretorius' voice chimed in. The bride slowed her descent and cocked her head to listen to the words only she could hear. *They're not here by chance. They hoped to find something valuable, no doubt the very remains of Frankenstein's creation. Imagine the plans they've discussed. To display him in some vulgar carnival, charging the masses a few pennies to see the corpse of your groom.*

"That was a long time ago," said the widow. "Before my time." Thinking: *You were my true groom, Pretorius.*

"I think not," said the fortune teller. "Lead me to my children. No tricks."

As the widow resumed a normal pace, she caught a glimpse of Napoleon sitting on an alcove, as still as a gargoyle. She said, "You hear that, don't you, Napoleon? No tricks."

The fortune teller followed her gaze but saw nothing. "Don't mock me. I take my people's lives seriously. Their trust in me won't be in vain."

"I wouldn't dream of mocking you," said the widow, not looking back. "I admire your imperiousness."

"My what?"

"Nothing. We're not far." But she hoped Pretorius heard her use the word correctly. She listened for his praise but heard nothing.

They reached the ground, but the stairs continued downward, going into the earth. Before rebuilding the tower, Pretorius' creatures had tunneled into the ground, and during what little hours they slept, they took their rest down there. If not for the promise of a spectacular tower, the widow would have joined them. Something so peaceful about the idea of sleeping beneath the dirt, where she could entwine herself with the roots of long-dead trees and sleep for ages.

The widow started down the steps, expecting the fortune teller to follow. When she looked back, however, the other woman actually looked afraid. This apparent fear disappointed the widow. Perhaps she should have thrown her off the tower after all.

The fortune teller read the widow's expression. "I'm not frightened. There's no light down there, and I suspect a trick."

"I told you. No tricks. Do you have your matches?"

The fortune teller didn't reply, instead taking a step back and, while still holding the knife, she extracted the matches from the folds of her skirt and lit one quickly.

The flare excited the widow. "I'll hold the match if you'd like."

The fortune teller agreed to this proposition. She handed the whole box to the widow. She'd never lit a match before in her life, but she'd watched and observed and knew what to do. As she led the way down the steps, the walls of the tower gave way to tunneled dirt illuminated by the match flame. Holding the fire excited the widow. She let each match burn all the way down to her fingers before lighting a new one.

She lit five matches before they reached the bottom, and she wished they could keep going so she could continue to light them. Already, she decided that the fortune teller wouldn't get these back. The card, maybe, but not these.

They arrived in hollowed earth, the ground beneath their feet littered with bones and half-eaten carcasses of deer and wild pigs, their images aglow in the matchlight. Entranced by the power of the flame she held, the widow felt truly imperious and realized that she hadn't really understood that word until now. As she walked about the enclosure, she nearly tripped over remains she'd not seen previously. Human, she realized, a man with the colorful clothes favored by the Romany people. She lit a new match and held it close so she could study him, sensing the fortune teller close behind her, still holding the knife and looking along with her.

The man looked half-eaten, his intestines dangling from the open cavity of his stomach.

You've invited invaders into our home, said Pretorius' voice. *As I suspected, they intended to pillage our belongings, including the body of your husband, that other misbegotten creation, without whom you wouldn't exist.*

The widow said to the fortune teller, "Did you come here to steal from me?"

At first, the woman couldn't reply. Though her mouth hung open, no words came forth. As the match in the widow's hand burned out, she saw the look of horror and mortification. Quickly, with an expertise as if she'd done it for years, she lit a new match, and now the fortune teller turned that expression upon the widow. The knife looked useless in her hand.

"He's alive? The monster. He did this, didn't he?"

"So you did come for him. Did you plan to steal me as well?" asked the widow. She closed the distance between them. The size of the enclosure allowed her to stand at full height, and she intended to show the fortune teller how tall she stood over her.

The shadows around them began to move. Pretorius' other creatures had begun to gather. The widow noticed Lear, not afraid of the weather at all down here. Yonder, she saw Catherine the Great, her naked breasts pendulous and missing the nipples she'd bitten off herself when, in a moment of delirious hunger, she'd tried to suckle herself. Poseidon over there, and

Napoleon, too, hunched in a corner. They wouldn't make the first grab at the fortune teller. The widow knew who else lay in wait down here. From a far corner came the mewling of a child. As she suspected, Henry's queen had begun dining on the children. Using her formidable height, she began moving in that direction, the fortune teller cowering now, hoping to maintain their distance.

"Did you plan to put him on display? Make him a carnival attraction? Set me alongside him and proclaim me his bride? Well, I'm not his bride. He's not my husband. He's been blown to pieces. His remains are built into the tower, parts of him there inside the walls, still living, still breathing. Can't you see him in the shape of this tower? I hate looking at it because I always see him. He's all I see."

She hadn't meant to let her voice rise to such a level. The truth of what she'd spoken struck her for the first time and surprised her. The fortune teller dropped the knife now. Moving backward, she bumped into Lear. He grinned at her, and she saw him now. Behind him crouched Poseidon and his insane fins for arms. The fortune teller turned the other way, saw Catherine the Great who smiled broadly and licked her lips. None of them pounced though. They understood what the widow meant to do, and with their bodies, they helped her guide the fortune teller into the passageway that led to Henry's Queen, the largest and most hungry one of them all. She lived down here, and only the enticement of eating children could ever draw her away from her throne.

"My fortune. You only agreed to read my cards to distract me. So your kinsman could invade my home."

In her fear, the fortune teller looked incapable of answering. The woman turned in time to see the monstrous queen bite off the head of a child, her mouth large enough to hold it in its entirety. The widow lit a match in time for the fortune teller to see everything. Around the queen lay the bodies of other half-eaten children.

Before the fortune teller could scream, the others set upon her and made short work of her. They needed to eat, too, and the evening's work of rebuilding the tower could wait as they drew sustenance.

The widow sat on the ground and watched. For some reason, she felt suddenly sad. Pretorius had gone quiet and didn't offer any words of consolation to her in this terrible moment. For the first time, she felt truly alone, and not even watching those creations dine could provide any solace. She wondered if in another life, she and the fortune teller could have become friends. Smoked together, perhaps. If she did possess the corpse of the monster (not her husband, stop that) she might have parted with it as an act of friendship. *Here, take him,* she would have said. *Become rich.* But she couldn't tolerate acts of deceit.

She lit another watch and watched as it burned. In the light of the flame, Napoleon approached. In his hand, he held something for her.

The Tower card.

As his ridiculously long arm extended, he bowed that odd head of his, as if in supplication.

That lightened her mood. She smiled as she took it, bowing back.

"Thank you, Napoleon."

She could never consider herself as imperious as the queen who now gnawed on the bones of Romany children. When they finished with the fortune teller, the mad things would go to work on anyone who remained on the grounds outside. In their wild hunger, they displayed an undeniable imperiousness, one she couldn't match.

But that small gesture by Napoleon made her feel special for now. Pretorius' question now gnawed at her. What would she do when they completed the tower? She knew now she couldn't continue to live inside it, and she could certainly never rule it. She knew that now. Those things created by Pretorius would eventually throw her off the top of it, and she would tumble down to the ground like the poor fool shown on the card.

No, she corrected herself: she would fly.

What the tower card showed was not falling, not death, but flying. She must always remember that.

Thanks to Napoleon, that card belonged to her now. She would cherish it and allow it to remind her of what the tower truly represented. Let tomorrow bring what it would.

The Revenge of Katrina Bloodspell

First of all, they really did call it *Sex Camp*, that name appearing on the official records. Second of all, put all your expectations aside because it didn't live up to the name. At least not the way you'd think.

No skinny dipping, no orgies, no partnering up to lose one's virginity. Not even co-ed cabins. No, the Crosswood Methodist Church ran the so-called Sex Camp as a learning experience, one that would teach naïve teens a very sanitized version of how the body's plumbing worked, followed by programming designed to scare the shit out of you from ever doing anything with that knowledge. Not if you believed in sin and hellfire. You couldn't even touch yourself with a clear conscience after sitting through one of their slideshows.

But we endured and we could look forward to nightfall, when we could talk in the cabins without any adult supervision. They put the college-aged kids in charge, and you'd think that things would get more interesting then.

Except we had Brad in charge of our cabin, and he liked to sneak off on his own most nights. If we got "lucky," Brad, an accounting major, would let us sniff his fingers when he returned. Some of the kids went wild for this opportunity, but some of the more critical thinkers amongst us wondered if Brad didn't seem a little too eager to force his digits under our noses. Some of us wondered if he really could find a girlfriend with that wandering left eye of his and that hairline that seemed to be receding a little too early. Some of us, like me, who got a little too mouthy sometimes.

"How do we know you didn't open a can of tuna and rub it all over your hand?" I asked.

"Smell it, Parham," Brad said, after everyone else stood in line for a turn.

"I can from here," I said, "and it smells like Starkist."

"How would *you* know the difference between Starkist and pussy? Go on, Parham, tell us all about it," Brad said.

I shrugged. I didn't. I just didn't share in the adoration of good old Brad that seemed to occupy the waking hours of everyone else in my group. They even loved his pranks, like the first night, when he burst into our cabin with a potato sack covering his head, howling and waving an axe like a madman. A bunch of kids screamed. One nearly broke through a window trying to get out. Another literally wet his bed. But afterwards, everyone talked about it as some brilliant prank.

"Admit it," said Brad, "you're a virgin."

I was, but I didn't want to say it. Instead, I let my tendency to get mouthy take over. "I'll admit that you're one."

That got an audible response from everyone else. If Sex Camp didn't deliver on anything else, at least they might get to see a fight. And because I wouldn't call any of my fellow campers my friends on a good day, I felt certain that they hoped I would lose that fight. Though no weakling, I still hadn't reached my full height, and thanks to the fleshy inner tube around his waist, Brad outweighed me by a good fifty pounds. In other words, I didn't stand a chance.

Good thing for me then that Brad just decided to laugh it off. "You think so, Parham, but I lost my virginity right here in this camp. You all have heard the legend, right? I'm talking about the Whore of the Lake, Katrina Bloodspell."

From the excited sound around me, it became clear that everyone but me had heard of this so-called legend. Sure, I knew about the lake in the middle of the camp. In fact, on my first day there, just after being dropped off, I skipped decided to skip the round-up and go exploring on my own. I couldn't believe my luck when I not only found the lake, but also an old rowboat with rusted oarlocks. With no one around to stop me, I climbed in and pushed it out onto the lake, planning to spend a little quality time by myself, not realizing until I'd gone a good distance from shore that the craft was sinking. Apparently, I failed to notice the rotted wood on the bottom. When one of the counselors saw me, she shouted, "What the heck are you doing out there? It's dangerous!"

"Fishing!" I called back. Sure enough, a little minnow chose that moment to jump inside the water-logged boat. Quickly, I grabbed it by the tail and held it up. "See?"

That little escapade nearly resulted in an early trip home. Instead, I got to join the round-up anyway, late and with a towel around my shoulders. Maybe if I listened to all the spiels about rules and expectations, I might have heard something about the lake and its legend.

As things stood, I managed to piece together the fragments of what I'd heard: how just a few years ago, this Katrina Bloodspell came to the camp all hot and worked up on teenage hormones, ready to screw everyone and everything in sight. She started with the counselors, meeting them for one-on-one sessions in the showers and restrooms. She just couldn't get enough, though, eventually a single partner at time couldn't fulfill her desires. Finally, one night at the lake, she had a group of boys line up and take turns with her, right there near the edge of the water. At some point, though, her conscience overcame her, and the shame she managed to forestall rose to the surface and hit her hard. She looked down at her used, naked body and decided she just couldn't live with herself. So she walked into the lake and drowned herself.

But her spirit still haunts these grounds, still filled with mortal lust.

Or something like that.

"I was there," Brad said. "It's all true. And that's how I lost my virginity."

"No. Bullshit," I said. This time I think I spoke for others, too. Some of them, at least. I looked around at the other faces. But plenty of them looked gullible enough to believe it.

"It happened. I'm not proud, but that's how I busted my cherry," Brad said. "To the Whore of the Lake."

"Prove it."

He laughed. "It's not like it showed up in the papers. Well, her suicide did. You can look that up."

I surveyed the room. I had managed to smuggle in my smartphone, but guess what? My little excursion in the boat ruined it. Apparently, everyone else in the cabin decided to follow the rules about no cell phones. None of us could look up anything.

"How about a séance?" Brad asked. "We can call forth her spirit, and maybe she'll take pity on one of you. Show you a good time."

I didn't believe in that sort of thing. I didn't believe in much, to be perfectly frank. That made my whole appearance at this church-sponsored camp ironic, I know, but I belonged to parents who worried about my increasingly antisocial behavior, and I guess they couldn't afford any other camps. Maybe they worried about me not showing a lot of interest in girls or sex in general. Maybe what the school psychiatrist said about me showing an alarming lack of empathy for the hamster who died on my watch during sixth-grade science class worried them, too. You'd have to ask them.

In any case, some of my cabin-mates looked terrified at the thought of a séance. They'd heard all the church propaganda about the dangers of witchcraft. But an equal number of them got off on the idea of something forbidden, and their eyes grew wide when Brad produced a Ouija Board from his duffle bag, along with a candle.

"We'll wait until tomorrow night," he said, "and then we'll call forth her spirit. Then maybe one of you'll get lucky the way I did."

Based on what I'd seen so far at Sex Camp, I suspected a trick, some kind of elaborate hoax that would lead to a lesson about the dangers of lust. Since none of us could verify the existence of Katrina Bloodspell, you can understand my skepticism. Nevertheless, I found myself getting caught up in the anticipation the next day, especially when the sun began to set over the camp. That night would bring a full moon, and Brad said we'd have to wait until full dark, when its light filled the sky.

When the time arrived, he made us sit in a circle on the cabin's wood floor, all eight of us just a few inches apart, and he placed the candle in the middle, setting it aflame with a disposable lighter. Then he regarded us with his best attempt to look serious and spooky. I ought to hand it to him: he surprised me by not smirking the whole time. He even shouted at the kids who tried to make each other laugh with scary ghost sounds.

"Shut up," said Brad. "This is serious. If you want the spirit of Katrina Bloodspell to visit us, you need to quit the joking. So keep your fucking mouths shut. You especially, Parham."

"I didn't say anything," I said, looking around at the others, who, unlike me, snickered at Brad's profanity.

"I'm serious," said Brad, looking hard at us.

Everyone got quiet.

Brad held up the Ouija Board. "We don't need this cheap piece of shit." He tossed it aside. "It'll probably just call a demon instead of who we really want. Just sitting like this ought to do the trick. Now, close your eyes. Everyone needs to do it. And keep them shut. I mean you, Parham."

"Fine." I shut my eyes and let Brad continue his séance.

"Good." We heard him take a deep breath. "Now, I call upon the spirit of Katrina Bloodspell, the Whore of the Lake. Visit us humble boys in this lowly cabin. Reform yourself into bodily form so that we may look upon your shame. Reveal your defiled body to us."

He repeated this speech three or four times, like a mantra he'd memorized. I almost opened my eyes, another sarcastic remark ready on my lips, when I felt something strange. The room suddenly went cold. I actually shivered, which made no sense, given how we sat in an airless cabin during the summer months in one of the hottest, most humid states in the county. Still, I wished I had a blanket nearby. I would have pulled it around my shoulders, just like the time after I went in the boat. It became *that* cold.

I couldn't tell if anyone else felt it. Brad kept going with that stupid mantra of his. I opened one eye, long enough to verify that everyone else sat still with their eyes closed, not shivering like a bunch of fools.

I squeezed my eyes shut, wondering if I let this stupid spook show get to me. I willed my body to warm up, trying to imagine a hot, crackling fire, but somehow that only made me feel colder.

Then I felt it. I felt *her*.

Fingertips, like ice, on my cheek, the words she whispered, sending sharp tingles down my spine.

I leapt up, looking around.

But I saw no one except Brad's group, still sitting in a circle. Everyone's eyes opened, now looking at me.

"The fuck, Parham?" Brad said. "You need to take a piss or something?"

My mouth moved, but I couldn't get the words to come out. Someone *had* whispered something in my ear. A girl. But I saw no girl anywhere, just a bunch of boys my own age, along with a cranky counselor.

"No," I managed to say finally when Brad asked me again if I needed to piss. "I think I felt a spider or something crawling on me."

"Well, sit the fuck down. You don't have to be the goddamn center of attention every fucking second."

"Yes, sir." I cringed when I heard myself say that. I heard some snickers, too, and I wanted to die. I only said *sir* once in my life, and that was when the psychiatrist asked me if I killed the hamster. *No, sir*, I told him, wanting to make sure he believed me.

It took Brad a few minutes to get everyone back in position. Then he started again with that incantation of his. ". . . the Whore of the Lake. Come visit us humble boys . . ." And so on.

I clenched my eyes shut. My butthole, too. I waited for the icy coldness to return, the touch of those fingertips on my cheek. I thought about the words I heard the voice whisper.

But instead, we heard the cabin door slam. My eyes opened in time to see someone, perhaps Brad himself, blow out the candle. Several of the others screamed. Then, an illuminated face appeared outside the circle.

"Just a bunch of horny boys," the figure said. Most of its body remained hidden under a sheet, only the face visible, thanks to a flashlight. I recognized the voice, even though it spoke in an exaggerated high pitch, made to sound like a girl. It belonged to Brad's buddy, Marcus, the counselor in charge of the cabin next door. "I am the Whore of the Lake," said this fake ghost.

I looked around, surprised to see of my fellow campers actually looking scared, cowering in the corners, the circle broken.

"You want some of this?" said the "ghost." "Come and get it!" Then it threw off the sheet, and everyone could see Marcus standing there, grinning.

He wore nothing underneath the sheet, his nakedness just dangling there for everyone to see.

Then he laughed. So did Brad, who threw him a pair of pants.

"Got all of you," said Brad, clapping Marcus on the back as he got dressed. Marcus grinned wolfishly. "Got every single one of you." Most of the campers laughed along with him, aiding and abetting this stupid homophobic joke, even more offensive than when he chased us around with the axe and the potato sack. "I even got you, Parham," he said. Then he used that slur. The same slur my old man called me when he noticed that I didn't seem to care about girls.

But he hadn't gotten me. Something else did.

* * *

Late that night, once everyone fell asleep, I went down to the lake. I remembered what the voice whispered, and I followed its instructions closely. It wanted me there late. And alone.

Something in the voice and the way the fingers brushed against my cheek told me not to expect what Brad described. Rather than an insatiable libido, I heard and felt other things.

Sadness. Longing. Anger.

The moon lit the path for me. When I arrived at the water's edge, I watched the way the light dappled on the water. Though the air remarked still, little ripples disturbed the lake's surface, as if something had crawled from its depths only moments before I arrived there.

I saw no one, not at first, and I started to wonder if I imagined the whole thing.

But then I saw her standing near the water's edge, not even fifty yards from me.

Even as I approached her, she didn't move, standing with unnatural stillness, staring at the water as if posed a great question she could not answer. I could see the way the torn clothes hung from her body, damp

111

and muddy from sitting for years at the bottom of the lake. But she didn't scare me, not even when she turned at my approach, revealing gaping holes in her pale flesh, her eyes entirely white and her teeth blackened by mold. The wound just below her hairline stood out most of all, ragged torn flesh revealing a glimpse of a brown skull underneath.

I listened as she shared her story with me. How years ago, Brad and his friends invited her to the lake one evening, long after everyone had gone to bed. Thinking herself a tomboy who liked to swim and play rough, she showed up, thinking they wanted to challenge her to a swimming race. Things went fine for a while, until Brad suggested that they all take off their swimsuits and go skinny-dipping. She didn't want them to think her a square, but she didn't want to do that, no, not as the only girl there. She wanted them to treat her like an equal, just one of the guys, but them one of them grabbed her by the wrist, asking her she didn't just relax. Then they got rougher. Soon, all of them fell upon her at once, tearing at her clothes. When she tried to scream, Brad hit her with a rock, and then everything went black.

I listened to her tell the story. I could feel everything she described. Every bruise. Every scratch. The fatal blow that they would later blame on her trying to jump off the boat, hitting her head by mistake and accelerating her alleged plan to drown herself.

The school psychiatrist who said I couldn't feel empathy would have been amazed at my reaction. I actually cried.

Of course, he might not have liked what I decided to do about it. What *we* decided to do.

The basic idea came from her.

I supplied the means.

You see, I knew where Brad had stashed that potato sack, along with the axe.

She watched me silently as I covered my face with the sack, making sure I could see through the crudely torn eyeholes. As I hefted the axe, I listened to the names of the others who called her down to the lake on that fateful evening. She told me how they grew up to work as counselors and which cabins they now slept in.

But I would start with Brad, we both decided. My face concealed under the potato sack and the axe slung over my shoulder, I left her near her watery grave and walked back toward my cabin, where I planned to give Brad a rude wake-up call. I'd make sure he had time to see me, just to give him a good scare. I would say, "This is for Katrina Bloodspell, who you falsely call the Whore of the Lake" before I brought the axe down.

And I would bring it down hard, right in the middle of his face. For real.

The Stone Gate

No forethought went into unearthing the coral. When he cut it from the ground, he did so out of anger driven by betrayal, for he now knew for certain that Agnes didn't love him. First, she hinted that she might break off their engagement, and now she wouldn't so much as answer the letters he sent to her from America. After another day of no communication, he began cutting into the coral limestone like a madman.

Though he didn't stand tall, barely reaching five feet in height, and weighing only one hundred pounds, he had strength and determination. Most importantly, he understood weights and balances, so that once the pain and rage subsided and he could cut no more, he devised a way of lifting the block of coral from the ground by utilizing a hoist made from three beams of Florida pine. It took him some time, but the hot sun didn't bother him like it did those of weaker constitution. He justified it this way: without the love of Agnes, he needed some mindless labor to occupy himself with. Thus, he didn't rest until a block of coral twice his size sat on the dirt before him.

Exhausted by the achievement, he finally went inside his bungalow to rest his aching muscles.

Later, when he spied the block of coral through his window, he saw a female form seated upon it. At first, he mistook it for Agnes, and his heart leapt. Upon his approach, however, he saw a woman closer to his age, not quite thirty, but older than Agnes by at least a decade. He also saw a rounded stomach. A pregnant woman, he surmised, a stranger. He suspected that weariness from a long trek led the stranger to take a seat on the block of coral stone. It made a good, solid seat.

"Are you lost?" he asked.

"No," she said, "are you?"

He saw her dark red lips, and if his heart didn't already belong to Agnes, he would have found this woman's strange beauty enchanting. Besides, with a pregnant belly, she belonged to someone else.

"I live here," he told her, "and I have no close neighbors. So no, I'm far from lost."

"You seem lost," she said. Her hands bore long fingers, and he watched as they caressed the coral. "Did you extract this from the ground then? By yourself?"

He nodded.

"You know what it is, then. The remains of dead sea creatures from long ago. It's good you have no neighbors. I'm sure they'd hear your work and complain."

"I work quietly," he said, before adding in a secretive voice, "and where you see death, I see raw material that I can hone and craft." Indeed, he learned his techniques by belonging to a family of stonemasons before moving from Latvia to America. He knew how to work without expensive machinery, and as he just proved to himself, he could apply his skills to the limestone coral that lay under the ground of his new home.

Silently, he watched the woman touch the coral with her long fingers, stroking it as if it formed the scales of some giant gilled beast.

"It was cut with passion," she said.

"With rage," he said, and before he could stop himself, he began telling this stranger about his heartache. Before long, he found himself sitting by her side, and she held him as he wept. When he finished telling her the story of Agnes' inconstancy, he apologized.

"This is too much to burden a woman with child," he said.

"No, I understand this pain all too well. I've known rejection. But you need to do something with this talent of yours. If I had someone like you who could move stone, I would love him and never let him go." She gazed off toward a distant strawberry field, the property of the closest neighbor. "You should cut more stone from the ground and build a castle. For you and your future wife and all the children you'll have together. You won't be alone if you do this. You'll see."

At first, he rejected this idea, but in the days ahead, he began cutting, doing so in the early evening so as to avoid the heat of the day, as well as the gaze of curious onlookers who passed his property. The woman came back as well, always on foot, and she did so at a late hour. Since it was she who had given him the idea, he didn't stop working when she appeared, eventually learning her name: Nada. At first, he mistook her to be of Spanish origin but quickly learned from their conversations that she came from Eastern Europe like him.

"But you call yourself Ed now," she said.

"I do. New country, new life." He noted her belly. "How much more time?"

"Not long."

He hesitated in asking his next question. "Your husband. He doesn't mind you coming to me like this?"

"I have no husband. Didn't I make myself clear before?"

Her anger startled him, and he stopped working. Her eyes gazed at her lap, avoiding his. "You're not the only one who's experienced heartbreak," she said.

"I'm sorry." He could think of nothing more to add.

Nada shook her head before changing the subject. "Tell me what you're building today."

He told her how the pieces of coral he was cutting would form a series of chairs, all different sizes in homage to the story of Goldilocks and the Three Bears. One day, he would sit with Agnes and their child in these chairs, and they would tell this story together. Then he described his plans to carve out more coral into round objects, creating the likenesses of the planets to sit atop the castle's walls. It cheered him to describe these plans to Nada, and the more he talked, the more her mood seemed to lighten. Soon, he came to look forward to Nada's company as he worked, and eventually, she began contributing her own ideas, like a rocker which two people could sit upon and face each other, gazing into one another's eyes.

It was not long before Ed began work on this design.

"Maybe we could sit upon it together," Nada said as it grew closer to completion.

This suggestion angered Ed. In a sharp tone, he reminded Nada that everything he created, he created for himself and Agnes alone.

The next evening, Nada didn't appear. Nor the evening that followed. Ed began to regret rebuking her for such an innocent thought, fearing that he might never see her again. On the third evening, however, she returned looking different somehow, and it took Ed a moment to pinpoint the source of the change.

She was no longer pregnant.

"You've had your baby," he said, intending a note of congratulations.

Her expression betrayed no emotion. Flatly, she asked to see what he'd accomplished in her absence, so he showed her his new additions to the castle, including the nearly completed rocker.

"If you'd like to sit on it, you may. You'll find that it rocks quite well."

"I don't want to sit on it alone," she said. Her brown eyes contained a question: Would he betray Agnes and sit upon it with her?

With this question hanging in the air, they faced each other as the sun fell in the west. Now without her stomach, Ed could appreciate the shape of her body, with its full breasts and wide hips. She wore a dress made of thin, red fabric, and he could smell the muskiness of her perspiration. He found himself longing to taste her dark red lips, but he could not and would not betray Agnes.

Instead, he broke the silence with a question. "Where's your child? I don't even know where you live."

Nada looked off to the strawberry field in the distance. Ed didn't know the name of the owner, but he knew him as a Cuban bachelor who also kept a small herd of cattle nearby. Sometimes the cattle annoyed Ed by wandering onto his property.

"You must build the walls of your castle higher," Nada said, as if to distract him from asking more.

"Higher?"

"So that no one can see over them. How can you call it a castle if your neighbors can simply walk up and spy on you and your wife? A castle must be fortified."

At first, Ed rejected this notion, reasoning that no one but the Cuban bachelor lived in his vicinity. As luck would have it however, his sole neighbor appeared at his door the next day in his straw cowboy hat to deliver the news that he planned to sell all of his land to a developer.

When Ed asked him why he would sell such a profitable property, the farmer spat in the dirt and said, "Something has begun preying upon my animals. Attacking them and feeding on them at night. And now it's begun going after my men. It attacked one of my workers two days ago, tearing out his throat and eating his organs. Very bad. I'm selling and returning to Cuba. I don't know what it is you're building," he added, gesturing at the coral shapes on Ed's property. "It looks like some mad project to me, but whatever it is, I suggest you do the same and return home as well."

Ed reminded him that he'd found a home here. He was an American now. He didn't tell him the real reason he would never leave: that he was building a castle for him and Agnes.

"Suit yourself," said the Cuban bachelor. "I'm telling you as a courtesy. Also, to inform you that the land is cursed and that whatever is stalking my men and animals will turn to you next. Good luck."

Later, during a fitful night of sleep, Ed dreamed of himself in the future, an old man, living alone. He slept on a hammock inside his coral mansion—really, just two rooms built atop each other—and even though he couldn't find Agnes in his dream, the woman called Nada searched for him in the garden of coral sculptures below, calling out his name under a full moon. In his dream, he hid from her because she wanted to drink his blood. Eventually, she found where he hid under the covers, but instead of opening a vein in his neck, she let her dress fall from her shoulders. Naked, she straddled him, and they began making love in a way that brought Ed to an orgasm so thundering that it drove him awake. Still shaking, he found that he'd soiled himself and his bed.

Eventually, Ed did sell his property to the same developer. When Nada appeared around sunset that day, he stopped working. It seemed mad to suspect this woman of anything diabolical, but since the dream, he felt as if even talking to her marked a betrayal of Agnes. So he went inside his bungalow and hoped she would just leave.

Instead, she sat upon the rocker-for-two he'd created, as if to wait for him to return.

When he realized that she wouldn't leave, he cried out to her from the window. "I've sold everything. I'm moving away!"

In truth, he planned to only move to the town further south. He'd already begun making arrangements to buy a parcel of land away from any roads, hoping that would provide some privacy.

Nadia continued to rock silently in the stone chair he'd made for two as if she owned it, and Ed was unsure if she'd hear him.

This rocking infuriated him and he called out to her again. "Leave! Go back to your husband. Go take care of your child. Never come here again. Soon, I'll be gone from this place."

Again, she appeared not to hear, but gradually her head turned and Ed could see tears on her cheeks. When she finally rose to walk away, he noticed that her belly once more appeared distended, as if she'd become several months pregnant suddenly and quickly.

Hoping he'd seen the last of Nada, Ed spent the next few weeks organizing his move to the town to the south, a place called Homestead. The Cuban bachelor let him borrow some of the equipment he needed to move the heavy blocks of coral, as he still planned to build his castle.

"I'd loan you some men, too, if I could," the bachelor said. Before Ed could explain that he needed no assistance, the man added, "They've all left. Simply abandoned me. I caught one of them trying to destroy my fields with salt. He claimed he needed to purify the earth behind him. Said the devil was walking there. I don't know what to believe, but something is hunting and killing here."

Ed almost asked him if he knew Nada. He still didn't know if the man maintained some kind of relationship with the strange woman who visited him, and he didn't want the Cuban to consider him a romantic rival. That would jeopardize the good-will that his neighbor showed in loaning him the equipment he needed. It was thanks to his former neighbor's tractor, that he managed to cart each piece of coral miles down the road to his new location, where he set about constructing his castle in earnest.

There, he once more began writing letters to Agnes. Without divulging the secrets of his craftsmanship, Ed explained how he was creating a coral table on which they could serve meals to their children. He was shaping it into the form of a heart to represent his undying love for her. The garden now had a sundial that could accurately tell the time, and he added a megalithic telescope which he'd aimed with careful precision toward the North Star. These achievements had taken time, of course, and though he'd grown older, the passage of years hadn't robbed him of his youthful passion for her.

In these letters, he said nothing of Nada, who continued to visit him in erotic dreams.

Instead, he emphasized how this land of coral he created would become their Garden of Eden, if she'd only choose to make the voyage to him across the ocean. He signed his letters by saying that he eagerly awaited her answer.

In the meantime, he continued his labors. When curiosity-seekers came to watch him work, he would stop. As Nada suggested, he constructed a high wall, tall enough so that no one could peer over it. Despite this, news continued to spread of his work, and he decided to capitalize upon it. Outside the wall, he placed a sign designating a price of ten cents to view his work, and next to the sign he hung a rope attached to a bell. A visitor could pull the rope, and at the sound of the bell, Ed would answer. Or he might not, depending on his mood.

One night, Ed awoke to the sound of voices. At first, he mistook it to be animals, assuming that feral cats had found their way over his wall. When he heard the noises again however, he detected what sounded like human speech— or at least something close to it— then laughter. Strange laughter.

Determining that trespassers had gotten onto his property, he dressed quickly and grabbed a lantern, though he hardly needed it. As he walked down the coral steps which led from his room to the garden, he saw the full moon shining over the planets he'd carved. It provided him with just enough light to see a small form, the size of a child, jump from the heart-shaped table before scurrying off to a point beyond the well. Just then, he caught a glimpse of another movement, this time coming from the grotto he devoted to Goldilocks and the Three Bears. Whatever he'd seen now hid behind a palm frond.

He heard more of the sounds that awakened him. It *was* laughter, but unlike any Ed had ever heard. Cautiously, he approached the palm, leaning forward to better see what had invaded his premises.

Not a cat but a feral child perhaps? A monkey escaped from a traveling circus?

The lantern upheld, he leaned in for a better view.

Over the leaves of the palm, he saw the top of a bulbous head, obscene in proportion to the rest of the body. Red, glowing eyes stared back at him.

Then that laughter again, a sound that reminded him of a thousand lizard legs running across dried leaves. The creature leapt away, running on all fours like a jackal. Ed pursued, but he lost it when a cloud passed over the moon.

When the cloud lifted, he found himself standing near the lover's rocker. There sat Nada. She wore the same red dress she always wore, even in Ed's dreams.

She turned to him and smiled. "He just wants to play. Unlike the other one, he's yours. Why don't you play with him a bit? Read him the story of the Three Bears in the grotto? He would like that."

Thinking that his dreams of Nada had morphed into some kind of awful nightmare, Ed turned on his heels and hurried back to the stairs leading back to his hammock. There, he lay awake, willing himself to fall back asleep. That awful laughter and the sound of small legs scampering about his creations continued.

The next morning, Ed couldn't rouse himself from the hammock. He felt achy and exhausted. The bell sounded several times that day, rung by people who traveled miles in their wagons and jalopies to see the Eighth Wonder of the World. They called it the Stone Gate, his castle.

Word had spread of Ed's accomplishment, and though he'd once hoped that Agnes would hear people speak of it, he suddenly hoped that talk of it would dissipate.

But it didn't.

One day, the bell rang so insistently that Ed forced himself to answer. When he opened the door built into his wall, he beheld a young man wearing the kind of expensive clothes that had become fashionable in Miami. On his arm hung an attractive woman with bobbed hair. Both swayed there before him, obviously drunk.

"We've come a long way, old boy," said the man.

Ed didn't answer at first. He stared at the woman, who looked familiar.

"Agnes?"

"Victoria," said the woman, correcting his mistake. She held out a tipsy hand. "Charmed, I'm sure."

"How about it, old boy," her companion repeated. "You going to let us in? We drove all day to see this castle." With an unsteady hand, he held out two dimes.

Ed took the money, but he kept staring at the woman. He tried to estimate the age of Agnes today. No longer sixteen, but thirty? Even forty? This woman before him who looked so much like Agnes, couldn't be older than twenty.

How fast time went.

"You'll need to show yourself around," Ed said with a grumble, allowing them inside. "I'm not feeling well."

The couple barely seemed to notice, or care, as they made their way to the Three Bears Grotto. Ed listened to their tipsy laughter, hardly caring himself as he made his way back up to the coral chamber that held his hammock. There, he tried to ignore the sounds of the couple, and even as the light coming in began to dim, they continued to carry on. Once, he thought he heard the sighs and gasps of lovemaking, and almost roused himself to order them not to defile his property, but he eventually managed to fall asleep.

A different sound awoke him after the sun had set.

Blood-curdling screams.

When he made his way downstairs, Ed found the bodies of the man and woman laid out on the family table, their bellies slit and their guts exposed and hanging free.

Two pale creatures with bald oversized and deformed heads sat at the table like good children, one eating what looked like a liver, and the other, a heart still filled with blood. Gore smeared across their faces, they looked at him and grinned, displaying mouths full of razor-sharp teeth and shredded viscera. One even wagged a black tongue at him playfully.

That made the other one laugh, and they both began chittering to one another in some kind of private language. Hearing it made Ed feel as though tiny crabs had crawled up his back.

When they finished, they left the bodies splayed on the table, forcing Ed to later bury them himself. He used the quarry on a remote area of his property from which he'd recently cut coral. After covering the bodies with a thick layer of earth, he drove their car to a mangrove swamp and pushed it into the water, watching until it sank completely. He returned home by hitching a ride in the back of a truck filled with farm laborers, who laughed and joked about the women they'd left back at home. Ed couldn't even bring himself to fake a smile at their ribald humor. In truth, it made him sick.

When he finally arrived back home, he found people waiting for him. Near the bell-rope stood a man wearing a Panama hat. Next to him, a woman and a small girl in a frilly white dress.

Ed began to send the family away before he recognized the man in the hat. It was the Cuban bachelor, who embraced him as if they were old friends.

"Would you believe I've married?" said the former bachelor.

Ed tried to look pleased when the man, whose name he didn't even remember, introduced him to his wife Esme, and his daughter Flora.

"Even men like us can't stay bachelors forever," said his friend. "Will you take us inside to see this marvel you've created? As far away as Cuba, they talk of it. When I heard, I told Esme, 'I know this man. We must go and see what he's created in the name of love.'"

Reluctantly, Ed agreed to take them inside, and he waited impatiently as the family strolled amongst his mason work. Esme looked bored and smoked a cigarette while her husband talked with great animation about his new business in Cuba. Then he spotted the lover's rocker, the one Ed had built for two.

"You must take a picture of us on that. Will you do so?"

Ed agreed, taking the hand-held camera that his friend produced from a leather bag. He watched as the couple sat on the rocker he'd intended for himself and Agnes. Esme took several moments to fix her hair, and she complained when her husband insisted that they pretend to kiss each other on the lips as Ed snapped the photo.

Once completed, the husband's eyes squinted, looking into the sun at something behind Ed.

"I see that you've married, too. And congratulations, I also see that you're an expectant father. You must be so happy, my friend."

Ed held the camera tightly, afraid to turn and see what his former neighbor saw. Instead, he watched as the man's smile changed into something more serious. It was almost as if he suddenly recognized someone he'd forgotten and rather not remember.

"Esme, get Flora. We must leave now." He then said something in Spanish which Ed couldn't understand, and after re-taking possession of the camera, the former neighbor hustled his family back to the door in the wall.

Before they left, the Cuban hugged Ed again, this time like a brother, whispering into his ear. "Take care of yourself, amigo. And whatever you do, salt this earth immediately. I mean it. Salt everything. And as for those," he pointed at the carving of the planets and the moon which Ed had mounted upon the wall, "tear those down. They're probably evil, inviting an occult thing that doesn't belong in this world. The coral is probably rotten, too, full of death. Remember, use much salt. Before this becomes your prison."

As he watched the family leave, Ed knew that it was already too late.

As he suspected he would, he found Nada waiting for him inside his Garden of Eden. She wore her usual red dress, and her stomach showed signs of a new pregnancy. In creating the walls as high as she suggested, he had created a prison.

"I'm glad they're gone," she said. "After all, we didn't make this for strangers."

"I built this for Agnes," he said, knowing that it wasn't true somehow, and that he would eventually die without ever seeing Agnes again.

Nada reached for his hand. When he didn't accept it, she turned and walked toward the rocker built for two. There, she sat down.

Ed thought more about how tall he'd built the walls. If Agnes had ever answered the pleas he sent her in his letters, if she'd crossed the ocean to join him, she would have become a prisoner too. His prisoner. Perhaps he intended that from the start when in anger and frustration, he'd extracted that first lump of shapeless coral

Having nowhere else to turn and nothing more to complete, he joined Nada on the rocker. She smiled at him and once more offered her hand.

The sun began to set, and in a few hours, the North Star would appear in the sights of his megalithic telescope. Just one inch off and it would not have worked, but his precision proved true, and on a clear night, one would always see Polaris in it. How had he managed that feat? Even he didn't know.

At that time, his other creation— the misshapen marvel spawned from his loins and Nada's womb—emerged and joined its sibling to play amongst the rocks. Together, he and Nada watched.

She continued to offer her hand, and he finally relented, placing his into hers as they sat on the rocker. After a moment, she moved his palm to her pregnant belly to let him feel the stirring there.

"It will be a female this time," she told him. "They will have a sister."

The Baron of the Rails

There came a point when I refused to run the trains on my father's model railroad.

"Come on, Elise," he would say, "it's time for us. Come into the garage, and Daddy'll let you run that special locomotive, the one I know you love so much."

But I resisted, later worrying that I broke his heart. Even after everything that happened, I still wonder if he felt anything like that, or if he even could.

Saying no had nothing to do with age or puberty or old-fashioned notions that girls simply didn't play with the trains on their fathers' meticulously designed model railroads.

In fact, I loved the effort that went into making everything so perfect and realistic. So much detail, from the way he laid the tiny track, to the miniature houses with colorful roofs and the streets with tiny policeman directing traffic. Also, the town square with green bushes and people, their arms held up in a perpetual wave as the train went by, a perfect replica of 1950s America, the decade of my father's youth, when Americans still rode trains. He made the railroad big enough to fill an entire garage, his life's work practically, and one section even consisted of farmland, with tiny sheep that he made from scratch, shaped and molded with his strong, delicate hands to fit into the HO scale of the whole railroad. Nearby lay a pond that glistened with such blueness that it looked as though you could dip your finger into it and it would come out wet. I tried to do that so many times, fooled by the illusion my father crafted. Just beyond that lay a dense pocket of trees, a forest where I imagined unseen creatures hiding.

The real reason I began resisting his invitation to run the trains with him had to do with the house in the middle of that forest, situated right by the track that cut through the trees.

A house painted completely black.

Unlike the other areas of the model railroad, where he painted his miniatures with bright colors, this house contained no replicas of people, either inside or outside. Everywhere else on the railroad, you could find tiny people my father had painted with such care, all with little eyes and smiling mouths. Even the sheep meadow contained a herder, and the sheep had faces as well. The train station itself contained people with baggage and briefcases, all waiting to go to their jobs or on vacation. He even put a drunk on a park bench.

But not the black house.

And the track passed by it within just a few inches, and every time my special locomotive—a steam engine, of course—approached it, I would hold my breath, afraid that whatever hid itself inside that house would make it jump off the track.

I probably said something about this fear because I remember my father saying, "Don't worry, honey, I'll put it right back on the track if it derails."

It seems like it did just that every time. It would derail.

And true to his word, my father always did what he promised, putting his hand right by the door to that black house so he could lift the train and re-seat it on the track.

The worst feeling would come over me during these moments. I expected the black door to open up, allowing something large and snake-like to emerge and wrap itself around my father's wrist. Even though my father stood like a giant over the railroad, it would pull his whole body into the house, making him disappear inside so quickly that I couldn't even say goodbye, much less save him.

I hated that I couldn't see inside the opaque windows. The door, despite my dread, always remained closed.

"Why'd you paint the house black, Daddy?"

Instead of answering directly, he acted as though he couldn't see it, which was crazy. He designed every inch of that model railroad, laid all the track, built every model from scratch. "What house?"

I pointed to it, and he acted as though he noticed it for the first time.

"Oh, that house. Someone must've painted it black so I wouldn't see it."

"Who did?"

"The Baron of the Rails, of course. He doesn't want to be seen, so he lets the coal dust shroud his house in black."

I immediately became afraid of this Baron, imagining what he must look like and why he wanted to remain hidden. To match his house, he would dress from head to toe in pitch black, and with equally black eyes, he would watch the train approach from his window, judging my skill with the small controller that powered the electricity running through the track. Though powerful—the most powerful person on the railroad—some kind of deformity marred his features. I imagined that he kept some kind of machinery in that black house, and he kept it humming with infernal power, and on more than one occasion, he'd driven it past its limits, laughing madly even when it exploded in his face, further disfiguring him.

Worse, when the trail derailed close to his door, he would sneak out under the cover of the trees as my father worked to place the locomotive's wheels back onto the track. Sometimes I thought I caught a glimpse of him hidden under his black cloak as he scurried past the door, open and closed so quickly that one had virtually no chance of seeing it. Then, when my father turned his back, the Baron would jump aboard the locomotive, where hidden controls lay in wait for him to use.

"Go ahead," my father would say, "it's ready."

And I would always turn the throttle gently, so carefully, exactly the way he taught me, allowing the locomotive to start gradually and build momentum.

But the Baron of the Rails had other ideas.

Using those tiny controls, he would drive more power into the engine, causing it to speed faster and faster.

"Slow down," my father would say, using his outside voice, but he didn't understand that I'd already brought the throttle down to zero. Despite this, the train sped up. "Slow it down!" he'd say again, even louder, not knowing that inside the tiny compartment, the Baron of the Rails laughed insanely, the engine now entirely at his command.

Finally, the locomotive would run off the track in some horrible way, ruining a house or, most often, the church, a Methodist one, complete with a white steeple topped by a tiny cross that broke away time after time, along with a section of wall.

My father would lose his temper entirely. He'd grab my wrist, wrench away the throttle, and slap me for the disobedience that'd force him to rebuild the church yet again. On the railroad, the Baron would jump off the wrecked locomotive, the black cloak covering him once more, and he would run through the tiny village, hiding himself behind any available obstruction until he'd made his way back to the forest on the outskirts of his black house. Eventually, he would disappear back inside, still laughing at such a high frequency that only I could hear him.

Through tears, I'd catch glimpses of his movements as my father picked up pieces of the broken building. "You know how many times I've had to repair this because of you." He would never see what I saw—that black cloaked figure running on small legs. But he would see me, and the tears running down my face, and just when I thought he would pick me up and console me, he'd say, "Why are you laughing? Stop that, now, before I make you stop!"

* * *

As the years passed, I would look for signs of the Baron's whereabouts and realize what a long life he enjoyed.

Take Pemberton Ferry, for instance, a town virtually no one has even heard of today, but one that used to exist, somewhere just north of my father's house in Tampa. Now, it's a ghost town, with little more than the remains of an old rail station, along with a large section of weed-choked track, the remnants of a rail-line that went through it. Way back in the 1880s, the Baron haunted that line, and I know this because of what happened.

During that decade, a train rounded a curve, when suddenly a tree appeared where none existed before. The engineer had no time to react—in fact, I suspect that his train actually started to speed up, as he desperately tried to make it do. Nothing could stop the impact, which sent the engineer flying into the air. Rather than land somewhere safe, he managed to fall under the wheels of his own train.

It sliced him in two.

A year later, at the same bend in Pemberton Ferry, another train came across a tree in precisely the same place. Once again, the engineer couldn't slow down the train, so he braced himself for impact. Instead of hitting a tree, though, his train made it around the curve safely. He couldn't explain it. But he did hear a blood curdling scream—it sounded like a man being cut in half. When he stopped the train, he found no signs of any tree, nor any man.

The same thing happened again and again throughout the 1890s: the reappearance of the tree, and the sound of a screaming man being sliced in two.

When I learned about these incidents and the fact that the town couldn't stay alive, I knew that the mad Baron of the Rails must have had something to do with it.

Amazingly, the old station remained, and no one removed the track to build a road or use the pieces for scrap metal, so some historical society got the idea to open the area for short rail trips, the kind that train enthusiasts would pay to enjoy on weekends. They'd bring their families, including their daughters, and sit them down in an actual rail car and have an actual locomotive pull them over the miles of track that still remained, saying, *See, this is just what it was like in the old days, when Americans still rode trains.*

Even better, if you wanted to pay extra, you could reserve a special, private day and, under the supervision of one of the volunteers, operate the locomotive yourself.

Guess who decided to pony up for that opportunity, setting aside the money she'd earned running the till at the local grocery? Not for herself, but for her father?

By that point, my father had grown old, his hair thin and gray. I turned eighteen, and on the day I moved out, my father knocked down the wall between my room and the one adjacent to it, creating a newer, larger space for his railroad than the one-car garage. Hard not think of that as a kind of revenge.

Now he could expand it with more towns and buildings. He kept the forest, though. The black house, too, now surrounded by more trees, as if they'd grown in my absence. It looked different in ways I at first couldn't identify. Then I saw it—tiny pieces of balsa wood now covered the windows, as if someone had come along and nailed up plywood to block the Baron's view of oncoming trains. A strange addition. Something hung from one of the trees, and at first I thought it looked like a noose before my vision corrected itself and I realized that it was just a dried strand of glue clinging to one of the branches.

Time seemed to soften my father's mood and temper, though I didn't test him the way I could have. He tested me though.

"Don't you want to run your old locomotive? I still have it—your favorite."

He asked me as if we'd only stopped yesterday.

But as I said, I didn't test him, instead begging off to show him the brochure clasped in my hand, the one mailed to me when I paid for his reservation to drive the locomotive in Pemberton Ferry. I thought receiving this would excite him, the novelty of it make him beam with joy. In the past, I'd never bought him gifts. For one thing, I never had enough money, and for another, I never knew what he'd want. No surprise, since I never know what people want, especially myself.

I expected enthusiasm, but he regarded the brochure with disinterest.

I began talking quickly, explaining the circumstances of how they'd reopened the line for family excursions, how they managed to come by an old locomotive and two or three passenger cars to give people an understanding of how travel worked in older, simpler days. A museum on rails, practically. I pointed to the picture of the locomotive. "And you get to operate it. Like a real engineer." In my hand, I held a bag. I used this moment to open it, unveiling an engineer's cap I bought for him. He let me position it on his balding head.

"What's the matter?" I asked.

"It's not a steam engine," he said. "Your favorite locomotive is a steam engine."

"I don't have a favorite locomotive."

"Of course you do. You kept running it off the track and breaking it."

I could have reminded him about the Baron then, but I went on. "This isn't for me. It's for you. It's a gift."

"You could have just brought me flowers. When I had that heart thing, I mean."

He meant a heart attack. When he went into the hospital, I cried for days, but I hadn't gone to see him. I still had needed to resolve certain issues within myself, the punishments I used to receive that lasted for days, sometimes even including not getting meals. By the time I found myself prepared to let those things go, they'd sent him home.

"This is to make up for that," I said.

"It could be for both of us," he said.

"I'll go along with you," I said. "I checked, and I can ride along, but you'll be doing the driving. That is, with an actual engineer to guide you."

* * *

A month later, at the end of the long drive to Pemberton Ferry, that engineer welcomed us outside the remains of the train station. Though the brochure showed pictures of a refurbished station, brightened up for tourists, what we encountered still looked drab and gray, still very much a work in progress, even with patches of graffiti still showing on the walls. Most of it looked unreadable, with one notable exception. Someone had scrawled *BARREN* in red paint, leaving me to wonder if the person who wrote it wanted to comment on the lack of life in a ghost town like Pemberton Ferry or if they wanted to lament someone's lack of fertility. A third possibility loomed, one in which the artist simply didn't know how to spell *BARON*, and that possibility intrigued me the most.

Whatever the case, the engineer who stepped out of the station looked like someone out of the 1950s, donned in coveralls with a rag sticking out of one of the pockets. He wore an engineer's cap like the one I'd bought and which my father had left at home. The engineer met us with a nod.

"Name's Curt," he said, "and that's Greta." He pointed to a blue and gray locomotive sitting on the track.

"A diesel," said my father.

If Curt heard that as criticism, he didn't let it show. "Courtesy of the U.S. Army, circa 1951. A good one, too. Who's driving? Because I'm riding shotgun."

I pointed at my father. He smiled and held up his arms, like the victim of a hold-up.

"Room for me?" I asked.

He scanned me from head to toe, sizing me up. "You sure ain't skinny, but you'll fit." Then he spit on the ground, and while he extracted the rag in his pocket, he mumbled something else that I don't know if I heard correctly. "Let's get started before the weather turns ugly," he said before leading us to Greta.

I stayed back a beat longer, wondering if I heard right. Not the part about my stature, but the other thing he mumbled. I thought I heard him say, "Used to be skinnier."

✦ ✦ ✦

My father took directions like a pro. You'd never imagine that it usually worked the other way around, with him giving orders rather than taking them.

I stood in the corner of the cab, as close to a window as I could manage so that I could enjoy the breeze while Curt showed him the throttle, the brake, even the means by which he could sound the whistle.

"Don't know if you'll need that one though," Curt said. "Only one crossing to worry about, and if we see even one car, I'll get out and bed the driver in front of both of you." He looked at me as if he'd just remembered my presence. "If she's pretty."

The train started, and I could see the look of concentration on my father's face, his determination not to make a mistake indicated by his set jaw. Did I look like that when I'd tried not to let my train run off the track of his model railroad?

To show that Curt's comment didn't bother me, I asked, "Not much traffic out here?"

"Just a lot of nothing. Well, maybe not nothing. Go ahead, whip this pony harder. She can take it."

I didn't understand his meaning until my father adjusted the throttle and we picked up speed.

"Do her some more. She can't even feel that," Curt said.

Did he mean me or Greta? I couldn't tell, but my father gave the throttle more juice, and I felt the wind in my hair.

"What do you mean by 'a lot of nothing'?" I asked, wanting to know if he knew the story of the tree that appeared in the middle of the track and the engineer cut in half. I wondered how long you could live like that—cut in half. No doubt long enough to see the wheels passing over your severed mid-section, the other half of your body underneath the passing train cars, your insides spilling forth. Long enough to know what happened and to feel it.

As we gathered speed, I watched the trees pass by, so much thick forest, once the scene of turpentine stills and sugar mills.

Curt said, "You'll see once we get around the bend. Look that way and you'll see some signs of life now."

I leaned toward the window, expecting to see a deer or wild pig, but instead I saw what looked like gravestones sticking up out of the weeds like rotten teeth.

"What was it?" my father asked. He missed it because he kept his eyes fixed on the track ahead.

"Old family cemetery," said Curt. "You'll see more of those if you keep your eyes peeled. My favorite's up a-ways." He looked at me, his lip curled into a smile. He kept his cap pulled down over his brow so I couldn't tell if his eyes joined in. "You get my joke?"

"'Signs of life,'" I said. "Yeah."

"A lot more where that came from." Then to my father: "You think your little girl's going to fly out if you give Greta here more speed?"

My father's hand moved the throttle and the increase in velocity forced me to catch myself as I fell back.

"That's better. Now blow the whistle. Wake up those folks back in yonder graveyard. Let them know who's been here."

The whistle sound filled the air around us. With the increasing speed, the woods outside the locomotive became a blur or green and brown.

"Should he slow down soon?" I asked. I knew from my reading that somewhere up ahead, the line ended at the remains of an old bridge.

"You getting tired of standing?" Curt looked at me, and I caught a glint of a single dark eye beneath the bill of his cap. His face remained visible long enough for me to notice other features, like scarring. Curt's face bore several scars, especially around the nose, as if a long time ago something had exploded in his face. I shifted my weight, feeling the iron of the locomotive press into my back.

"I'm fine," I said. "I'm just wondering how long this trip's going to take."

"We got a good section of track to work with. No reason not to put some fire under these wheels. Assuming your daddy here wants to. Go ahead, her name may be Greta, but she's no lady, so stop trying to treat her like one."

My father's hand remained fixed to the controls, his eyes on the track. He spoke without looking away from what lay ahead in the distance: the bend in the track. "You sure?"

"Hells, yes, I'm sure. If she were a lady, she'd be wondering when you're getting around to taking off her drawers."

Our speed increased.

Curt worked a finger into the neckline of coveralls, trying to scratch at something. That exposed an area of skin I hadn't seen before. More scarring and what looked like some kind of rope-burn.

I asked, "This locomotive ever been in an accident?"

Curt kept scratching, as if he wanted me to have a better look at the rope burn.

When Curt didn't answer immediately, my father looked over to see his reaction. Just a brief glance, not long enough to see what I saw: the mark left by a hangman's noose. Sweat had formed on my father's brow. He didn't want to leave the track out of his line of sight for very long. The trees whizzing by seemed closer, as if the woods had begun closing in on us.

Curt licked his lips and smiled before finally answering. "One or two. You want details?"

"Sure."

"Well, now. This very machine your daddy's driving right now collided with a bus full of illegals, sometime around '63 or '64. The bus tried to cut in front of the train, and when they collided, the train dragged the bus about three-thousand feet, leaving a mess of body parts in its wake. Get this: the bus was full of farming equipment, so throwing all those blades and sharp edges around made it all the worse. You should've seen how the blood actually flowed out of the doors of the ambulances." He paused to study my reaction before adding, "One illegal was cut in half under these very wheels. What do you think of that?"

We gazed at one another for a moment, and I started to ask him about the accident that took place on this very railway, but I didn't have time.

Curt began shouting.

We'd entered the bend without slowing down, maintaining the speed that Curt wanted, but up ahead, he saw something.

He kept shouting, commanding my father to apply the break, but in his confusion, my father actually *increased* our speed, and for a moment I thought I could hear Curt laughing as he barked orders, eventually twisting the throttle himself and applying the brake on his own.

I knew the cause of the panic. A tree was ahead of us. As the wheels ground to a halt that seemed to take an eternity, I braced myself for the noise that would follow. I knew the story, after all.

The sound of a man screaming as the wheels cut him in half.

Instead, a different sound met my ears. Curt's yelling. "That was a goddamned traffic crossing back there! I never seen nothing using that road, but did either of you see what I saw?"

With his hands away from the controls, my father blinked at the track ahead of him. A light rain had begun falling, and the air became thick with mist. I squinted, struggling to see anything other than trees and iron rails.

"A pedestrian," Curt said, "a goddamn pedestrian, right in the middle of the track. I seen him in the distance, all huddled up, just casually taking his time, like nothing's going to be coming along except a two-hundred-ton locomotive." Then, more quietly: "I think you may have hit him. I can't swear to it, but I felt something. We better get out and look." He regarded me sternly. "You asking me about accidents brought this on. If I find a dead man under this machine, it'll be your fault."

I gasped my reply. The words came out mangled by fear and anxiety. I don't even remember what I said. Imagine that, he blamed me for what happened, a ridiculous accusation. I looked at my father, who cleared his throat.

"She didn't mean nothing by it. She's just excited about me getting a chance to drive a locomotive. This was a present, me coming out here. What did you call it, Elise—a Father's Day or a birthday gift?"

I didn't answer. There I stood, listening to him try to come up with excuses for me, as if the blame really did fall on me. I bristled at his confusion over what to call the gift I'd given him. I stared at Curt, who stared back.

"Been an engineer all my life," said Curt, "and never had no accident, not a single one." He pointed at my father. "You're coming with me. I'm not looking for an accident victim all by myself."

While I watched, the two of them climbed down to the ground and began circling the locomotive, gazing under the wheels, sometimes pointing and saying things that got lost in the wind. Occasionally, my father would look up at me with guilty eyes. He knew the depth of his betrayal, and he knew that I wouldn't forgive him, not this time. Their facial expressions told me that they hadn't found anything.

But then Curt pointed toward the trees. My father looked that way, too, and started nodding. I leaned over the railing, trying to get a better look at what drew their attention. That's when I saw it.

A black house.

Nearly concealed by the mist and the trees.

But once you saw it, you couldn't discount its presence.

As the wind rustled the trees, more of it came into view: the remains of an old Victorian home, the paint worn by time, peeling in places, but the color still clearly evident. Black as night, with opaque windows not covered by boards of any kind, but unobstructed so that whatever inhabited it could see us and watch us, even as everything inside remained invisible.

The Baron. Those words formed on my lips, just as the two figures below, Curt and my father, began walking toward it. What drew them, I couldn't tell, whether a sound they detected, someone calling them, or maybe just a suspicion that if the train really hit someone, then perhaps they'd flown off in that direction, maybe staggered toward the house on injured legs looking for help.

Vines covered much of the house, the greens blending in with the chipped black paint, making it hard for someone passing by on a train to see it, especially one going at the rate of speed we traveled. At first, I entertained the notion that Curt didn't want us to see it—hence why he kept urging my father to increase the speed. The faster we went, the more quickly it would flash by, decreasing our chances of ever observing its presence.

I watched Curt lead my father closer to that vine-choked house, stopping even to lift aside a dangling branch for him. At that point, I expected the door of the house to swing open and a vine branch to emerge, wrapping itself around my father's body like a tentacle and pulling him inside so that I'd never see him again. It became real now, that childhood fear, and I realized with a rush of discovery that all those years ago, I didn't actually see a tentacle in my visions, but rather a monstrous vine.

As Curt turned to let the tree branch he held swing back in place, he looked back for a brief instant, and I saw a change in his expression. A smile? Did I see a contemptuous smile?

Then I could see them no longer. Alone, I stood on the back of the locomotive, my hands gripping the railing, not sure what I should do now: follow, or wait.

The answer came when I felt the locomotive lurch and begin to move. I fell against the side of the railing, looking about in panic as I realized that the woods had come alive with movement and color.

So easy to hide amongst the vines, the rocks, the trees, and so simple for someone to jump aboard and put the engine into motion.

As the locomotive accelerated, those two familiar figures stumbled out of the woods and onto the track, Curt and my father, both of them shouting and running toward me, with Curt in the lead. Never a fit man, my father struggled to keep up, but I could see from the strain in his face that he didn't want to stop running. I tried calling back, but the sound of the engine drowned out my voice, so he probably couldn't hear me telling him not to run because of his heart.

Something they found in the house must have shocked them, their eyes grown wide with fear, and no doubt they thought I meant to abandon them. They wanted me to save them.

I called out to them even louder, hoping they would see that it wasn't me driving the train, that it had started on its own.

My father stopped, his hand clutching his chest. Curt hurled one last slur in my direction before dropping to his knees to help my father, who began gasping and heaving. Finally, he stretched his body out on the track, like a man waiting for the wheels of a train to cut him in half.

Curt raised his fist at me.

No, they didn't want me to save them. They intended to save me. They knew it wasn't me operating the controls of the locomotive.

I stepped inside the cabin, and there, I saw *him*.

The Baron of the Rails, wearing that black cloak of his and working the controls my father had manned just a few moments ago. His back to me, he kept his features hidden. Black gloves even concealed his hands.

"We need to go back." I used as much command and authority as I could muster. "Stop this. Now."

But his gloved hand gripped the throttle while his head remained fixed on the track ahead. In the distance, the faint outline of a bridge, barely visible in the mist. Underneath that, the creek. The end of the line.

"We're going back," I said. "We are." I'd watched Curt's instructions. I knew how to operate the controls. I pushed my way next to the Baron, ignoring the stink of the engine oil and grave dirt that soiled his cloak. I put my hands over his to test his resistance.

In that instant, he looked at me, allowing me to see his ruined face, his eyes, nose, and mouth, all mangled by flying steel and boiling fuel, the results of hundreds of explosions. If he could have smiled with that mouth, he would have. He loosened his grip and let my hand slide under his. Then he tightened his fist, nearly crushing the bones in my hand. But he allowed me to do what I wanted to do: bring the locomotive to a stop.

He showed me how to put the engine into reverse, and with our hands working together as one, we increased the speed again, only this time going backwards, toward the place where my father's body lay on the track, his heart struggling to work.

"We'll have to slow down soon," I said. "You'll need to help me slow down as we get closer to him. So we don't ride over him and cut him in half."

I closed my eyes and saw my father's prone body still there, struggling for life, and I wonder if Curt knew what to do, if he could move his body off the track before the train arrived.

"We should slow down now, shouldn't we?" I said to the Baron. "It's time to slow down and stop."

But he maintained his grip, his hands enveloping my own. I could no longer move. Instead, I watched as he increased our speed even more, and I couldn't stop him. I braced myself for the scream that would come from beneath the wheels.

Papa's Night (or the Short, Happy Life of Elena de Hoyas)

". . . I continued to give the body nourishment as long as possible."
—from *The Lost Diary of Count Von Cosel*, entry dated 1933.

Maybe it was Vincente who first asked about the bull's ear. Papa couldn't remember, the evening having gone hazy, not just because of the drinks, but also because of the fist that landed on the side of his head. Damn stupid of him for not protecting his left flank. Now his skull rang, and he needed to keep blinking his left eye to keep things in focus. On top of that, they wanted to hear the story again about how the Spanish matador killed the bull and presented Hadley, Papa's first wife, with the bull's ear, pestering him about whether that made him jealous.

Some stories you get sick of telling.

"But did she eat it?" Vincente wanted to know. "Do tell us if she ate that ear in front of you."

"Shut up, Vincente," Papa said, and everyone at the table laughed.

They'd all enjoyed a good day of boxing in the courtyard of Papa's house on Whitehead Street, and now, while cooling off with drinks in Joe Russell's bar, they wanted a good story. But Papa still couldn't see straight. Did Vincente hit him, or one of the others? He couldn't remember.

Papa looked for something further away to focus his eyes upon, and he saw the little German seated at the other end of the room, gazing upon their group through thick spectacles.

"Go on, tell us," said Vincente.

Papa slammed his glass on the table. "No, she ate the goddamn book I wrote instead. Remember, I gave her all the royalties."

They all laughed uproariously at this, but Papa didn't join them. Instead, he began to feel uneasy under the German's gaze. The man looked damned peculiar, his bald head mottled with age spots and a chin sporting a pointed white beard, but his most telling feature were his eyes, magnified by the round glasses, fixed squarely in Papa's direction. He looked like an undertaker, even wearing a black suit with a matching bow tie, a fashion not at all conducive with the heat on the southernmost tip of the United States. A small island at that, where many knew the German as an employee at the Marine Hospital. He called himself Count something or other, though Papa figured that name was bullshit. He also heard the man had fallen in love with some Cuban girl who came to the hospital years ago, though the details proved cloudy after the boxing and drinking.

And with Vincente refusing to let such an old, tired story go, now Miguel offered quips about the girth of Hadley's throat. Vincente pounded the table with laughter, and once more Papa's head throbbed with the memory of the fist striking his head. These men had wives and ex-wives of their own, except for Pelayo, who had a prostitute who visited him regularly. Still Pelayo referred to her as his "wife," but only Papa found this amusing, the others willing to grant the fisherman his illusion. Papa tried to bait them into some good-natured needling, but they wouldn't bite. For some reason they found Pelayo's feelings sacred, but a decade-old story about Papa's being cuckolded with a bull's ear made them burst into riotous laugher.

Now he watched Pelayo saying something to the bartender, his face animated with frustration. The bartender cut the air with his hand, as if to end the argument.

"What's that conversation about?" Papa asked Miguel.

"Pelayo's wife didn't show up last night. Pelayo's worried she found a new man."

"You mean a new customer," Papa said.

No surprise that no one laughed. Everyone loved Pelayo and became piqued whenever Papa tried to shatter his precious illusion. "No one has seen her for days," said Miguel.

Now they watched as Pelayo grabbed the bartender's arm. The bartender responded by slapping Pelayo across the face.

"Hey now," Papa said. Papa staggered his feet. Nobody manhandled his friends, even Pelayo. Miguel followed his lead. Vincente shouted at the bartender, demanding him to go gentle on Pelayo since the poor man suffered from a broken heart. They all rushed forward to defend Pelayo, except for Papa, who had to steady himself against the table, his head still buzzing. He wanted to follow them, prepared to tell the bartender that any new mark on Pelayo's face would only make him uglier, but he slumped back into his chair. Vaguely, he became aware of the chaotic throng moving outside, leaving Papa by himself.

Except for the little German, still staring at him through those thick lenses. The man stood and walked over to where Papa slouched. He spoke in halting English.

"Sir, if you could forgive the intrusion, I wish to introduce myself. Count Von Cosel at your service." He clicked his heels and bowed.

Through squinting eyes, Papa considered the little man's formality. Vaguely, he recalled someone telling him the German's real name. Carl, or something like that.

When Papa offered no reply, the count continued: "No need to introduce yourself to me, of course. Everyone knows you as the famous writer. The greatest in the world. I've hoped to meet you one of these evenings. I have a wonderous story to share with you. A story about the love of a beautiful woman. When you hear it, you will want to write it down. I wish to grant you this amazing story. Will you come meet her?"

Papa found a glass still containing some liquid. He drained it quickly and looked around the room. Where had the others gone? Spilled out onto the street apparently. The funny little German awaited his answer.

"Meet who?" Papa asked.

The count smiled, revealing a mouth full of tiny teeth. Papa didn't trust men with tiny teeth. "A beautiful woman. The most beautiful woman on the whole island. Nay, in the whole country. Nay again: in the whole world! I wish to introduce her to you. Her name is Elena de Hoyos."

Papa searched his memory. The name rang a bell. He looked around the room.

"I see no one here but me and a German with an assumed name," Papa said.

As impossible as it seemed, the man's smiled widened and revealed more teeth. "She's at my home. Will you come meet her? Tonight will mark a glorious occasion. Trust me, you will want to tell this story."

Papa looked for signs of his comrades. It seemed almost as if someone had closed the bar for business and left him here alone with the German. Fuck them, Papa decided. They crushed his skull with their fists and now they had abandoned him. He thought about it. He could in fact use a new story to tell.

It took him several tries to get to his feet, and he needed to lean on the German to walk. Despite's the man's stature, he proved sturdy enough to keep Papa from falling over. "So be it. Take me to this beautiful woman of yours. What did you say her name was?"

"Elena de Hoyos," said the count, joy reverberating through his voice.

* * *

Count Von Cosel continued to support Papa's weight as they walked through the darkened streets of Key West. The count talked non-stop the whole time, describing his job at the Marine Hospital and how he worked behind the scenes to find cures for ailments, both common and uncommon.

"And that's how I met Elena de Hoyos," he said.

"The beautiful woman," said Papa.

"You'll see that I'm right." He went on to explain how Elena came to the hospital in a terrible state, suffering from the ravages of tuberculosis, and how the count recognized her as someone he'd seen in his dreams and visions. "Before I saw her in the flesh, I dreamed of her walking with me on these streets as I do now with you. She would sing to me the most beautiful songs in Spanish, and I would sing back to her."

The count demonstrated a few bars, but that only made Papa's head hurt worse. The street before them loomed dark. Had power gone out on the island somehow?

"No more singing," Papa said. He stumbled, but the German somehow kept him from falling on his ass.

"She likes my singing."

"I do not."

So the count went on to describe how things looked very grim for Elena, necessitating some novel strategies to ensure her survival.

"What did you say you were a doctor of?" Papa asked.

"I am a radiologist. I have access to sophisticated machines. When the hospital tried to limit my resources, I brought my equipment to her home. I used X-rays and electronical currents. Oh, her family thanked me effusively for my efforts. Her mother brought me teas as I worked, and when Elena grew tired, I sang her lullabies. I dressed her in colorful clothing and adorned her in fine jewelry. Later, her family gave me permission to build her the finest mausoleum on the island. Ah, here we are. This is my home."

Papa tried to process what he just heard about the mausoleum as he took in the bungalow. Not much more than a shack by the looks of it. It sat nearly hidden in the darkness underneath the branches of an impressive banyan tree, a short walkway leading to the door.

The count proceeded up the walkway, pulling Papa behind him. The night air did help rejuvenate Papa a bit, so he didn't need to lean on the count nearly as much.

"Did you say *mausoleum*?" asked Papa.

The count fumbled with the key, apparently not hearing him. He seemed to remember something about Elena de Hoyos now. The information might have come from Vincente, who considered himself an expert on beautiful women. Papa told him that he found that no surprise since Vincente was practically a woman himself. Vincente just laughed and told Papa that a woman who broke his heart with her beauty had sadly died, and that some poor sap built her a mausoleum with one odd feature: a telephone. It all started to come together.

The count disengaged the door bolt and looked at Papa through his thick lenses, his face serious. "I funded it myself. The finest on the island. Only the finest would suffice for her. Come inside."

A growing sense of unease settling over him, Papa hesitated. He couldn't see the little German any longer thanks to the bungalow's lack of lighting. But he also couldn't resist. Didn't the man promise him a story? And besides, Papa had survived battlefields, wars, untold violence. A little bungalow on this sleepy island should not fill him with such trepidation. He crossed the threshold just as the count lit a candle, its flame causing the lenses of his glasses to appear opaque.

"The power is out," said the count, "and I've retired my generator: perhaps an unwise decision given how many storms strike the island. But Elena no longer requires electricity nor ultraviolet rays. I have another, more simple means of rejuvenation, one that should prove more lasting. I'm delighted for you to bear witness."

"So I can tell the story."

"Indeed."

Following the little German, Papa began to berate himself for becoming involved in something so strange. The candle flame guided them past what looked like an old church organ and toward a bedroom at the back of the bungalow, where Papa anticipated seeing truly awful. Hadn't that fop from Mississippi written a story about a woman who kept her dead lover in a bedroom for years? Certainly Papa could write about this experience, and not only write a finer story but do it in fewer words.

But when he stepped into the doorway, he saw no desiccated corpse lying in a state of putrefaction. No, in fact, the candle lit the face of a woman who did possess a peculiar beauty, her face far from skeletal but full-fleshed, her hair flaxen and spread across her shoulders. Dressed in a wedding gown, she sat positioned upright on the bed, her unblinking eyes already turned toward the men who appeared at the threshold of her chamber. She seemed almost expectant. A floral scent permeated the whole room.

Holding the candle, the count introduced Papa, who established his position in the doorway. The count, meanwhile, took the seat next to the bed and rested the candle on a nearby table. In the dim lighting, Papa also saw an expensive-looking radio-phonograph. Near that sat several bottles of perfume, the source of the room's thick scent.

"Here is the writer I told you about," the count said to the figure on the bed.

"How do you do?" said Papa.

The woman neither spoke nor moved. In fact, Papa didn't see so much as a blink, her eyes remaining fixed and almost comically wide. The count lifted her hand and pressed it to his lips as he gazed with love upon her strange face. Such an uncanny sight reminded Papa of when he and Pauline, his current wife, bought the house on Whitehead Street, a scene of dilapidation at the time. Pauline took one look at the crumbling walls of the house and deemed it haunted. What would she think of the scene before him then? Papa felt that he'd found something truly uncanny in this woman who didn't move or talk.

Then it hit him. He said, "You've taken me here to see some sort of doll."

The count's bespectacled eyes turned to regard him. "Oh, she's no doll. She's real. Isn't she beautiful?"

Papa smirked, but he crossed the threshold to see more. The hair seemed real enough. A wig, perhaps? The skin looked made of putty, as if he could press his finger against the cheek and have it sink all the way to the knuckle. Clearly, the count was barking mad, but Papa found himself growing amused. Maybe he did find something he could write about.

"Forgive me," said Papa, "I obviously don't know a real woman when I see one."

"She's very real. Aren't you Elena? She even sings to me. Ah, that reminds me." He reached for the radio-phonograph, and Papa watched as the man turned several dials, but of course, with the power outage, he could find nothing. What a daft man, thought Papa. The count continued: "She dances, too. Just the other night, she got out of the bed and danced with me around the living room. I even let her lead."

"You don't say."

"Oh, yes, but such animated moments don't last long. Tonight, however, I shall try something new. Something different from electricity or X-rays. Tonight, I try a special diet. To see if she likes it and see if it gives her more lasting energy. Will you keep her company while I prepare it?"

The German stood and left the room before he received an answer. Papa considered his options before finally settling himself in the vacated seat.

The voice of Count Von Cosel came from outside the room, startling him momentarily. "Hold her hand, would you please? She doesn't like to be alone. And to feel the hand of a great author? I know she would love that."

Papa grimaced, but curiosity compelled him to do as instructed. He touched the hand, cautiously at first. The texture of the skin repelled him initially. It reminded him of molds applied to the damaged flesh of men mutilated during the Great War, those missing eyes and noses, even whole sides of their faces. Papa realized that he felt more clear-headed than he'd felt for much of the evening, and his sobriety allowed him to overcome his revulsion, so he lifted the hand. It fit pliantly into the form of his own, almost like a real hand. Such a small, delicate hand, and such a convincing likeness that he could imagine that he felt muscle and cartilage. But in the candlelight, he saw no evidence of such things, not even the ridges of blood vessels. If forced to identify its texture, he would say some kind of oiled silk. Maybe beeswax.

In the count's absence, he studied the face, too. The fixed staring eyes shone like glass, the orbs too wide to appear natural. They were obviously painted to look like the real thing. Leaning in, he realized that the face did not possess eyelids.

In time, he detected the aroma of something cooking. It cut deliciously through the thick smell of perfume in the room, and Papa's stomach growled. When had he last eaten? He couldn't remember.

He might have relaxed in anticipation of a meal, if not for the sound that startled him. Static. The radio, he realized.

Good. They finally restored power to the island. He expected music, but what he heard sounded like muffled conversation, the soft murmurings of a female voice. Then the singing began, as if the talking served as the preamble to a song. A lonely one, too, in Spanish. Papa guessed the broadcast came from Cuba, just ninety miles to the south.

He found himself listening, enjoying the respite from the quiet.

"Lovely voice," he said out loud, though he knew this strange doll, this effigy to a woman named Elena, could not hear it. "I suppose you want to get up and dance."

He felt pressure applied to his hand, as if the doll replied with a gentle squeeze.

Startled for a second time, Papa dropped the hand and stood, staring at the strange, fixed face.

But he must have imagined it.

In that moment, the music stopped, the radio going dead. Did the power go off again?

"Getting to know one another?" asked the count, who appeared in the doorway, holding a plate of food.

"What game are you playing?" Papa said. He remained on his feet as Count Von Cosel sat. The count set the plate on the nearby table and began cutting with a knife.

"No game, I assure you," he said, holding up a fork, its tip spearing a hunk of what looked like cooked liver, the source of the smell that made Papa so hungry. "Do you have ideas for your story yet?"

"I have ideas," Papa managed to say, still recovering from the shock of feeling his hand squeezed. But he obviously imagined it.

"Very good, very good," the count said. "Now, for what I wanted you to witness. I've tried using food before, but I realized she might require a special diet. Let's see if it has the effect I'm hoping for." Papa watched as the count placed the fork near the doll's prone lips. Of course, the mouth did not open.

"Strange," said the count. "She refuses. I thought for certain she would like this dish." He pressed the meat against her mouth, as if that would make a difference. "Perhaps she needs some assistance." Using his finger, he gently pried her lips apart.

The inconstant light cast by the candle made it difficult to say for sure, but

Papa thought he saw the form of brownish teeth when the lips parted. More of his mind playing tricks.

The count made a frustrated noise. "She will not eat."

"Perhaps she isn't hungry."

"Oh, she is."

Once more, Papa heard a woman's voice, but it did not come from the radio this time. Instead, it seemed to come from outside the room—outside the bungalow, in fact.

"Tanzler!" the voice said. "I know you're in there! Show yourself!"

But the count just sat there, the fork still poised in the air. Papa now recalled that as the count's real name—*Tanzler*—and it seemed as if the sound of it had left the man frozen.

"Come out and face me." The voice sounded slurred. "You have my sister. I know it!"

His curiosity aroused even further, Papa watched the count to see what he might do. The fork still upraised, the count swore. He looked at Papa through his thick lenses. "I apologize for this interruption."

"Who is that?"

"Elena's sister. She does not share the gracious, benevolent heart of her family. Would you?" He held out the fork and the plate.

Papa saw the food and heard his own stomach growl.

Perhaps the count heard it as well.

"See if she will eat, I mean. I'll take care of this…interruption."

Papa shrugged, accepting the fork and the plate. Though impatient for the evening to end, a mischievous idea came to him. "Don't be long," he said.

The count smiled and promised he would return without delay. He left Papa with the food. Papa knew he shouldn't drink on an empty stomach. He considered the expressionless face on the lifeless effigy before him as he sniffed the meat still impaled on the end of the fork. "This will be our secret," he said out loud. Then he ate it.

And it was delicious.

He recognized the recipe from his travels—*saure leber*, from the southern region of Germany. Though Papa would have chosen a better wine, he had to hand it to the little man. He'd proven his German credentials with his culinary skills.

Papa used the knife to cut a second bite, then a third, savoring the texture of the liver. He would have to ask the count where he came by his meat. He'd nearly finished the whole thing when he heard more of the conversation outside.

"I'll call the authorities," said the drunk woman. "Everyone knows that the mausoleum sits empty."

The sound of a slamming door followed, then the patter of feet. The count appeared in the doorway, looking flustered. But his face immediately brightened when he saw how little of the meal remained. "Oh, you've had luck! I knew she would respond to you. May I?"

Feeling slightly guilty and more than a bit perplexed by the words of the visitor, Papa nodded. He relinquished his seat to the German and handed him the plate.

"I knew she would be hungry," said the count as he carved off one of the remaining bits and held it to the doll's lips. "She'll need more. This will be a glorious night indeed. Would you?"

"Would I what?"

"Go into the kitchen. Bring back another plate."

Papa nodded, his appetite growing. He wondered what the count might have in the way of drink. His eyes now accustomed to the dark, he found his way to the kitchen, where he found the stove, along with a frying pan with meat still simmering in sauce. Papa stood over the stove, using his fingers to help himself to more. It really was delicious.

Still chewing, he saw the ice box. He opened it, hoping to find a bottle of beer that had not gone warm yet.

But he saw nothing of the kind.

Instead, he found the source of the liver.

Bits of it, at least.

At first, he stared without comprehension, not sure what to make of the pale skin. Had the count bought a whole pig? He regarded the rough signs of butchery, the jagged cuts in the flesh suggesting haste. The animal had a tiny head, too, with one large eye that seemed to consider Papa imploringly.

He leaned in for a closer look.

When he recognized what he saw, he nearly toppled over in panic and confusion.

Not an eye at all. Not a head. A woman's breast, the areola of her nipple.

Perversely, he remembered Pelayo's "wife," the prostitute who had gone missing.

He suddenly knew why, just as he knew the source of the liver still simmering on the stove.

Papa vomited on the floor.

Once he emptied his stomach, he steadied himself and made his way back to the bedroom, where he planned to murder the German. He heard the little man's voice before he arrived.

"She's doing it," said the count. "She is eating. She really is!"

Papa stopped in the doorway. He stared at the scene before him.

The thing on the bed, the doll, was in fact leaning forward and eating from the fork held in the count's hand. Papa blinked, trying to make the image go away, but it would not. The thing's mouth chewed, and once more Papa saw brown teeth, clinging with bits of a dead prostitute's flesh.

The count looked over his shoulder at Papa and smiled. "She loves it. She'll truly dance now."

Papa stumbled away, his hands fumbling for purchase on the walls as he rushed toward the front door of the bungalow. He didn't know what he'd just witnessed. He just knew he needed to get away. The count's voice called after him as he practically fell into the street outside. There was still no power, so everything lay in darkness. He looked about, hoping he would see the sister of that thing in the bed. He thought of what she said. *Everyone knows that the mausoleum sits empty.* Not a doll, but a corpse, its putrefaction disguised by layers of cloth and perfumes.

But Papa found himself alone, no sign of the sister. He paused to establish his bearings and began walking the darkened avenue in the direction of home. His stomach roiled, still holding remnants of his meal. He resisted the urge to stop and vomit again, wanting only to see the lighthouse that stood on the opposite side of his house on Whitehead Street. Surely, he reassured himself, it would come into view soon.

Not only had he eaten the flesh, but he'd seen that madman feeding it to the corpse, its jaws moving. If only he could say that the darkness played tricks on his eyes. What would Vincente say to that? If he liked the story of the bull's ear, he would go on and on about this one.

Papa thought about what he hadn't told Vincente—how he offered to fry up that bull's ear for Hadley, teasing her that if she ate it, it would make her a better lover. Give her more energy, as the Spanish said the flesh of a bull would.

What then would eating the butchered flesh of Pelayo's "wife" do for that corpse covered in cheesecloth and beeswax? As he walked, the night air did little to help him contain his revulsion.

In fact, the wind seemed to carry a voice. At one point, he slowed his steps, hoping he would find the sister behind him. She could talk sanity to him.

But the voice sounded familiar in a different way. It sang the notes of a long song popular in Cuba a few years ago. Papa didn't know all the words, but he recognized the song as the one heard playing on the madman's radio earlier, even without electricity. Something about passion in the breeze, a love that would not die. Then the smell of that perfume, a scent he would never forget. The sound of steps, too, feet moving in rhythm with the song. Dancing. Waiting for a partner to join in. One who would not feel opposed to letting her lead because she felt so fresh and alive tonight.

Papa did not turn to look. Even though the voice and steps and that awful scent followed him all the way home.

Gatortooth Sam

Phillip hoped to wake up to howling winds and a day off.

Instead, his dad told him the bad news about the storm changing direction. "Sorry champ, it's not coming here. Gotta go to school."

So Phillip stumbled into the kitchen where they all ate breakfast like any other day, as if a Category Four hurricane churning offshore in the Gulf of Mexico didn't mean anything. The television blared behind them, showing a reporter standing on a beach in a raincoat. That encouraged Phillip to keep pleading his case. "Nobody else is going to school," he told his dad while his mom wiped down the kitchen counter. He knew this for certain because everyone said so the day before. Everyone knew this storm looked worse than the one that hit a few years ago, and no way would they keep the schools open.

But open they did. Phillip's family finished breakfast, his mom kissing his cheek and running out the door in her work clothes because she never missed a day, his dad hustling him to the car, ready to drop him off at the bus stop because *he* never missed a day of work either, though he often ran late and made no effort to disguise his impatience with Phillip's slowness.

Phillip moved especially slow today because he knew he'd be the only one at the bus-stop.

He didn't want to see Gatortooth Sam today. Not if he had to ride the bus by himself.

Only he turned out to be wrong again.

They arrived to find one other person waiting for the bus. *Shit*, thought Phillip.

"See," his dad said, "you're not the only one here. Tomorrow you get out of bed sooner—you hear me? I can't be late again. They're going to fire my ass eventually. And you know whose fault that'll be."

"Mine," said Phillip, because he knew better than not to answer. From its size, he recognized the figure standing in the morning mist. Devon. It figured. If anyone else had parents who would make him attend school on a day everyone else got to skip, then that person was Devon. That kid's parents worked more than job each and usually didn't even drive him to the bus stop.

Exiting the car, Phillip nodded at the other kid. Devon didn't nod back. The rain matted his hair against his head, and his clothes looked damp. No telling how early he arrived out here, probably standing alone in the dark as the outer edge of the hurricane brushed their side of the Florida coast.

Phillip wanted to talk about Gatortooth Sam, but not with Devon. Anyone but Devon.

Sightings of Gatortooth Sam depended upon the weather. They never happened on sunny days. Just on wet days like this one, when the sun struggled to break the morning gloom.

With enough people on the bus, kids can distract each other, talk about videogames or whether the Bucs would ever figure out how to win. When the distractions fail, someone usually looks out the back of the bus, along the section of road lined with untended woodland and the wrecks of houses lost in the last storm. "Oh hell, there he is," a voice would say, and everyone else's head would turn.

And they would all see him running after the bus. Gatortooth Sam, pale in wet, tattered clothing, teeth gleaming.

Phillip always tried not to look. When the silence around him became too much, he couldn't help himself. It hurt to see him, to remember what made him that way. Still he would half-stand in his seat and look out the back window at the loping figure chasing the bus. It hurt to see what made that name so right, so perfect.

"Hey, sit down back there," the driver would yell. The driver never saw Gatortooth Sam. Or maybe he did and misidentified him as some poor kid who missed the bus. Either way, everyone took their time following his instructions so he'd have to repeat the order to sit down, but by that point the figure in pursuit would have sauntered off into the woods. Probably to make his way back to the house with the pool. Phillip tried not to think of that house as much as he tried not to see Gatortooth Sam.

* * *

That house seemed older than all the others in the neighborhood, with its rounded portico windows and two stories. Stone steps marked the walkway to the house, and once you got close enough, the broken tiles on the flat roof became visible, as well as the missing panes in the trellis windows. Cardboard and scrap wood covered a section that once held a window unit air conditioner. Empty, trash-strewn lots marked the bumpy road leading to the house, adding to the pervading sense of rot and sadness.

Whenever Phillip rode past it on his bike, he wondered about the original occupant of the house and what led him to settle so far away from everything. Alone, he lacked the courage to get off his bike and approach the house. Toward the rear, he could see stonework that suggested a pond of some kind. Rumor had it that an old man lived there, probably since childhood. Phillip tried to imagine what it must feel like inside that house. Probably a place where mold and bad dreams grew.

In the presence of others, he found the courage to get closer. They could protect each other, this group of kids who rode bikes in a tight cluster and shared stories, and by tacit agreement, they preferred not to include Devon. Whenever they passed his house, they would see Devon sitting on his brother's broken-down Plymouth. On one occasion, Phillip nodded and sort of waved. In response, Devon held up his middle finger, keeping it there as Phillip passed by.

"Fuck you, too," said Phillip, barely audible. He didn't want Devon to hear. He'd seen what Devon did to smaller kids who gave him shit.

"He's too poor for a bike," said Gary, who rode a nice mountain bike his parents bought him. "Sorry, Sammy," he added when Phillip gave him a look, but the third kid in their group either didn't hear the comment or pretended not to. Sammy rode the shittiest bike. Where Gary's sparkled with silver polish, Sammy's had no luster at all. Like his clothes, it came from a thrift shop.

* * *

The first time Phillip stepped foot beyond the gate of the house with the stonework, he did so in the company of Gary. Brown patches of dirt and weeds marked the area where the stone steps led up to the door and around the side of the house. "I want to see the pond," Phillip said, pointing toward the stonework.

"What about the crazy guy who lives there?" Gary said.

"He's probably really old—too old to do anything to us. We're kids," Phillip heard himself say, and to even him, it sounded like bluster. He'd never admit that he felt too afraid to go alone. He needed someone with him.

Gary looked unconvinced, but he said, "Fine, only if I see a rifle point through one of those windows, I'm hiding behind your fat ass."

"Deal."

They left their bikes on the street. Sammy stayed on his.

"You coming?" Phillip said.

"No way," Sammy said. "I heard stuff about this place."

"What stuff?"

Sammy's mouth moved, but nothing came out. Gary and Phillip stood there, gesturing for him to spit it out. Finally, Sammy said, "The guy who lives here goes fishing. With a gun."

"Jesus," Gary said. "I thought you had something scary to tell us. I know like five guys who go fishing with a gun. Though if I see that gun…" He finished the sentence by giving Phillip the stink-eye.

"Fishing with a gun *is* scary," Sammy said.

"No," Phillip said, "it isn't."

They left Sammy and their bikes behind, Phillip feeling emboldened, almost like he didn't need Gary to do this. As they walked toward the house and around the side, they could see the house's flaking yellow paint and the layers of rust on the porch railings. Odd bulges marked the surface of its

157

walls, like pustules fit to burst. Regardless, he felt more and more immune to any threat that might come from inside.

When they came to the stonework, they could see that it didn't line a pond, but rather an old swimming pool—square and bordered with black tile that probably once looked white. A closer look revealed the details of the stonework, evidently meant to represent planetary objects, perhaps astrological symbols, though he knew little about how star signs worked, beyond the imagery associated with his own sign: Gemini. The Twins, his mother explained. She had him look at his horoscope every morning before school. "You need all the advantages you can get," she said in that tired tone that, Phillip had learned, adults used to indicate how much they hated their lives and the choices they made.

He didn't see Gemini amongst the stone carvings. Several looked ominous, even perverse in the acts they represented. A naked horned figure appeared noticeably aroused, while another set off amongst the leaves bore a large overbite and huge fangs. One frog-like monstrosity with an enormous head and wide grinning mouth crouched, as if prepared to pounce. Gary pointed out that it had human anatomy below its waist and made a jerking off gesture while grinning at Phillip, who didn't smile back.

Instead, he reacted to the prickling feeling on the back of his neck and looked over his shoulder, back toward the house. He sensed someone watching them. Opaque windows returned his gaze.

"Holy jeez," Gary said, and Phillip returned his attention to the water. Inside the battered border of stone grew clumps of weeds and sawgrass, breaking through the concrete floor of the neglected pool and extending all the way above the surface of water so brackish they couldn't see the bottom. Moving branches drew their attention, a sign of circulation in the water. On closer inspection, he realized what they saw.

Baby alligators, dozens of them, swimming between the stalks and reeds growing out of the water.

"I don't believe it," said Gary. Neither did Phillip. He leaned in for a closer look, putting his hands on his knees, his toes right be the edge—stupidly leaving himself vulnerable to the kind of prank Gary pulled. Phillip felt his friend's hand on his back too late to avert the push.

He would've fallen in if the hand that pushed him hadn't also grabbed his belt.

"Got'cha," said Gary, laughing. "You don't want to fall in there, dude."

"No way. I mean, they're not big enough to hurt you."

"Right. But swimming through all that crud, probably swallowing it—you'd get gonorrhea."

"I already got it from your mom. I just don't want to swallow a baby gator."

"He'd just eat his way out of you," said Gary.

They both laughed and turned around to walk past the house, toward the street.

A glance at one of the windows stopped Phillip cold.

A fanged face looked out at him, a pink tongue frozen near the window, as if in mid-growl. For a second, he expected it to lunge through the glass and come after them. Gary didn't see it at first, but once his eyes tracked to where Phillip was looking, he froze too.

They stood still, not saying anything, afraid of courting attention.

Finally, Gary spoke. "It's a stuffed bear, I think."

Cautiously, they began to move, more slowly this time.

"Looks like a bear, except for the mouth."

"Yeah, like a reptile mouth."

Phillip agreed. They passed the window, each imagining what sort of taxidermist would fuse together the faces of such disparate animals. They didn't look away until they ventured out of sight of the window, unable to decipher the meaning of the object's placement. Did someone intend to scare them away? Maybe it was there all along, and the reflection of the sun just made it hard to see.

When they got to the street, they couldn't find Sammy or his bike. "Sonofabitch," said Gary, because his own bike wasn't there either.

"Stolen?" Phillip said, though he already knew the answer.

Saying nothing, Gary began walking up the street, his anger showing in his accelerating pace. Phillip got on his bike and pedaled slowly behind him.

As they passed his house, they saw Devon still sitting on the Plymouth. He flipped them the middle finger again.

Without saying anything, they both avoided meeting the bigger kid's gaze.

Until Devon started laughing.

Fed up, Gary stopped and turned. "Fuck you!" he yelled before Phillip could stop him.

He knew Devon wanted this reaction. Gary should've known too—or maybe he did, and he wanted the confrontation. He should've hopped on Phillip's handlebars so they could both ride away to safety. He should've known that just standing there, in the middle of the street, heartbroken over the stolen bike, invited the bigger kid to stride out into the street and plant his fist against Gary's head.

Sure enough, Devon threw a punch so savage that Phillip cried out as if it had hit him. Gary went down, hard, and didn't get up back up for a long time.

They wouldn't find his bike that day, nor did Sammy turn up. When he finally wobbled to his feet, Gary needed Phillip's help walking home, the two of them taking one of the handlebars on Phillip's bike and moving very slowly. Twice, they needed to stop so that Gary could sit down in the street. When he spoke, he did so in a slurred voice. "What do you think was in the window?" Gary said.

"I don't know." Phillip wondered if he should leave Gary sitting there in the street and run for help, find an adult somewhere. Each time he came to that resolution, Gary would stagger to his feet and grab the handlebar again and start walking. It took over an hour to reach Gary's house. The sun had already gone down. Phillip knew he'd catch hell when he finally made it through his own door. He knew his parents already called all his friends' parents, asking if they knew where he'd gone. For once, he didn't care. They could call all they wanted. He didn't like how Gary kept needing to sit down and how glassy his eyes looked. "You ok?" he said outside Gary's house, the two of them still holding onto the handlebars. The way Gary hunched reminded Phillip of the way his grandfather's posture as he shuffled around the house with a walker.

"Yeah, I'm fine. Why?"

"Because Devon Smith just kicked your ass, that's why." Phillip tried to smile, an effort that went unreturned. One of Gary's pupils looked bigger than the other. "I won't bring it up again," Phillip said. "I won't tell anyone."

But Gary didn't answer. He didn't say anything. Phillip watched him walk toward his front door. "I promise," he said to the back of his friend before he disappeared inside.

* * *

On Friday of the following week, they buried Gary.

Phillip's parents offered to buy him ice cream after the funeral, but Phillip said he didn't feel like it, and he sat in his Sears suit and looked out the back window as they drove home. His mother wouldn't stop talking about how Phillip needed to report any persistent headaches, that if he ever developed double vision he would tell her immediately, that if he ever died of an aneurism like poor Gary, she didn't know what she would do with herself. Just come apart completely, maybe.

Phillip never told anyone about how Devon slugged Gary. He kept the promise he made and kept his mouth zipped. Even in death, he imagined, Gary would feel the embarrassment of getting his ass kicked, and if he could find a way, he would take the form of a ghost and haunt Phillip forever.

Mentally, he replayed that day's events over and over. Kids punched each other all the time, and no one ever died from that. He argued with himself about whether or not such a thing could have killed his friend. Everyone said it was just a natural defect, and no one ever questioned him about what happened to Gary on that afternoon. No one ever brought up the missing bike, though Phillip wondered where it went. Just thinking about it made him mad.

A few days later, he got his answer.

Riding his bike to the quarry, he expected to spend an afternoon throwing rocks into the water by himself. He spent a lot of time by himself now. He just didn't expect to find Sammy in his spot, as if waiting for him. There with him, he saw Devon. With Gary's bike. The two stood motionless on their wheels, as waiting for him to make a move.

Phillip stopped but didn't drop the kickstand. He held the bike between his legs like a horse ready to bolt. "You need to return that," he said.

"I'm keeping it for him," Devon said.

"You're not keeping it for anyone but yourself." He regarded Sammy. "You. You stole it that day."

Sammy's mouth opened and closed, but no words came out. Sammy had terrible teeth, brown and yellow with receding red gums, reminding Phillip of his grandfather's tobacco-stained teeth, only Sammy didn't get that way from smoking or drinking. Phillip imagined striking those teeth with his fist. He pictured the teeth breaking off, some of them embedding into the flesh of his hand, Sammy choking on the rest.

Then he looked at Devon just sitting there, hunched over the handlebars of a bike that once belonged to his friend, seeming to dare him to do something about it. He grinned at Phillip, predatory and malicious. "We're going to catch snakes," Devon said.

"Yeah," Sammy said. His face brightened. "Come with us, you always know where to find snakes."

"Help us find snakes, and I'll give you the bike. I'm just borrowing it," said Devon.

"No. You give it to his parents. You tell them what you did."

"I took care of his bike. That's what I did. You want it, help us find snakes."

Phillip grimaced. He knew he couldn't just take the bike away from Devon. Turning direction, he started riding toward an area full of empty lots. Just pine trees and tall grass. He rode ahead of the other two by three bike lengths, his rage simmering. Devon had longer legs than Gary did, so he rode awkwardly hunched, his knees coming up too far. Apparently, he was too stupid to raise the seat. Sammy huffed along next to him, his smallness exaggerated by the size of the older kid.

At one point, he peddled harder to catch up with Phillip. "Hey," Sammy said.

Eyes ahead, Phillip didn't answer.

"I just want you to know," said Sammy, "that I didn't do anything bad."

"You stole. That's pretty bad."

"He followed us that day. When you guys went into the yard, he just grabbed the bike and started riding. I didn't know what to do."

"You could've yelled or something."

"I rode after him," Sammy said. Then he used the dumbest phrase Phillip ever heard. "I gave chase."

"You gave what?"

"I gave chase. I rode after him. Told him to stop. But he said it was just a joke. Said he'd give it back later. I told him he better."

"Well, he didn't. And now you two seem like best friends."

"He's going to give it back like he said. We were looking for you to do that. I swear."

Distracted, Phillip stopped paying attention to where he was leading them. At some point, he missed a turn and he realized that he'd brought them back to that house with the pool and overgrown weeds. He stopped riding and looked at the structure before them, the yellow-brown paint that seemed somehow duller in the fading light. Maybe he intended to take them here all along. The scene of the crime. The house seemed to breath, vaporous, wrapped in tumorous secret.

They wanted snakes, but Phillip decided to give them alligators.

"There snakes here?" Devon said, pulling up next to them, out of breath. He eyed the weeds like a cowboy appraising the suitability of a prairie for a homestead.

Without answering, Phillip got off his bike, momentarily considering its safety. But anyone who would steal it, he thought, was coming with him now, following him as if enthralled in the spell of the house. As he passed the questionable window, he turned his head, but he saw no animal face peering back at him. Instead, it held a garland of some sort. Teeth, he realized. He didn't draw attention to it, nor did he stop to consider it more closely. If someone in the house spied them, then so be it.

He led them to the edge of the pool, the statues and carved astrological signs still standing there along the darkening concrete. Except certain details looked different, slightly off. Some of the statues had changed position, some in subtle ways, others more drastically, like the horned creature, which now mounted the frog-thing. Someone must have repositioned them, thought

Phillip. He noticed another garland of teeth, this one tied in a necklace around the neck of the frog-thing. "Sweet," said Devon, following him.

Devon reached for the necklace of teeth as Phillip turned to the reeds growing out of the bottom of the water, now much taller, thicker. "Look," Phillip said, pointing out the tiny, baby alligators swimming in tight circles amidst the reeds.

"Holy fucking shit," said Devon. Grinning. "I need one of those."

"This is what we saw," Phillip whispered, as if talking to the unseen presence in the house. "With these here, you never have to go to a store to buy food. You come out at night and collect what you need."

"What I need," said Devon, "is one of these. You can keep one alive in a bathtub, I bet. Feed it until it won't fit no more."

"I wouldn't know what to feed it," Sammy said.

Devon crouched and reached out with his hand. The closest baby alligators moved further from his reach. "Goddammit," he said, "come back here." But they all kept their distance. Devon straightened and moved to the opposite end of the pool, where the water looked most brackish and where the thickest clump of weeds grew. Sammy followed, with Phillip moving warily behind them both.

A baby alligator surfaced close to the pool's wall, and Sammy, probably in imitation of Devon, leaned over and reached out his hand, his toes at the water's edge.

Phillip was the one who pushed him.

He acted on impulse, putting little thought into the way he pressed his fingers into Sammy's back. Later, he would tell himself he meant to pull Sammy back at the last moment, just like Gary did to him the first time they saw the pool together. Maybe he just underestimated the weakness of Sammy, how it took just the slightest nudge to make him topple into the water. He didn't have time to grab him by the belt the way Gary grabbed him. Under the interrogator's bright bulb, he would say, *It all happened so fast. I had no time to react at all. That kid was so small for his age, so weak and light. I barely had to touch him at all.*

Maybe enough time would elapse before the police took him in to convince himself that he really meant those things, that with practice saying it over and over again to himself, the lie would become true.

In truth, he stepped back as Sammy fell and Devon laughed. Below them in the brackish water, Sammy's arms flailed, his head popping up above the surface and spitting out a mouthful of polluted water. "Get a good one," Devon shouted as Sammy struggled to keep his head above the surface, his hand reaching for the lip of the pool, where the other two stood.

Just standing there? the interrogator would ask.

Like I said, it happened so fast. I barely believed it when I saw it.

What was "it"?

Every day, Phillip prepared himself for this question. No police car ever arrived for him, and that moment under the bright light in the interrogation room never arrived. But he knew what he would have said because he practiced it so often, especially as he lay awake in bed night after night, unable to sleep.

Sammy yelling for help. Devon double over, laughing. The smaller boy's arms stirring foamy black water. Phillip stepping back because he didn't want to get splashed.

Maybe he glanced back at the window, wondering what this might look like from the perspective of someone looking from the other side. The feeling that someone else watched never went away, along with the certainty that no one would ever question the presence in that house.

Something else he knew: that this presence enjoyed the show. Inside his head he heard the voice of that presence: *This is what growing up feels like. You watch other people struggle and enjoy the fact that it isn't you.*

As if in response to that voice, the reeds parted suddenly, and something enormous moved through them. Phillip watched and enjoyed as an enormous dark green body moved toward Sammy. He watched and enjoyed as gigantic jaws parted, and a mouth crowded with teeth closed around Sammy's head.

A shrill scream filled the air, Sammy not using words anymore, just a sound of animal horror as the gigantic form thrashed about before disappearing beneath the surface, taking Sammy down with it.

Devon stopped laughing and joined Phillip in silent shock. For several endless seconds, they watched the surface of the water, undulating like a stage curtain snapped shut, waiting for Sammy to re-emerge. When he failed to do so, they both turned tail and fled back to the front of the house, taking their bikes and riding away in silent fear.

The voice of that presence grew fainter in Phillip's head as he put more and more distance between himself and that house. *That's how it's done*, the voice said.

They left Sammy's bike there.

Days later, when Phillip found the courage to return, he discovered it gone.

In stillness, the house sat like a fattened monster.

* * *

Until the day of the storm, Phillip avoided going back there. He thought he could choose to never see it again, maybe even get to the point where he could pretend it didn't exist.

Except Gatortooth Sam wouldn't let that happen.

With the bus empty but for him and Devon, the specter of Gatortooth Sam would appear for sure, sprinting out of the mist to pursue the bus.

Or not the bus itself. In truth, Phillip knew, he appeared because of *who rode* the bus. And not just anyone.

Phillip thought a lot about that stupid phrase Sammy used, how he *gave chase*. He would always give chase now, pursuing the people who spoke not a word when Sammy didn't turn up at home later that evening. Who kept quiet when the authorities visited the school, questioning everyone about his last whereabouts. Who said nothing to contradict the official story that this undersized kid had no real friends, that other kids only picked on him, that he made for easy prey for whoever kidnapped him one day after school, around dusk. Who last saw Sammy disappearing into a loathsome pool, arms waving, his head inside an alligator's mouth and did nothing, said nothing.

No one ever found Sammy's body. How would they even know where to look?

They'd have to open up the gator's belly to find him.

But what Phillip feared most was the possibility they'd only need to look inside that window of the tumorous house to see what became of him. Not a distorted bear-gator anymore. A new design would await them.

The first time Phillip heard that name—Gatortooth Sam—he thought that, oh god, someone knew, that Devon had told.

Yet it only took one look at the misshapen form following the bus for someone else to come up with that name, and it stuck.

As the bus passed all the familiar landmarks, Phillip made furtive glances out the window. Certain thoughts tempted him—that their pursuer had somehow called down the inclement weather, crafting the kind of moment where the bus would have only the two of them aboard. With each glance, he expected to see the figure looking back at him, small eyes glaring over that crowded mouth of teeth. When Gatortooth Sam failed to appear, he finally started to relax.

Until the bus driver made an unexpected turn.

"Gotta turn here," the driver said with a brief glance over his shoulder. "Some flooding up ahead." As the bus rounded a corner, Phillip saw the yellow cones barring them from their usual route. A sign blinked orange letters: DANGER: STANDING WATER. FOLLOW DETOUR.

Realizing where this new road would take them, Phillip risked a glance in Devon's direction. If it troubled Devon to come this close to the house again, it didn't show. As silent conspirators, they spoke only once after Sammy died in the pool. That conversation happened in the bathroom after an assembly where a police officer addressed the student body about the importance of reporting suspicious strangers. The officer held the microphone too close to his mouth, and feedback kept distorting his voice, every other word obliterated by an electronic screech. Covering their ears, everyone had to fill in the blanks the best they could. "Every one of you will get molested," he seemed to say, though Phillip thought he may have heard it wrong. "If you see someone about to molest you, run for the nearest house and scream as loud as you can, and I will personally come to help. Do not be afraid, but run as far as possible. Any questions?" Afterwards a grief counselor asked if anyone would like to share anything about Sammy. No one volunteered.

"They were talking about us," Phillip said to Devon afterwards, as they stood at neighboring urinals.

"I don't know what you're talking about," Devon said. He shook off the last drop of urine and zipped.

"You were there. If we don't tell anyone, no one'll ever know the truth."

"I don't even know you. And stop looking at my dick." As he walked away, he shoved Phillip into the urinal, not giving him a chance to say no, he wasn't looking down there at all. Instead, he had been gazing upon what Devon had around his neck: the garland of gator teeth. He didn't see Devon remove it from frog-thing's neck, or had he gone back another time and taken it? Wasn't that an admission of guilt?

The next day, the start the rainy season, Gatortooth Sam appeared for the first time.

And now, here they were, following a detour that would take them past the house again. Phillip closed his eyes, hoping the driver would accelerate, pass by it quickly.

Instead, they slowed. An audible curse from the driver's seat prompted Phillip stand up and look ahead. Before the bus lay another obstruction, a river of water moving across the roadway. This time no sign redirected them, so the driver idled forward. To their left, Phillip could see what amounted to a new river. Water gushed over the steps leading down from the house. It came from the pool behind the house, Phillip somehow knew.

The rain picked up, along with the wind, and the waterline rose as the bus pushed forward. Phillip willed the driver to go faster. He glanced in Devon's direction but saw no break in his bland disinterest. He wished he could shut off like that. Feel nothing. It was no act either. Of course, Devon would feel no worry, no guilt, and he could keep Gary's bike forever. Gary didn't need it anymore. All Devon did was punch him. Everyone heard about how Gary was born with a ticking time bomb, an undetected birth defect. From the moment of his birth, Gary could have gone to sleep and not waken up. No reason for Devon to think punching him had anything to do with it. He did nothing wrong to Gary, and he did no wrong to Sammy either. He didn't push him into the pool. Phillip did that. And only Phillip had to live with that guilt.

At that moment, Phillip realized that Gatortooth Sam gave chase after him alone, not anyone else.

With a shudder, the bus came to a stop. The driver cursed even louder this time and beat his fist on the wheel. They didn't even make it past the house with the pool. Three more times, the driver yelled *goddammit*, once when the bus engine refused to turn over, once when the radio couldn't get a signal—probably because of the weather, the driver said—and once more when the engine still refused to turn over. He looked over his shoulder at Devon and Phillip. "You boys got shoes on?"

Both kids said yes at the same time, as if neither one of them found the question stupid.

"Well, take them off and pull up your pants legs as high as they'll go. You're getting off."

"But the water," Phillip said.

"It ain't that high. If you were girls, I wouldn't recommend this. But you got balls, right? I hope I'm not mistaken about that."

"You're not," said Devon. "At least not about me." His shoulder bumped Phillip's as he pushed down the aisle, a move so typically Devon. It threw Phillip off-balance, but instead of getting angry, Phillip noticed the sneakers in Devon's hands. They looked so surprisingly juvenile, embossed with a cartoon character logo, the kind a much younger kid would wear. No way he could actually like that sort of thing, not Devon. That didn't fit into the profile he and Gary worked out to explain Devon's constant bullying. They never pictured him this way, a kid not just mean, but maybe a little slow. One who knew how to tell time only by the shows that came on TV and who loved some goofy cartoon character so much that he wanted his sneakers to reflect it.

He trailed behind Devon, seeing him as small and weak. He would talk to the driver, argue for a sensible alternative, anything besides stepping into the spreading body of water outside, appearing as deep and as unknowable as the waters of the gulf far off shore. With the storm, there was no real difference, the winds pushing the sea's bony fingers inland.

The driver seemed to sense what he wanted to say and opened the door. "I'm doing you a favor, kid. You could be waiting here all day."

"It's a hurricane though," said Phillip.

"That's no hurricane. It's just a band of rain. The storm landed miles from here. Didn't you see the news? Look, I'll say I never saw you. I don't even care if you go to school or not."

"I'm not," said Devon.

"Yeah," the driver said. "Go jump some puddles together. I never saw you."

The water came through the bus door and climbed almost to the top step. Phillip would have stepped in front of Devon if he could have, but his wide body blocked him. Around Devon's neck, the necklace of teeth grinned at him. They looked like they could bite. Phillip thought again of the squat frog thing that once held the necklace and the garland hanging from the window. Such things, movies say, ward off evil. At one point he would have tried to take it from Devon. Now, he wanted to Devon to keep it on.

First Devon, then Phillip, jumped from the landing of the bus into the water still filling the street, already high enough to reach Devon's waist, while on Phillip, it covered his stomach. Phillip looked back at the driver, hoping that he could see reason now. This wasn't safe. But the door closed against the water, and he could see nothing through the foggy glass.

He trudged behind Devon, not sure at first where they should go. The landscape around the house marked the highest ground, the ongoing rush of water creating a waterfall on the steps. Intuition told him where it came from. Without looking he knew spewed in an upheaval from the pool, just as he knew the statues had disengaged themselves from their stone moorings. The frog-thing would love this weather. The frog-thing would be anywhere. Even below the surface, near their feet.

They needed to go toward the house. At least they'd be out of the water. He called out to the figure walking ahead, but Devon pushed on stubbornly through the water and didn't look back, either not hearing or refusing the hear. Maybe like Phillip, he believed the teeth around his neck would protect him.

As if hearing his thoughts, something jerked Devon underwater so suddenly he had no time to call out. He simply vanished beneath the surface.

Phillip had to fight against a current to reach the spot where he disappeared.

He called out Devon's name, used his hands in a stupid attempt to part the water, struggling to see where he went, but his own reflection met him, smeared with the film of street oil and roadkill.

Into the water he reached with his hands, hoping to grab a loose article of clothing. Something snagged his fingers, the rough bristles of twine and something hard and pointed.

The necklace of teeth.

It would save him, Phillip thought, tugging on it.

But he couldn't get it to break the surface, something holding Devon down with incredible strength.

With one final tug, he felt something give, and he thought he had him, he would rescue Devon, thanks to that garland of teeth. He thought about how Gary pulled him back from falling into the pool, and if only he did the same thing when he pushed Sammy, none of this would have happened.

Maybe no storm would have formed and the street wouldn't have flooded and the driver wouldn't have made them get off the bus.

Even if it didn't make things right, he could at least save Devon.

The bite ruined any hope of that.

Maybe his hand never held the necklace of the teeth.

Fortunately, he wouldn't remember feeling the sharp, jagged teeth chomp through his flesh. The doctors somehow managed to reattach the thumb, though it would never work right, and without fingers, it couldn't do much on its own anyway. No one ever found the four fingers he lost.

The driver supposedly pulled him from the water, though Phillip couldn't remember, nor could he remember the way he screamed over and over, *He's under there, he's under there*, and the driver, assuming he meant Devon even dived under the water, but he could only save Phillip.

His mom and dad both took days off to sit with him in the hospital. Never the same days though. The boss might sympathize, his dad explained, but that didn't mean they could bend the rules, and they needed the paychecks. Thus, his parents alternated shifts, sitting by his bed, soothing him, answering his questions. Like what happened to Devon? His mother hushed him and encouraged him to drink the milkshake she brought him. "It's a good thing," she said, "that you still have the fingers on your right hand. When you're better, you can write the bus driver a letter thanking him for saving you." But he still needed to know what happened to Devon, and while his mother avoided the question, claiming not to know, his father looked at him grimly and told him what he knew.

"Something bit his head off. An alligator, they think. Your mom made me promise not to tell you. But it's been such a terrible year, but I think you need the truth. You've lost another friend, and I just hate, hate, hate that for you." Tears welled up in his father's eyes. Phillip looked up in wonder. He'd never seen him cry before. "But one other thing you ought to know, and it's the most important thing. You're also goddamn lucky. You just lost some fingers. That could've been your head inside that thing's mouth."

"Did they find it?" Phillip said.

"Find what?" His father's tears dried up instantly. "The kid's head? That's a morbid question to ask."

But Phillip meant the alligator, the thing that did the biting.

He doubted they ever would find the thing that bit off Devon's head.

And it would do no good to tell his father about how sure he felt that he had that garland of teeth in his hand, about how certain he was that wearing it around the neck would protect Devon.

Later that night he would wake up in the hospital bed, sweating and crying and alone, because this one time the chair nearby was empty. He wouldn't remember whose turn it was to sit there, his mom's or his dad's. But he wished he could tell one of them about his sudden realization: that in pulling on that necklace, he had probably cut off Devon's head himself. How he pulled it on it so hard that he drove the teeth into Devon's neck and ripped his head away, along with his own fingers.

At night, such explanations made sense. He didn't think of the impossible strength this act required, to sever flesh and bone so suddenly. In daylight, especially on days when he rode the bus again, he thought of the things that could accomplish such a feat, the things with sharp enough teeth, and he always refused to look behind him, even when the other heads turned.

Children of the Goat Man

Charlie heard nothing from Elsa in years, but he promised to drop everything and come over when she called him. She provided no explanation. "Just come over," she said. "There's someone here you need to see."

"Someone I know?" Charlie said, feeling the weight of years and the ache of a decade's absence. He started counting when no immediate response came, making it to thirteen before she said anything else.

"That's hard to answer. I can't really say one way or another."

Charlie didn't know what that meant, but he verified that she still lived with her father, though she declined to call what her father did "living." More like waiting out the effects of smoking four packs a day since forever, she explained. His chief reward for a diligent habit: congenital heart failure and a slipping hold on reality. Elsa stuck around and helped him pay whatever bills he couldn't cover with his police pension.

Charlie said, "This person I'm coming to see—is it your dad? Because I doubt he wants to see me."

"Just come over," she said, hanging up before he could reply.

On the way, Charlie recognized the neighborhood, though it looked a little worse than he remembered, with more than a few cars on blocks and plenty of listless people sitting on doorsteps, taking a break from doing nothing.

He found Elsa waiting outside for him, taking quick puffs from a cigarette that looked all filter. He didn't know if she should hug her after not seeing her for so long. They did a lot more than hug in the old days. She crossed her arms after throwing away the cigarette, so he just gave her a little wave.

No greeting in return. Instead, she led him up a walkway overgrown with weeds, toward a side garage door. She paused with her hand on the door and looked at him. "You remember Cole?"

"No," Charlie said.

"Me neither." She opened the door and gestured for him to follow.

The person called Cole sat in a chair in the middle of the garage, surrounded by tools and broken machinery. At first, Charlie misread the scene of the skinny man sitting so straight and rigid, thinking that ropes held him bound to the chair. But he stood up when he saw Charlie and beamed like a million dollars just walked in.

"I can't believe it's you, really you. Jesus Christ. I never thought I'd ever see either of you ever again," the man said. Charlie took in the height of the stranger—well over six feet even with hunched shoulders. Impossibly thin, too, like he never ate, with a chest so hollowed out a bird could nest inside it.

Charlie looked at Cole, then Elsa, then back to Cole again. "Do I know you?"

"Yes, you fucking know me, and she knows me, too. You left me in the fucking woods, in that fucking place, but I finally got out. And the part that sucks is we need to go back, and I mean right away."

* * *

Cole meant the woods behind the high school, a refuge for scrub jays and empty beer bottles and weather-torn porno mags. With the Internet, nobody bought porno mags anymore, but somehow, they kept finding their way to the woods for teenagers to find, because only teenagers went into those woods, looking for reprieve from adults and of course to find trouble.

Cole said they had a gang back then, and on occasion they liked to explore those woods together. On a cool October day, they cut school early just to see how far back the trees went and how long it would take before they ran into any sign of civilization.

This led to them finding the hospital.

It sat there, nestled among the trees with broken windows and wild vines

175

nearly covering it entirely. None of them expected to find it, nor did they know it even existed. Except for Elsa. She recalled her dad talking about some abandoned hospital off the beaten path, but she didn't remember him saying anything about it existing so close to where they lived or how it could sit back here in the woods without them even knowing it. I mean, there's not even a road leading back here. Or maybe the hospital went so far back, perhaps all the way to the 1920s, that over time, nature just reclaimed everything. That suggestion seemed to jar more memories for Elsa, and she remembered her dad saying something it served as a convalescence home for people with TB, later becoming an orphanage or mental hospital—she couldn't say which—but she also remembered her father warning her not to follow any of her dipshit friends into it.

"This is the one," Cole had asked.

"How many abandoned hospitals are there?" said Elsa. "I'm not just being sarcastic. How many are there really?"

Cole started to say, "Probably a lot," but the words didn't have time to come out because he saw the first goat. A large white one, with magnificent horns, grazing, just at the far corner of the building. This discovery at first delighted them, but they soon began to feel uneasy. To find some farm animal grazing out here in what otherwise seemed unoccupied land made them feel vulnerable, watched. Then Max pointed in another direction toward another goat, this one partially obscured by a tree, but grazing just like the other one.

("Wait," said Elsa. "Who's Max?")

("You don't remember him either, I guess, but he was part of our gang. An important part. You forgot all about us.")

Soon enough, two more goats appeared, them two more after that, and they began to realize that a whole herd of goats occupied the area, many of them camouflaged by the surrounding woods but gradually becoming visible as they stood quietly, stricken by what Cole described as a feeling of both awe and terror.

Those feelings only increased when they saw the largest goat of them all— the apparent lord and master of the rest, one that stood out because of its pure whiteness, though that alone couldn't explain how magnificent and large he seemed, with horns that dwarfed all the rest, standing long and rounded to intimidating points. This one stood before an empty doorway, and unlike the other goats, he regarded the teenagers with intelligent curiosity. Perhaps to show his lack of fear, this goat sniffed the air contemptuously and turned around to disappear through the open doorway, as if daring the teenagers to follow him inside.

No one spoke. Cole searched each of their faces for clues to their thoughts. All of them seemed to feel the same magical rush, a sense of having stumbled upon something forbidden. However, something buried within Cole's consciousness began sending him warning signal. A thought struggling to form.

Before he could pinpoint it exactly, Max took a step toward the entrance where the goat had vanished. "Well, who's coming with me?" he said, looking over his shoulder.

No one else moved, and though Cole couldn't say for sure what went through everyone else's minds, he found himself approaching a stubborn, resisting thought, a memory really, and before anyone could take another breath, it finally broke through completely, a phrase forming in his consciousness.

The Goat Man.

There it was. He spoke it, and Max halted his movement and turned.

Yeah, all he knew about the Goat Man came from crazy Uncle Larry, a guy who liked to drink beer, ride motorbikes, and shoot the shit. He told Cole the story—how he went camping in the Everglades one night during one of his many treks to find the Lost City, where Al Capone allegedly hid a bunch of money, though Larry never did find any such thing. It happened that Uncle Larry pitched his tent and settled in with a good fire going, eventually nodding off after enjoying a few cans of beer. A full moon lit up the surrounding area pretty well, so when he awoke and saw what he saw, he saw it pretty clearly. The Goat Man. Sitting on his haunches on the other side of the fire. Just looking at him. *He was the devil, kid, I swear it*, Larry said. *Pure evil, through and through.*

When Cole related this story to his friends, they laughed and reminded him that every single one of them had an Uncle Larry—a delusional drunken relative. Max told him to calm down and follow that goat into the building. "Stay close and keep me safe if you're so worried," Max said.

But Cole remained rooted to his spot, unnerved by what seemed like an unnatural determination to follow the goat into that building. No discernible purpose in that. Nobody ever took Cole to church, but he grew up with what he considered a healthy fear of the invisible world—he had a grandmother who made sure of that, believing that only a lingering fear of eternal damnation would keep him from the kind of life his dear uncle lived. That strategy didn't work out as well as she would have liked, but it did make Cole think that only evil machinations could explain Max's determination to follow a goat into an abandoned building.

But what did Elsa decide to do? She suddenly ran off in a different direction, apparently transfixed by the appearance of a baby goat. Charlie ran after her—as usual, he only had one thing on his mind, and Cole could hear him making all sorts of promises about how he'll catch one of those babies for her. Cole realized then that none of his friends took anything he said seriously, and none of them respected the obvious *gravity* of their situation. Not even Max, his best friend in the world, who smiled at him just before disappearing into the empty doorway.

What else could Cole do? Their doubt in him proved contagious, and he didn't want to stand there alone in front of that creepy building. No other choice but to follow Max. Which he did.

* * *

Charlie forced himself to laugh at the end of all this. But nothing in the story struck him as funny. Something felt wrong.

"Look, I'm sorry. I just don't know you. I've never met you, and I don't know anybody named Max. I've never even heard of an old orphanage in the woods."

"It was a hospital," said Cole.

"Whatever. Right, Elsa?"

Elsa said nothing. She watched Cole, searching for something.

"We've got to go back," said Cole. "Max is still there."

"Still where?"

Cole looked at Charlie as if he had just discovered the dumbest person alive. *The hospital.* He and I were kept there. As slaves."

"Slaves to the Goat Man? The Devil?" Charlie looked at Elsa just to verify that she heard all this. But she continued to regard Cole with a blank expression.

"Does your Goat Man want something?" she said, as if she sensed something. "In exchange for Max?" She avoided Charlie's questioning gaze.

"Yeah. He does. He wants his offspring back. The one you stole."

* * *

Elsa loved animals. Charlie remembered that. He remembered any number of cats that varied with indoor or outdoor status, at least two dogs, and at one point, a rabbit and a parakeet at the same time. In the backyard, she also kept a goat.

Leaving Cole in the garage, Elsa led him to the backyard, where they stood quietly side by side watching the goat graze on grass long overdue for cutting. Around the goat's neck hung a bell—a quaint touch without any practical purpose. Elsa just thought a goat should have a bell.

"You remember where I got Farnum?" Elsa said.

Charlie didn't even remember the name of the goat until she mentioned it. "A fair?"

She shook her head and chewed on her pinky. "Maybe. I'm struggling to remember. I can tell you the complete biography of every animal I've ever owned—but Farnum here, I can't rightly recall. I feel like I'm waking up from a spell. Like I've been clobbered over the head."

That last comment made Charlie look away. He understood that Elsa knew what clobbering felt like. Charlie had promised to pick her up that time her father got drunk and laid into her with his fists, calling her a whore. He should have met her at the corner like he promised, and then they'd have both escaped this miserable town. He struggled to remember his excuse. Cold feet? Nervous about their prospects for finding jobs and living on their own? When Charlie didn't show, she took her bags and went inside, where

179

she'd stayed for the remainder of those years.

But maybe that miserable excuse of a father could finally serve a purpose.

"Your dad remembers, I bet," said Charlie.

She snorted without humor. "You won't like what he does remember."

* * *

Elsa's father wore a dress shirt with boxer shorts, along with a hose of oxygen going up his nose. According to Elsa, she preferred he wear boxers because he liked to squirrel things away in his pockets. She especially had to make sure he didn't get hold of his car keys—he'd likely kill himself and anyone unlucky enough to get in his way if he ever took the wheel of a car again.

That subject apparently weighted heavily on the old man's mind when Elsa reintroduced Charlie to him. Her father sat at the kitchen table with his legs spread, a tuft of hair showing through the fly of his boxers. "Saw a report on the news," he said, "there's a new law—you got to wear a helmet while you're driving any sort of vehicle. I'd love to be a cop now. Know how many people I'd pull over for not wearing a helmet?"

Charlie looked at Elsa for help. Her expression told him to just roll with it. The dementia.

"Zero?" said Charlie.

"Zero! That's fucking right. What'd you say your name was?"

"Charlie Panchuk. We've met before."

"You fucking my daughter? It's OK if you are, I just don't want to know so I don't come barging in her room and see nothing."

"We're not fucking anymore, Dad," Elsa said.

"That's probably a good thing. All sorts of new diseases these days. Got to know who you're fucking. Who was that boy you were with before?"

"That was Charlie, Dad. He's right here." Elsa signaled to Charlie with her eyes. Over by the kitchen entrance stood Cole, out of her father's sight. "Dad? I'm going to leave you for a while. I'm going to take a hike with Charlie here, and we're going to bring someone else along. Someone you might know."

She gestured for Cole to come closer. Looking hesitant, he complied.

"Hey there, Mr. Campbell," said Cole.

"Why, how you doing, Cole?" said Elsa's father.

* * *

The three of them stood just behind the high school on the forest's edge, regarding the path that Cole insisted would lead them to the abandoned hospital. Elsa carried a satchel and held a rope that led to the neck of Farnum the goat.

At first, Elsa resisted taking Farnum, but Cole insisted, explaining that without Farnum, they'd have nothing to bargain with, and thanks to them, Max would find himself abandoned to a living hell for the rest of his life.

"What exactly is this living hell you're talking about?" Charlie had asked before they left.

Cole said, "He likes to do things to us. Make us do things to each other."

"What 'things'?" said Elsa.

Cole answered by pulling up his shirt and turning around. Charlie and Elsa gasped when they saw the scars crisscrossing his back. "I could show you more, but I'd have to take off my pants. I'll spare you that, Elsa. You never liked me that way. And you'll never have to worry about me."

"Did I have to worry about you before?"

"Not really," said Cole. He glanced quickly at Charlie. Charlie noticed it, but he couldn't tell if Elsa did. He looked closely at the marks on Cole's backs, and they did look real. He noticed that they constituted more than random patterns—that some of them consisted of what looked like deliberate shapes and designs. "They're called sigils," said Cole, as if reading his thoughts. "He carved them into me. They're everyone has forgotten me."

"Not everyone," said Charlie, thinking of Elsa's dad.

"There's these, too." Cole sat down and showed him the dirty bottoms of his feet, where cross-shaped scars appeared. "I can never step into a church now. I'll burst into flame."

"You could've done these yourself," said Elsa.

"I couldn't have done the ones on my back though."

"Let me talk to Charlie alone for a second. You can go wait with my dad. Give us just a minute."

181

She led Charlie to her bedroom and closed the door. It had changed a lot since Charlie had been there. Fewer posters, no stuffed animals. She didn't seem stuck in the past at all, not like Charlie felt. He waited for her to say something, but she began rooting through her closet until she found what she wanted. She presented it to him: a high school yearbook. "Look him up," she said. "If he's in there, I'll bring Farnum. But only if he's in there."

Charlie flipped through the pages meant to commemorate their senior year together, both of them having just turned eighteen at the time. Had he written her something, even though they'd both gone separate ways by the end of that year? He couldn't remember, and the book contained few markings or notations. Elsa didn't have many friends then—at least so he remembered—and probably didn't now.

"Here he is. I think." He showed her the image of a skinnier, less-grubby version of the person now sitting in the other room. *Mark Cole*, read the name.

So, Elsa found a bit of rope in the garage, and Farnum the goat joined them as they pushed their way through vine-covered pines and wild-growing sable palms, Cole leading without any objection from Charlie or Elsa. Thunder rumbled from someplace distant, and the air felt wet and heavy.

"What's this Goat Man—this Devil—look like?" said Elsa when a black snake crossed her path.

"You've seen him," said Cole, not looking back.

"Excuse me?"

"You saw him. That day. You stood outside and called for me and Max to come out. He showed up in the doorway, and one look made you run away." He looked back and nodded toward Farnum. "You ran away with him in your arms."

Charlie exchanged a quick glance with Elsa. "If you were inside, how would you know what we saw and did?"

"I watched from a window. I thought you'd come back for me, but you never did. You forgot it all—everything—just like he promised."

* * *

The sky itself seemed to change as they came upon the hospital ruins. The air already felt hot and sticky, but the presence of the building seemed infect its surroundings with an ugly yellow smear. Its ivy-covered intrusion made Charlie feel ill. He thought he'd have remembered such a sight, with its graffiti-covered siding and shattered windows.

"I don't see any goats," said Elsa. Attached to the rope she held, Farnum the goat began feasting on the shrubs near her feet.

"He's hidden them. He doesn't want you stealing them."

"This is just an old hospital," Elsa said. Something in her voice told Charlie that she didn't really believe that. "Tell your friend to come out and stop playing games."

"Games? I thought you believed me. We have to get Max out of there."

"I don't believe anyone's held prisoner in there," said Elsa. "I don't remember this place at all. I admit it, I might've known you way back, but you obviously made zero impression on me. And just so you know, in case you thought that this would be a good way to rape and murder me, I brought this." From her satchel, she withdrew what looked like her father's old service gun. "I don't like it when people show up at my house, acting like they know me." She pointed the gun at Cole but then paused as if to reconsider something. "Here, Charlie, you take the gun. I need to hold Farnum."

"Your dad knew him," said Charlie, not taking the gun.

"My dad's a retired cop. Cole probably got arrested for doing something stupid or for being an asshole. What'd you do, Cole? Diddle little girls? Take the gun, Charlie."

When Charlie still wouldn't take the gun, she turned her head and saw him leaning over, his hands on his knees. He began to dry-heave. "Now what the fuck is wrong?"

She didn't see Cole lunge at her. Even if she had seen him, he did so with a speed she couldn't have expected from someone who looked so malnourished. Even Charlie stopped being sick so he could marvel at how supernaturally fast Cole moved.

Not to mention how strong he proved. He held off Elsa's blows as he twisted her wrist and wrenched the gun away. Then he threw it as far as he could into the forest.

Elsa swore at him and rubbed her wrist. Farnum barely moved during the struggle, just kept on chewing.

"I'm sorry, I'm sorry," Cole said. "You never liked me much, but I always liked you, and I never lied to you or let you down." Shooting Charlie a dark look, he added, "Not like some people."

That made Charlie's heart skip a beat, but then the dry-heaves returned. Something about this place made him feel sick.

"Know who else never let you down? Max. He'd have done anything for you, and you ran off with this lying motherfucker, leaving me and him trapped in this place for a whole fucking decade. All for a goddamned goat. Charlie grabbed a baby goat, and you both ran off with it. You took it, and you paid with your memory, and I'm guessing, a whole bunch of bad luck. 'Just leave them,' he said, and that's what you did."

The dizziness and nausea finally began to abate, and Charlie found himself able to focus. He saw Elsa staring at him. A look of memory and regret. He remembered that look.

"He needs his child—the animal—back. I served him for a decade, earning his trust. Those carvings on my back allowed me to hide in shadows, to sneak into places when we needed food or supplies. Sometimes he needed blood to spill, and I did that for him, too. At first he told me he used to be a doctor in the hospital. Then he told me he was really a magician who transformed himself through a spell. Finally he revealed the truth—that he was the Devil, and I mustn't ever disobey him, even if he told me to spill *your* blood. But I pleaded with him and begged him. Please, please, not you, not someone close to me. 'But she abandoned you and took my offspring,' he said. 'She needs to pay,' he said. And I begged and begged, and he whipped me for being insolent, and he carved more of his spells on me. Once, he made it so I couldn't eat, and I lived on goat's milk for a week, but still I refused to hurt you. Finally, he told me if I could get you to come here of your own accord and bring his offspring, he would let me go. 'What about Max?' I asked. He thought about it. He has no love for Max. Max refused to bow before him. So he made Max eat his own eyes."

He paused to let that sink in.

"Max is blind and suffering. He'll probably die soon. I asked again, '*What about Max?*' and he finally said that he would let both of us go—if we brought someone in return."

He gestured toward Charlie, and Charlie felt the heaviness of Elsa's gaze. The time had come to speak up, to say that they needed to turn around and go back, leave this forgotten ruin to decay into nothingness, to get away before the path vanished in the darkness. There arose a rustling sound, and in an empty doorway appeared a massive white goat. He stood still and regarded the three of them. A memory fought its way to Charlie's consciousness, and he fought it back. He didn't want memories.

"I suppose that's the Goat Man," said Charlie, though he knew it wasn't. They all knew because they all remembered now.

"It's the emissary," Cole said. "He wants to know what word to bring."

Charlie wished he had the gun now. He and Elsa looked at each other. He pleaded with his eyes, but her expression remained unmoved.

"Let me see Max," said Elsa.

"You won't recognize him," said Charlie. "He could be anyone. Anyone working with this lying cocksucker."

"He has dark shoulder-length hair," said Elsa. "Olive skin. Brown eyes."

"That's all correct, except the eyes. He doesn't have eyes anymore," Cole said.

"That could be anyone," Charlie repeated, though he knew the description would prove correct. He remembered, too.

A clattering from inside the building. The white goat stood motionless and alert.

"You need to drop the rope," said Cole. "Let it go. He'll follow the other one inside."

Elsa held the rope, her turn to look resistant.

"He's yours," said Charlie, "don't do it. Don't let go." As if to punish him, another wave of nausea struck him. He thought, *I'll say anything I want to say, you fucker,* and a voice deep inside replied, *Not if you're going to lie.*

The sky grew a shade darker, and a single horn of half-moon appeared over the husk of the building.

"He'll reward you with better things. Your freedom. My freedom." Elsa allowed Cole to approach her. He touched her wrist. "It has to be your choice."

Elsa dropped the rope. Then she began to weep.

The white goat turned and walked back into the building, expecting the other one to follow.

But Farnum continued to chew grass, untroubled by the commotion.

"He doesn't want to leave," said Elsa, her voice filled with hope.

"He has to," Cole said.

"He has a choice," she said.

Farnum remained in his spot.

"He's been spoiled," said Cole. "Corrupted." He reached behind his waistband and drew forth a knife that no one knew he had. "I'm sorry. There's no other way. You have to do it."

Elsa tried to reply but produced only a choking sound. She wouldn't take the knife.

"Take it," said Charlie, nearly standing erect now. "Or I'll take it."

Ignoring Charlie, Cole whispered, "I can't do it for you. It has to be you."

"Take it and kill him," Charlie said. He meant Cole.

Elsa ignored him, too. Everyone watched Farnum in silence.

Finally, acting quickly, Elsa snatched the knife. She cut quickly and deeply into Farnum's neck. The goat bleated in surprise and tried to run, but the blood ran thick and quick, and before he could go far, he slowed and fell, bleating in betrayal. From a distance, they watched him die.

A sound from the building drew their attention. The white goat reappeared, leading out a stumbling figure, a man with matted hair, olive skin, and empty pits that once held brown eyes.

"Cole?" the figure said.

"It's OK, Max. Everything is going to be OK again. Elsa did it. She's saving us."

Cole looked at Elsa. Her eyes shone brightly.

"There's just one thing left to do. Before we can go." She nodded her understanding and with the knife approached Charlie.

"We don't know who the fuck that is, Elsa," Charlie said. She didn't reply. Instead, the voice inside his head answered. *Yes, you do.* More pain wracked his insides, and he doubled over.

Behind Elsa, Cole said, "Not the neck this time. Just make sure he can't run."

The pain made it so Charlie couldn't fight, but Cole held him anyway as Elsa cut both of his Achilles tendons.

He collapsed onto the ground and screamed. He screamed so loud he couldn't hear Max saying he would need help navigating the path and Cole assuring him that he would never make him do it alone.

Charlie screamed after them. He begged them to come back for him. He screamed until both horns of the half-moon appeared above the roof of the building and filled the clearing with glorious light.

When he finally fell silent, Charlie could hear clattering from within the abandoned building. Then he saw it, tall and cloaked, standing just outside the empty doorway—a doctor, a magician, the Devil, he wasn't sure. Maybe all of them at once.

He saw its horns, long and curved, with tips as sharp as knife blades. As it reached for his eyes, he knew it was the Devil.

Wonce Was a Woman

I t turned out that they all had not only heard of the poem, but they'd read it, each one of them. While leaning against the sink and chuffing a cigarette, one of the older secretaries even recited the opening line from memory. When she finished, she said, "Your hips really will feel like a desk some days, what with the way they run you off your feet."

Carla pretended to laugh. She still found herself trying to remember all their names, but she knew this one went by Alberta. On the mirror's surface, just above Alberta's silver-streaked hair, she saw a "Good Luck Jerry" bumper sticker, but someone had used lipstick to cross out *Good* and scrawl *Rotten* instead.

Another secretary (*Trish*, Carla now recalled) saw Carla's eyes and gestured toward it. "Hope that doesn't offend you. We're all voting for Carter. We have to get that ERA passed."

"Amen to that," said Alberta. "The head honchos would have a conniption if they saw our non-endorsement up there. They're assuming we're all pulling the lever for Ford. If they ever came in here, they'd probably fire all of us."

"Or worse," said Trish, without elaborating.

Everyone nodded. But Carla didn't want to talk about presidential politics. Instead, she wanted to talk about the poem. These women knew something they wouldn't say out loud.

"But it's not just metaphor, right?" Carla asked.

They all looked at her quizzically, their ignorance clearly a put-on. Julie, the one who hardly ever spoke, asked, "The Equal Rights Amendment, or our political preferences?"

"No," said Carla. "I mean the business about the hips. Likening the hips to a desk."

They continued to gaze at her in a clueless way, until Alberta, the cigarette dangling from her lips, looked at her watch and said, "Shit. We need to get back to work, ladies—or we'll give those bald Vikings a reason to storm our sanctuary."

The other two nodded and stubbed out their cigarettes, waving away the smoke as they left the bathroom in single file. Carla trailed behind them, trying to stifle a cough.

Maybe she simply needed to better discipline herself, not make it too obvious what she sought by asking such direct questions. At least not so soon after starting as one of the many secretaries at Peabody Brokerage.

Not that she found it easy to land her new job, even with a resume full of embellishments, distortions, and outright lies. Fortunately, before he bit down on the wrong end of a gun barrel, her father worked for Decker Wetherell. Well into his nineties now and quite senile, Decker had met a much younger version of her when she visited her father at work, and he maintained enough of a blurry memory of her that he recognized her when she visited him at the Gray Oaks Retirement Facility. He nodded enthusiastically when she reminded him how she served as his personal secretary for five years. Not at all true, but by the time he started eating the chocolates she brought for him as a gift, he reminisced right along with her and eventually used a shaky hand to sign the reference letter she'd already written for him. The letter praised her diligence and work ethic, though she tried not to overdo it. When she got up to leave, he actually managed to get that shaky hand up her skirt and use it to squeeze her ass before she could bid him a good day. When the letter did the trick, she could almost, but not quite, forgive him for groping her. In this world, they all did that. If only she could bring the wrath of Eris down on them all, starting with him.

Eris. Who knew what name she really went by, or if she had a name at all. Absent one, Carla thought of her as Eris, named for the goddess of destruction.

The women returned to their desks and their typewriters, but Julie slowed her progress and pretended to extract a troubling piece of lint from her sweater. She whispered something Carla couldn't hear. When Carla asked her to repeat herself, Julie shushed her.

"I know what you meant," Julie said, indicating they needed to keep their volume low. She gestured toward the coffee machine. "Help me make some more. They'll want their afternoon fix soon."

Carla nodded. As Julie measured grounds, she said, "That goddamned poem about the woman turning into office material—that's the only reason you're here, isn't it?"

Julie's expression nearly made Carla wither and give up the ruse. As the youngest of the secretaries, Julie originally struck her as innocent and naïve, but she now realized her error. A façade, and more effective than her own. Maybe they all needed one to endure.

"It's not just a poem full of metaphor, is it?" asked Carla as she helped Julie arrange coffee cups on saucers. "She's *real*."

Julie let her pursed lips answer for her, and Carla pressed on.

"I want to see her. Where is she? Where does she hide? When does she come out?"

"What makes you think she gets to come out? If she does, you wouldn't want to be around her. Trust me."

"But why?"

"*Why?*"

By that point, they'd failed to keep their volume low enough for the others not to notice. Alberta arched an eyebrow in their direction, causing Carla to bump one of the cups out of Julie's hand. It fell to the floor and shattered.

A string of profanities flew from Julie's mouth. It shocked Carla how incorrectly she'd read this woman. Perhaps she'd found the high priestess of this little group.

She knelt next to Julie and helped pick up broken shards of porcelain.

"Please, I *need* to see her."

"Well, you can't. None of us see her. But we know if she's been let loose, and *oboy*, that usually spells trouble."

"Girls?"

They both froze as a bald head appeared from around a half-opened door. The head might have belonged to Hidey Fish, one of the senior executives, but they all looked alike to Carla with their spotted, hairless scalps. "Trouble out here?" asked the bald head.

Carla and Julie used their happy voices in unison. "No, sir."

"Well," said Hidey Fish, "get that cleaned up. We're awaiting our coffee. And Julie?"

Julie looked up with a smile so false that Carla wondered how Hidey couldn't see it.

"A little something extra in mine." He winked at her.

"Of course, Mr. Fish."

The bald head started to disappear, but it paused. "You know I always like something extra."

Julie's false smile widened. "I know you do. I'm here to please, sir."

"You certainly do," said Hidey Fish. As he withdrew his head like a fed eel, the man's gaze lingered a bit in Carla's direction. Her skin crawling, she tugged at the hem of her skirt as she stood up.

She tried to engage Julie further, but the appearance of the bald executive caused everyone's lips to tighten. Everyone now seemed hyper-focused and even a little scared. Alberta typed furiously while Trish went to a file cabinet she kept guarded behind her desk. Opening a drawer, she withdrew a bottle of bourbon and handed it without comment to Julie. Everyone instantly became a cog in the machine, fearful of appearing anything more.

Carla wanted to scream at them. Didn't they know that the poem warned them not to act this way? Not to allow themselves to become absorbed into the soulless environment of the office, becoming just another piece of furniture or office equipment? But the poem didn't just speak in metaphor. Julie believed that more than ever now. The woman in the poem composed of office parts was a messiah, a beacon of resistance. Her transformed body functioned as a weapon, and if they chose to follow her, the men would find themselves cowering for a change. She more than believed this—she *knew.*

After her father's suicide, her mother tried to survive on a job like this one, and Carla watched as it took her to her own early grave. It was one of her mother's co-workers who gave Carla a tattered copy of the poem at the funeral, saying "This is who could have saved her. Who could have delivered her and saved her from dying."

Puzzled, Carla read the poem and struggled to understand it. A chant for secretaries, one that described a woman whose body bore the features of office equipment, culminating in the birth of a Xerox machine. It struck her as absurd at first. But its images persisted in her consciousness, and during a brief stint of homelessness, she wandered the city, reciting it quietly to herself. Soon, she began noticing echoes of its lines in unexpected places—often as graffiti in subways and bathroom walls, perhaps scrawled there by despondent secretaries trying to summon the being to rescue them from their suffering. Carla came to understand it as not so much a shapeshifting entity like a werewolf, but something more like a golem, charged with championing an underclass of sorts.

Later, as her searches for it became more focused, she found that she could pry more information by offering booze, drugs, even sex on a few occasions, once she found the right people. In bed, one woman told her that she had actually seen it. "It comes out at night." Though Carla had never thought of herself as gay, she enjoyed letting the woman stroke her hair as they spent a post-coital moment together. "The time has to be right for it to be summoned."

"How do you summon it?" Carla asked.

"Anger? Sadness? Hurt?" The woman said she didn't know as she went on stroking Carla's hair, but she told her where she'd seen it.

The Offices of Peabody Brokerage.

* * *

It turned out that Hidey Fish, the firm's most senior executive, did in fact take note of Carla. He closely scrutinized her work as the day slogged along, finding flaws in her typing that needed innumerable corrections as well as missing data that required her to thumb through files as ancient as himself. When Trish, Alberta, and Julie began gathering their things to leave for the day, Carla tried to do the same, but before she could grab her purse, the bald head of Hidey Fish appeared once more, his brow furrowing at the document in his hand.

"I can fix it in the morning, Mr. Fish," Alberta tried to say, but he waved her off. Alberta regarded Carla, not with disapproval but with genuine concern.

"It needs to be corrected right away." He meant these words for Carla. She accepted the document, her eyes fluttering over it, trying to puzzle out the errors. Judging by the looks she received from the three other secretaries, she suspected there weren't any.

"It's okay." She smiled at them as they stood near the door, their coats already snug around their shoulders. "I've got this."

"You don't," Alberta quietly said. "Trust me."

"It's alright. Really."

Nodding ruefully, they filed out the door, though the last one, Julie, lingered a moment longer. "Don't let him tell you about his name."

"What?"

"Just look away when he does that thing." But Hidey Fish appeared again, and Julie shuffled away without elaborating.

In truth, Carla approved of her situation. Without the other women watching her, she could explore the office a bit more deeply, including a rather imposing looking file cabinet snugged behind Trish's desk. Aside from booze, Carla didn't know what they kept in there, but she sensed that they kept it largely inaccessible for a reason. It held the air of something forbidden, and she felt herself drawn to it.

But at the moment she could sense Hidey Fish leering at her.

"Would you like me to go over the errors with you?" she heard him say. "Are my notations clear?"

She shook her head and affirmed he had made them quite clear. She just needed to freshen up a bit, she said, indicating the restroom.

"You all go in there so often together. Are you afraid to go alone? I could accompany you."

"No," she said, smiling with the same fakeness she'd learned from the others.

"Female bodies are amazing in how they all seem to work in sync. Your bladders, colons, menstrual cycles."

She continued to smile, waiting for him to leave.

"You're not experiencing a menstrual cycle, are you?"

"No, sir," she said.

Their stand-off continued until Hidey seemed to understand that she wouldn't enter the restroom until he returned to his office. When he finally did so, Carla exhaled the breath she'd been holding.

Instead of the restroom, she turned toward the file cabinet. All day, her intuition had whispered to her that it held something special, something that involved the poem and the being it described. No telling how much time she had before Hidey reappeared. Her eyes scanned the markings of the drawers, each one corresponding to the letters of the alphabet. She finally decided to start with the one marked with "E"—for *Eris*, even though she'd conjured that name on her own.

Sadly, she found it full of documents that looked mundane and ordinary. Quickly, she tried another drawer: "S" for *Secretary*. The results mirrored her first attempt.

She paused, remembering the poem.

"*File me under W*," she recited to herself, quoting the last line, "*because I wonce was a woman.*"

On her haunches now, she opened the last drawer.

At first a musty scent filled her senses, as well as faint traces of perfume. Then came the odor that the perfume was meant to mask. Not a pleasant one at all, but cloyingly organic, like wet straw and rotting leaves. She coughed and shielded her nose, but her spirits rose when instead of files she found wads of tissue and the kind of muslin one might use to create a funeral veil. Waving the air around her with one hand, she used the other to poke through the mess. Hidden underneath these layers, she felt something solid. She pulled it out to investigate.

A cigar box, likely owned by Hidey Fish or one of his associates. She opened it.

And recoiled.

Nested within, she found four human fingers, their skin wrinkled and parchment gray. Blackened fingernails with hints of red polish on one end, a fragment of bone on the other.

Somehow, she managed to not spill the box's contents.

Instead, she found the poise she needed to set aside and continue digging through the drawer.

Which led to finding the book.

Ragged in appearance, it sported an ancient-looking leather cover and crinkled yellow pages. She thumbed through it and encountered a curious script as well as the occasional artfully conceived illustrations. Unable to read the script, she at first took it for someone's eccentric cursive. Closer scrutiny led her to a series of different conclusions, first that it constituted some kind of shorthand, then that it was a different kind of alphabet altogether. At times, the script devolved into confusing sequences of lines, crosses, and circles. She couldn't make heads or tails of it.

Just before giving in to complete frustration, she finally came across a word she recognized, spelled in all-capital letters:

BASEMENT

Underneath the word appeared what looked like a floor plan.

If someone meant to beckon her, that did the trick.

Anticipating that Hidey Fish might reappear at any moment, she quickly closed the cabinet drawer and, book in hand, made her way to the elevator. What she sought, she now believed, lay in the basement of this very building.

Thanks to the late hour, she had the elevator to herself—at least until it made one stop before descending all the way to the basement. On the third floor, a woman stumbled through the door, crying, her glasses askew. She glanced at Carla as she struggled to find something in her purse.

"Run while you can," the woman said. "This place'll chew you up and spit you out."

Carla clutched the leather book against her chest and watched the woman extract a tissue from her purse and use it to dab her eyes.

"I showed the fucker though," said the woman, as if Carla had asked a question. "I got him good in the balls. With my knee. Then I ran. They don't expect us to fight back. The balls—that's supposed to be their weak area, but he just looked surprised for a moment, and then he laughed. Sometimes I wonder if they're even human."

She watched Carla for a response as the elevator door opened on the ground floor. She paused when it became evident that Carla didn't intend to follow her out.

"Seriously, don't stay here a second longer. They're all monsters. I mean it—literally."

She stepped out and maintained eye contact as the door closed, leaving Carla with a pang of regret. She could have shown the suffering woman the book in her hands. She could have told her what she suspected—that it held the key to summoning the one who would bring down justice and revenge upon a sick system. Eris: the one who would bring retribution so fierce that a kick in the balls would seem like nothing. Carla truly believed it. In the basement she would decipher the key to bringing down a holy wrath upon them all.

Darkness met her eyes when the elevator finished its descent, and she regretted not having the foresight to take a flashlight. She stumbled about, willing her eyes to adjust, and she wondered if she would ever find her way back to the elevator, until finally her fingers brushed across a light switch. It powered a dull yellow light, barely enough to illuminate a partial area of the basement consisting of an uneven floor and overturned furniture. Beyond the circle of light lay a well of darkness too thick for her eyes to penetrate.

Standing still, she heard sounds though, what reminded her of a desk leg scraping a rough surface, the squeak of a wheel.

"Hello?" she called out.

As if frightened by the sound of her voice, whatever made the sounds went quiet. Mice perhaps? The single bulb hanging from the low ceiling cast enough light for her to see scratches and smudges on the floor, evidently made with chalk. Some of them suggested a sort of design, a notion she confirmed by comparing the markings to what she found in the pages of the book. More than ever, she believed she'd found a grimoire of some kind. She shuffled through the pages and found one that roughly matched the design on the floor.

She studied the two and determined that the markings on the floor only needed a few touches for completion. Amongst the refuse she found an ancient chalk tablet with a nub of chalk tied to it. Falling to her knees, she set about completing the diagram on the floor. Her intuition hadn't failed her yet, so she continued to trust it. She noticed more scurrying as she set about her work.

But she failed to notice the ding of the elevator.

"Well, this is where you went," said Hidey Fish.

She looked over her shoulder to see him smiling at her rump. Next to him stood a younger, larger, more brutish-looking man. Her intuition spoke to her again, telling her that he might be the owner of the steel balls. Carla hated him instantly.

"You didn't give me a chance to show you how I got my name," Hidey Fish said.

As he approached, he held his hands over his face, peek-a-boo style, opening and closing them to reveal comically wide, unblinking eyes as well as puckered lips, like those of a fish. He repeated the movement over and over as he walked closer. The effect proved not only grotesque and childish, but also hypnotic.

As if by some magic, the spectacle held Carla stunned and motionless. By the time he and the other man came close enough to grab her, she had to wonder if he *had* hypnotized her.

She struggled as their hands grappled for her, and she dropped the book. It drew their attention long enough for Carla to kick, and she landed her foot in the crotch of the younger man.

He grimaced. "Why do they keep doing that?" he said.

"They're told it's our only weakness," Hidey Fish said. He picked up the book while the other man secured her in a headlock. "No pain at all?"

The younger man shook his head. "Scar tissue."

"I thought it was impotence."

Instead of arguing, the man grunted from the effort needed to keep Carla still. She fought, reaching for his eyes with her fingernails, but before she could cause any damage, he lifted her from the ground and slammed her down onto the top of a dilapidated desk, which collapsed from the impact. She lay atop the fragments, struggling to recapture the air that escaped her lungs.

Hidey leaned over her with the book, tsking her. "You've been naughty. And this basement is full of naughty girls like you."

Once more she detected the scurrying noises. Something appeared at the edge of the light. Her vision blurred by pain, Carla caught a glimpse of it.

The pale face of a woman. Instead of eyes, two large, round objects protruded from her skull. They looked like chair wheels. The mouth consisted of a small table drawer, stuffed into a broken, unworking jaw.

Hidey turned in the thing's direction. Quickly, it scurried back into the darkness.

"You see that one?" he asked. "Always hungry. It eats paper."

"Whole reams," said the other man. "Can't get enough." With Carla subdued, he looked at Hidey. "Where should we start with this one? Hands? Feet?"

"You, always keen to use surgery. I like more nuanced methods." He gestured with the book.

Yet the other man seemed unpersuaded. "How about the arms? What should we replace them with?"

They both looked about the basement as Carla continued to gasp. Something else appeared at the edge of the light—another figure hobbled by a gruesome modification. This one had a face studded with typewriter keys. Naked and emaciated, a thick, black ichor leaked from its pale nipples. She opened her mouth as if to speak, but no sound came forth. Instead of teeth, bent paperclips lined her gums.

"Get back," Hidey said, waving the book at it.

This one hesitated, but after Hidey took a threatening step forward, it retreated.

As she felt her strength ebbing, Carla thought again of the poem. She uttered a line out loud. "My breasts are wells of mimeograph ink."

"Did she say something?" Hidey asked. "Is she trying to perform a spell?"

The other one twisted her wrist. "We perform the operations around here." He looked around. "Give me something to cut off her leg."

"We need to do the ritual first," said Hidey, "or she'll just die."

Not a spell, thought Carla. *A summoning.* She knew in her heart that the poem functioned as a chant of defiance. A call for deliverance from the curses cast by these men. "Eris," she said, "come to me! Mother of us all!"

She only had a poem and an assumed name. No liturgy. So she began making one up, reciting lines from the poem, adding her own flourishes, her own metaphors. But even to her ears it sounded contrived, inauthentic.

Even worse, Hidey and his cohort laughed at the effort.

"Listen to that," said the brutish one.

"It's pathetic," Hidey said.

"Where's . . . the thing? The one that cuts paper. The one like a machete attached to a steel board." The big man held Carla down with one hand while he used his free arm to make a cutting motion. "Let's use that and start carving."

Hidey surveyed the clutter around him. Carla noticed that as much as those creatures didn't want to come into the light, Hidey and the other man didn't want to go into their domain—the darkness.

"Eris," she said, pleading, "don't forsake me."

No comment this time from the men. Instead, a disturbance from elsewhere drew their attention. Something grated along the floor in the shadows, the sound coming from several directions at once.

"You know the thing I mean," said the big one, clearly flustered. "You see it?"

"I have it. I have it in my hand now." Did Hidey sound nervous now? He held nothing but the book, nothing like the tool the other one sought. Maybe he misunderstood.

But Carla sensed it: a presence stirring in the shadows. Listening to her pleas. Responding to her needs.

Two more malformations appeared at the edge of the light, the one with oozing breasts, and a different one. The new one that appeared looked smaller and more machine than any other. A Xerox machine with a baby's face, glistening with fluid as if recently birthed. It pulled itself forward with an appendage made of wires. This time, instead of stepping away at Hidey's command, they continued their slow advance.

"Smack the small one for me," said Hidey's companion. "It's been disobedient lately."

But Hidey only shouted for them to get back. Carla saw why. More of them began appearing, each with a uniquely modified, grafted body. The torso of one consisted of a water cooler, its sloshing organs visible through clear plastic. Another wobbled forth, belly distended with protruding wires and gadgets, its thin arms ending in staplers rather than hands and fingers, making Carla think of the fingers she found earlier. All of them, nearly a dozen or so, moved slowly, hampered by disfigurements. Carla's captors appeared increasingly unnerved.

"Use the book," said the one holding her down.

Hidey shuffled through the pages before he settled on the correct one. He began reading aloud, enunciating speech that sounded to Carla garbled and unnatural. Eventually, the other man began repeating the same speech in a kind of call and response. At the same time, his grip on Carla loosened a bit.

She managed to lift herself slightly and realized that the shattered wood under her back concealed something metallic. And sharp.

What they couldn't find before, the object they couldn't name. Arching her back, she managed to touch it with her hand.

Carla had used one before, usually to make even cuts in big stacks of paper. She found the handle of the blade and gripped it, realizing it had come unfastened from the board used to line up straight edges.

She exhaled, summoning all the strength she had left. She used it to push the man off of her. Then she swung the blade as hard as she could toward his neck. She realized the truth in his words. It did remind one of a machete.

It didn't sever his head as she hoped it would, but it cut deeply. The look of surprise on his face filled her with satisfaction. It made her feel like a goddess of destruction.

Hidey Fish still chanted away, but his words failed to slow the slouching approach of his creations. They now poured from the shadows, all of them bearing unique disfigurements. One of them looked like an amalgamation of office parts, its whole head made up of a tangle of rubber bands. All of them *wonce women,* doomed to this existence by the arcane magic and cruel surgery of men like Hidey Fish.

The bald man continued to hold the book and chant. He failed to see Carla standing behind him, her clothes and face streaked with fresh blood.

He finally did notice her in time to see the blade in her hand fall. It sliced cleanly through the top of his skull. As he died, his lips puckered and his eyes grew wide, resuming the expression he used in his peek-a-boo routine.

"It's called a *guillotine trimmer,*" Carla said to his corpse. "Learn the proper fucking name."

She gripped the bloody blade. It had fused to her body, a permanent part of her now. Even if she wanted to let it go, she couldn't. But that seemed just fine to her.

She looked upon the slouching forms around her, some of them shaking visibly, perhaps from pain, perhaps from excitement at her conquest, the prospect of revenge. Knowing they would follow, she turned to the elevator. She would lead them to the light of the upper floors, where they would eventually complete their liberation. She had found Eris. Herself. For them all, wonce and for all.

The Coat Closet

On a trip home from college during the winter break, I lost my coat on a train.

I would never have taken the train in the first place, if not for the fact that my car showed signs of falling apart completely, everything from worn brakes to leaking gaskets, and my parents worried that I'd never make it alive if I drove from Virginia to Florida. My father came up with the idea of the train—specifically the Auto Train, where passengers could load their automobiles into special oversized cars and take them along for the journey.

I'd never traveled by train, but my father assured me I'd enjoy it. "I'll even pay for a sleeper," he said. "It's a unique experience, one you'll never forget. And you'll be happy you won't have to sleep in coach."

I didn't understand why I'd need to sleep at all, but he explained that the train took a full day to make the trip from its starting point in Virginia to the Sanford station in Florida. "Trust me, you'll love it," he said. Dad preferred trains over flying, and, I suppose, he expected everyone to share his sentiments. "Get the car here safely, and we'll work on it together over the holiday. You and me, like old times."

I didn't bother to ask what old times he meant. We never did much together, and I suppose that fact led to feelings of regret on his part, resentment on mine. But we never talked about such things. On top of that, a heart attack over the summer scared him, and he resolved to work less and make up for lost time. I saw no reason not to indulge him and let him make my travel plans.

I did enjoy watching the crew load my car onto the train, marveling at the sheer size of the auto carriers, as well as the length of the train. Nearby stood a family, and I overheard the father proclaim that as far as anyone knew, this train was the largest in the world. "Europe might be smoother and more efficient, but leave it up to Americans to come up with something this audacious."

Either way, I felt happy I didn't have to drive the car, especially since it developed a new rattle on the way to the station. Plus, snow began to fall, adding an additional road hazard. I imagined myself breaking down then freezing to death while I awaited help.

No fear of that on the train. In fact, the heat worked all *too* well. If not for the garlands of holly hanging from the handrails or the notes of "Jingle Bells" playing over the staticky speakers, no one would ever guessed that winter had long ago arrived. All attempts to make things feel festive seemed in vain, foolish. The porter even apologized for the temperature as he led the way to my compartment. "Isn't supposed to be this hot," he said. "You'll probably wish you brought a fan along with you." Sensing an inexperienced rail passenger, he showed me how the tiny bathroom stall functioned as both a shower and toilet. Then he asked me what time I planned to go to sleep.

I didn't expect such a personal question, and my expression made him laugh. "I ain't trying to get up in your business," he said. "I just need to know when to come back and fix your bed." He tapped the bench, pointing out how he needed to unfold it and get it arranged so that I'd have something to sleep on.

Laughing at my own embarrassment, I provided him with a time. Beads of perspiration formed on my face, so I took off my outer garment, a light brown coat I'd owned since high school. That prompted the porter to show me another feature of the compartment: a tiny door I failed to notice at first. A closet, roughly the size of an infant's coffin. "Most folks don't even notice this is here," he said, holding open the door as I hung my coat inside it.

"I wouldn't have seen it," I said.

"Nice and compact, you bet," he said, shutting the door that now contained my coat. Then he indicated the opposite wall. "Normally, you could open that up and double your space, but someone's bunking in the other side."

"Oh?"

He nodded. "A sick old lady. She's the reason for all this heat. She boarded early and started complaining about how cold she was. Even now she wants me to raise the thermostat. I say, 'Lady, it can't go no higher.' She says she understands, but then two minutes later she rings me again and tells me she can't get warm. I suppose she forgets."

I wiped the sweat from my brow, and after the porter left, I settled down to wait for the train to begin moving. Outside the window, I could see the snow falling harder while bundled passengers continued to board the train. Maybe because of my own restlessness, the heat seemed only to increase. I couldn't imagine sleeping under such conditions and I considered not even trying. I thought of the sick old lady in the compartment adjoining mine and the miserable conditions she created for everyone. I wondered if the porter gave in and found a way to make it even warmer for her. Maybe I ought to lobby for cooler temperatures, no matter how absurd that notion seemed considering the snow falling outside.

Moments later, I heard a knock at my compartment door.

Expecting the porter, I instead found a diminutive woman with white hair, nearly half my height. Her pale, mottled skin hung from her face like soaked rags, and her eyes looked rheumy and unwell. Around her shoulders hung a thin shawl.

She spoke with a faint backwoods accent and offered no introduction or greeting. "I'm cold."

I stood there, wondering how to respond, feeling tired, and vaguely irritated at this elderly woman for making it almost unbearably hot on the train.

"Is there a coat or sweater I can borrow? I'm freezing," she said, and as if for emphasis, her body shivered.

I have no justification for what I will say next. Confessing it here now brings only shame. Even a self-absorbed college student should garner sympathy for someone obviously very ill. But I resented her for the misery she brought on me and everyone else on the train. I didn't even consider my coat hanging in the tiny space of the closet. Had I offered it to her, she would have vanished inside of it, her stature so small compared to mine. It would have warmed her for sure. So selfish I was in those days, so uncaring and focused only on my own needs. The freezing temperatures she felt only existed in her mind, I believed.

I don't recall exactly what I said to her. Something about not having anything I could offer her. Maybe I wished her a good night. I'd like to think I did. Then I closed the door, leaving her shivering outside my compartment.

Sweltering, I sat there, doing my best to put her out of my mind. Eventually, the train began moving, gradually picking up speed. From the window, I watched the snow continue to fall. I fantasized about what it would feel like to bury myself in it. The porter came and went a couple of times, once to bring me my dinner, and once to arrange my bed.

"These windows don't open, do they?" I asked before he left the second time.

He laughed and shook his head. "Don't we all *wish*."

Remembering the advice of my father, I tipped him. After he thanked me, I asked, "What's wrong with her?"

"With who?"

"The woman next door," I said, wondering how he could possibly not know who I meant.

"Oh," said the porter, "just old and under the weather. Happens to us all." Then he left.

Sleep didn't come easy that night. The train's jostling and its clacking wheels helped keep me awake the entire night. But the heat alone was enough to keep me tossing and turning all night. Even stripped down to my boxers, I perspired heavily, soaking the sheets. I gazed out the window, searching for some indication of how far we'd traveled. We would reach the Sanford station at some hour in the morning, but that seemed like an impossibly long time to continue suffering. Outside, the snow continued to fall.

Once more, I heard knocking at my compartment door, followed by a slight voice I knew belonged to my elderly neighbor. "Hello," she called out plaintively. I thought she might go away if I ignored her, but she kept knocking and calling out with that warbly voice of hers. "Hello. Hello?" Unable to take any more, I opened the door while muttering curses under my breath. At the sight of her, my volume rose. The words I spoke next should never have left my mouth. I don't recall them exactly. Or maybe I don't want to. I probably said, "What can you possibly want now? You're making everyone miserable. Absolutely fucking miserable."

No reply at first. She simply stared without comprehension. To an observer, it would have looked like a strange stand-off: a tall young man, sweating and wearing nothing but boxers, looking down at a shivering old woman. From the speaker in the passageway, the absurd lyrics to "Frosty the Snowman" became audible.

Finally, she said, "But I'm cold."

"I heard you. I truly did. But you know what? I don't think you're cold enough." My voice rose into a cruel laugh. "Not even close. Maybe when you're finally stone-cold dead, the rest of us can have some peace."

I'll always remember how she looked at me then, her expression finally registering recognition. She finally saw me for the first time. She nodded, showing she understood the individual before her. Not a good person at all.

Without another word, she turned, and I watched her walk away. Already the guilt began to surface, but I ignored it, instead slamming the door closed and walking back to the bed where I let my body fall onto the soaking sheets.

Still, sleep still refused to come. With the heat, I now felt nagging guilt.

In the morning I would apologize, I told myself. I would make it better.

Not long after, the train started to slow. Finally, it came to a dead stop.

With fresh irritation, I sat up, certain the woman had something to do with the train halting.

Sure enough, I heard voices outside my compartment door, along with the static of walkie-talkies interfering with the piped-in Christmas music, as well as the patter of anxious footsteps.

Bleary-eyed, I opened my door. That brought me face to face with the porter.

"Sir," he said. Nothing else, just *sir*, as if that word contained both a statement and a question. He looked nervous.

"What's going on?" I asked. With him standing in the way, I couldn't exit the compartment, and he made no effort to get out of the way. In the narrow passageway behind him came the source of the walkie-talkies, two paramedics squeezing past him. Through the window above them, I saw flashing emergency lights illuminating the snow.

He took a breath before answering my question. "Something pretty bad."

"The old woman?" I asked.

He stared at me. "Mrs. Hazel. She has a name."

"Oh," I said. "I didn't know her name."

"I thought I told you."

He hadn't said anything about her name, but I conceded I'd forgotten.

"Did she come to you at all?" he asked. "For help?"

"No," I said, attempting to convey concern with my eyes. "At least I didn't hear her if she tried."

Studying my face, he nodded. I held my breath, wondering if he'd detect the lie.

"She died," he said, "right here in the passageway. No telling how long she was lying here."

I couldn't imagine how that could be true. Only moments ago, I'd spoken to her. I made a sound of protest, almost admitting my lie to the porter. But then he reached out and squeezed my shoulder, a very fatherly gesture that brought forth a surge of regret. "It's good you didn't come out and find her this way. She looked . . . well, in pain. And when I touched her, she felt so cold." A pause before he added, "I should have increased the temperature for her."

I didn't know how to reply to that statement. The paramedics completed their work and lifted a gurney that held her body. It looked as if they carried nothing at all, her form underneath the sheet so slight that one could barely perceive anything at all. To make room, the porter stepped into my compartment, where we watched them carry away her corpse. Once they departed, he tipped his hat to me and promised the train would move again soon. We said goodnight.

I returned to my bunk and stared at the ceiling. Eventually, as promised, the train began chugging along again, but sleep remained impossible. With the woman gone, I wondered if the porter would lower the temperature, but it only grew hotter. A bit later than scheduled, we crossed the state line into Florida. I continued to lie there awake and watched the sunlight work its way through the window. Finally, we arrived in Sanford, where I disembarked with the other crabby passengers, all of us scowling and ill-tempered as we watched the vehicles slowly unloaded, one by one.

Because of these delays, I forgot all about my coat hanging in that tiny closet.

* * *

I finally remembered it on Christmas Day after exchanging gifts with my family. We'd just sat down to the first home-cooked meal I'd enjoyed in weeks, and I found myself relating the story of the dead woman. Already, I'd revised my narrative and perhaps also my memory of the event, casting myself in a more sympathetic light. I described how I did my best to find her something to wrap around her shoulders, and my parents congratulated me on my selflessness.

"Is that where your coat went?" asked my mother during dessert. "Did you give it the woman to keep her warm?"

That stopped me cold. My expression must have become readable because they showed concern. I wonder what they saw more of, the guilt or the sense of loss.

"What is it?" my father asked.

I confessed to them that I'd foolishly left the coat on the train.

"They have a lost and found," said my father. "Or they should." He reached for his phone and began dialing the station. But because of the holiday, he reached a recorded message.

"No matter," he said. "We'll call Monday. I'm sure someone found it."

But I thought about the small dimensions of the coat closet and how easily one could overlook it. I had doubts I would ever see my coat again. If I could so easily leave it behind, why hadn't I given it to the dead woman? Another even worse thought nagged me: that if I'd given it to her, she might not have died. But I would never know that, not for sure.

My pessimism about ever again seeing my coat only increased then next day, when we finally reached someone at the station. They did have a lost and found, but no one turned in a coat. Recovering it, they said, depended on the train schedule and someone finding the time to check the compartment I'd booked. Did I remember my car number? I did not. I left a number for them to reach me on the off chance it ever turned up.

But it didn't. Eventually, I came to accept the fact that I would never see that coat again.

* * *

A few years after I finally graduated, my father experienced his second heart attack, the one that finally killed him. At that time, I'd just taken a job at a consulting firm in Virginia. While sitting at my desk, I received the tearful news from my mother.

"That car," she said. "What do you want to do with it?"

She meant the automobile I'd transported on the Auto Train all those years ago. Dad and I never could get it running properly, so it just sat in their garage for years. Every so often, we talked about working on it, but we never found the time.

Now my father was gone forever, and my mother wanted rid of it. Though she never told anyone before, it turned out that she never liked that car or what it represented.

"What do you mean?" I asked.

"It killed him," she said, almost matter-of-factly.

I thought I misheard and asked her to repeat herself.

"That car killed him. He wanted to keep working on it with you, but you never had time. All that worrying and planning on his part. He thought it wasn't about the car. He thought you didn't want to spend time with him. He talked about it all the time."

I felt sick. "Well, he never said that to me." Instantly I regretted those words.

"Well," she said, "he said it to me. Come get the car."

* * *

At the time, a winter flu made its way through the office, but thus far, I'd managed to avoid it. The date for the funeral luckily coincided with management's decision to close the office a little early for Christmas in the hopes that the extra time would give everyone a chance to recover. That gave me more time to work out how to get the car from Florida to Virginia, and after considering several options, I decided to take the Auto Train, regardless of the unpleasant memory of the last trip.

Or maybe *because* of that unpleasant memory. Maybe I intended to punish myself. Maybe I hoped it would offer penance for the terrible things I'd done or, even worse, not done. The lies I told.

So, on an unseasonably warm day in December, I boarded the train. Hours before, my nose started running and my throat was sore, but I attributed these symptoms to the unusual weather and not the flu, which I felt certain I'd escaped. Even when I felt myself shivering, despite everyone around me complaining about the heat, I thought I was experiencing an allergic reaction of some kind. I regretted not bringing anything heavier than the sweater I wore, and I tried hugging myself to retain as much warmth as I could.

The train felt even colder as the porter showed me the way to my compartment. My hands trembled and my teeth chattered, causing me to fumble for my wallet as I handed him an extra twenty-dollar bill and asked him if he could please lower the air conditioning.

He raised an eyebrow, showing none of the affability of the porter from the first trip. "It's not even on," he said. "In fact, it hasn't been working well."

I trembled. The air felt freezing. I pointed to the wall dividing my side of the compartment from the other. "Maybe I could go in there," I said. "Maybe it's warmer."

He shook his head, but he accepted my money. "Afraid not. It's all on the same system."

"It wouldn't hurt, would it? Just to find out?"

Again, he shook his head.

"Is someone on that side?" I asked.

He continued shaking his head. "It's empty. And you paid for one compartment, right?"

We both knew the answer to his question.

"I'm afraid it stays closed sir," he said. And then he left.

Through the window I watched the boarding process continue. White hot sunlight filled the scene, but I felt colder still, so I sat on the bench seat, drawing my legs to my chest in the hopes I could generate more heat. I continued to sit in this position as the train lurched into action, my teeth chattering and my sore throat worsening. No more denying I had the dreaded flu that went around the office. I debated calling the porter and asking him to raise the heat on the train, but I clearly annoyed him before.

I recalled my previous trip and how I treated that elderly woman with contempt. If I believed in that sort of thing, I might have attributed my current state to recompense of some sort. Punishment I deserved.

I thought also of the coat I left, and its long absence filled me with fresh regret. Shivering, I wanted nothing more than to feel its thick, reliable fabric against my body. I could think of nothing else except the paralyzing cold as the train clattered on and night began to fall outside. At some point, the porter delivered a meal, but I didn't tip him, though I asked him once more about whether he could increase the temperature on the train. He looked at me with an expression of half worry and half disbelief, and he left without making arrangements to lower my bunk so that I could go to sleep.

Not that I could sleep, not with that pervading chill. My growing sickness made it impossible to eat, too, so I left my meal untouched. At one point, flies buzzed around the plate, an unbelievable thing to see in a freezing atmosphere like this one. Not only that, but I detected a noxious odor and wondered if the porter had served me spoiled meat.

But maybe I could no longer trust my senses, because next came the sound of knocking, along with a small voice that sounded eerily similar to the one I heard years ago on that journey. Despite my stuffy ears, I clearly heard the voice say, *"I'm freezing."*

I thought I must be hearing things, but I managed to gather myself and check the passageway outside my compartment.

Relieved, I saw no one there.

After sitting again for only a few minutes, I once more heard the knocking, followed by the voice. This time, I thought I heard the word *coat.*

No question it any longer—whatever ailment I suffered from must be causing hallucinations, I reasoned.

At that moment I heard the knocking again, only louder, more insistent.

The door between compartments, I realized. The sound must have been coming from there. Maybe too the bad odor only seemed to worsen. Maybe someone let a meal go bad in there.

Once more, I struggled to my feet. Placing my ear against the dividing wall, I listened.

And listened.

Finally, I heard it again, but realized the sound didn't come from there at all.

Instead, it came from *within* my own compartment.

Again, I worried the flu caused my hearing to go haywire. But then my eyes found *it*, and I remembered how, long ago, the other porter showed me the closet. How he paternally assisted me with taking off my coat and hanging it up inside.

There, off to the side, barely visible, I once more beheld the slim door.

I dared to imagine the impossible—that I could open the door and find my beloved coat hanging there. But what chance of that? It seemed inconceivable that I occupied the same compartment as the one from all those years ago. Even more inconceivable that my coat would still be hanging there after all those years. Someone would have found it and claimed it as their own.

Nevertheless, as my hand reached out to open the door, I clung to some distant hope.

Once open, darkness seemed to spill forth from the closet, along with stale air, clearly the source of the odor filling my compartment. My eyes burned and struggled to adjust, but gradually, my vision cleared.

And there it was. My coat. The same fabric, the same light brown color.

Even a coffee stain on the sleeve looked familiar. Still doubting, I reached out to feel its texture, as if that alone would verify it belonged to me.

And touching the sleeve, I knew. In every way, I was witnessing a miracle. I no longer cared about the terrible smell. My coat was still there, exactly where I left it years ago.

I would wear it, use it to blot out the cold.

But as I continued to touch the sleeve, it happened. Something terrible and inexplicable.

I froze with my hand outstretched, once more in a state of disbelief. The coat moved on its own. Not only had I rediscovered a lost possession, but I found it animated somehow.

Or so I thought. Until I saw the roaches emerging from the sleeve, four of them, wiggling their way out, each one as black and angry as the grave. Then I saw the skeletal worms attached to them, and realized that they weren't roaches at all, but fingernails, each one followed by a gnarled finger. A gray, bony wrist followed.

Then I saw the legs curled up inside the coat, extending themselves so *she* could crawl out of that tiny closet, and I recognized the body wrapped inside my coat. I remembered the features of the wrinkled face, as well as the eyes that locked upon my own, no longer rheumy but completely black. Her lips bore the same color, and I imagined if she used them to kiss me, they would feel as cold as the hand gripping my arm with an iron firmness.

Instead, the lips formed a smile as the thing in the closet spoke in a scratchy voice. "It's my coat now, but I'll share it with you." As I sunk to my knees, feeling the arms enfold themselves around me and the odor of the grave envelop me, I felt no relief from the cold, only a bitter iciness that remains with me still.

What Finally Ended the Jessup Curse

Eddie first heard about his family's curse—the "Jessup Curse"—when Grandpa Earl lost his eye. After that, everything finally made sense. Not that curses made sense. But Eddie finally understood that everything had a reason, even Grandpa Earl losing his eye the way he did. This injury resulted from a fight that transpired during a game of billiards at Squeaky's, the local titty bar, where Eddie's older sister, Felicia, happened to work.

Grandpa Earl went there solely to play pool with the boys and certainly *not* to see Felicia shake it on the stage. That didn't stop some people from getting the wrong idea. Earl corrected such misconceptions by explaining that her work hours coincided with him shooting pool because he needed Felicia to give him a ride on account of him losing his driver's license years ago. That unfortunate incident occurred after he fell asleep behind the wheel, skunk drunk, and went barreling through the front window of the corner grocery store.

One can find a silver lining in just about anything, and in this case, it so happened that the accident took place during slow hours, so only one fatality resulted—a retiree crushed under the car's wheels. Good thing that Earl remained unconscious through the whole ordeal or he'd have experienced the trauma of seeing the old woman's head burst like a watermelon under his rear tire. A mere glimpse of such a catastrophe could scar even an old man for the remainder of his life, so good thing Earl didn't wake up until two hours later, handcuffed to his bed at the hospital without a scratch on him, though he didn't care for losing his license.

Thus, to get to his favorite watering hole and Felicia's place of employment, he found himself leaning on his own granddaughter for transportation. But credit the old man for making a point of keeping his eyes averted when Felicia plucked off her G-string and spread those long legs of hers. Somehow, at these moments, Earl always found himself concentrating on lining up a difficult shot with his pool cue.

That didn't stop his sworn enemy and billiards rival, Curly Pomefroy, from making a remark. A fight ensued, and Earl received the worst of it in the form of the broken shaft of a pool cue sticking out of his left eye. Curly Pomefroy merely ended up with the eight-ball stuck in his gullet, but Felicia herself leaped down from the stage and managed to extract it with her fingers before Curly even lost consciousness. Curly later described it as the greatest moment of his life to have the fingers of Earl's own granddaughter inside his mouth.

As for Grandpa Earl, he found himself once more in the irritating position of being handcuffed to the hospital bed while they went about removing the wooden shaft from his eye socket. "Why am I being held prisoner when my assailant didn't die?" he asked the deputy stationed at his bedside. "I am the victim here."

The deputy explained that the altercation required an investigation, and they needed to ensure that Grandpa Earl didn't try to run off before they collected all the facts.

"You inbred numbskull," said Earl. "How far would I get with eighteen inches of wood sticking out of my eye?"

The deputy corrected his measurement, suggesting that it came to eleven inches at most. But the insult hit its mark, and the deputy left Earl handcuffed for the duration of the hospital visit.

"Make sure you finish your education," Earl said to Eddie, who sat in the hospital room with his history book open on his lap. "Get that diploma. Don't turn out like the rest of the panty-wastes in this town. I'm hoping you end the curse once and for all."

"Curse?" repeated Eddie, looking up from his book. He didn't know anything about a curse.

"The Jessup Curse," said Grandpa Earl.

No way could Eddie continue his homework after hearing this phrase. Not that it mattered since Felicia worked late and usually could not wake up in time to get him to the high school before the end of first period. Still, Eddie found history interesting, but not nearly as interesting as *family* history.

He told Grandpa Earl he wanted to hear more.

"Well, think about it. Where's your daddy?"

Eddie felt a twinge of pain at the mere mention of his father, but nothing he couldn't handle. He never knew the man, though others said he took after him with his large build.

"Killed in Iraq," said Eddie.

"That's right. Where's your mama?"

Now, that caused pain. Real pain.

"You don't want to say it, do you?" asked Grandpa Earl.

Eddie said nothing.

"She was my daughter," said Grandpa Earl, "and I can say it. She was butchered like a slab of beef by a no-good meth-head out on County Road 64. He followed her home from the pharmacy, and I never did get my oxy. He stole my oxy, and he stole your mama, too." Grandpa Earl experienced horrible pains after driving through the corner grocery. Without his oxy, he could barely get out of his recliner, except to play billiards. "So don't tell me that we're not under a curse. Our whole family."

Eddie thought about these words as a doctor and two nurses entered the room to get the shaft of wood out of Earl's eye socket. The doctor took one look at the handcuffs and started to order the deputy to remove them, but it turned out that the deputy needed a long bathroom break at precisely that moment, thanks to the gas station burrito he ate for lunch an hour earlier. This poor timing meant that the doctor and his nurses had to extract the wood with Earl still handcuffed to the bed.

"You in any pain?" the doctor asked.

"You're goddamned right, I am," Earl said. "I'm always in pain." He went on to question the doctor as to why he had not received any sort of tranquilizer.

The doctor studied the chart in his hands and shook his head. He went on with a lengthy explanation for why they could not provide Earl with what he requested. He used terms and phrases unfamiliar to Eddie. But Eddie only half-listened anyway. He still fought back tears over his lost mother, murdered by an evil meth-head, all thanks to a family curse.

He pondered the implications of this curse as the doctor pulled the shaft of the pool cue from the eye of Grandpa Earl. Despite the doctor's skill, Earl still thrashed and protested, but they managed to get the job done. It turned out that the handcuffs helped keep him stationary.

"Will I regain my sight?" Earl asked when he finally quite moaning.

The doctor and the nurses acted as if they didn't hear the question. Instead, they marveled at the length of the shaft that once projected from Grandpa Earl's eye. The old man repeated his question.

"Good lord, man," the doctor said. "You no longer have an eye. There's nothing I could possibly save. You experienced a major globe rupture in that foolish altercation. I hope it was worth it." He let those words sink in as he picked around the ocular cavity, removing stray fragments of ruptured tissue. Once more, Grandpa Earl squirmed, so the doctor did the best he could before signaling one of the nurses to begin disinfecting the area. Once she completed her task, the other nurse covered the gaping chasm with a piece of gauze secured by tape.

"So there's nothing at all you can do to restore my sight?" Grandpa Earl asked.

"You can see out of the right eye, can't you?" said the doctor.

"I use my left eye to line up shots when I'm playing pool."

"Good lord, man. You should know that you're lucky the wood didn't penetrate more deeply. I'm still not convinced it didn't cause brain damage."

"No, that still works fine. It does hurt like hell, though," said Grandpa Earl.

"Still, count yourself lucky. We'll refer you to someone who can fashion a glass eye for you to wear for cosmetic purposes. Or do you not have insurance?"

"I do not," said Grandpa Earl. To Eddie, who still sat in the corner of the room with his book, it sounded as if he spoke those words with pride.

"Well, then," said the doctor, "we shall provide you with an eyepatch." And with that, he left the room, the nurses following in his wake.

Grandpa Earl regarded Eddie with his one good eye before he finally spoke. "See what I mean? A curse."

* * *

Now that he knew about the curse, Eddie saw more and more evidence of its power. On mornings when Felicia managed to wake up in time to get him to first period, he found his teacher (a crusty old crow who delivered lectures on the "War of Northern Aggression" with a level of spite that suggested she'd experienced it personally, though she expressed no sympathy for the enslaved population at that time) unwilling to accept his late work or excuses. Already without friends, he struggled to withstand the way his classmates insulted him for peculiar behavior and poor hygiene, not to mention clothes that failed to fit him properly. Clearly, he suffered under the ignominy of a curse. He fully expected that in no time, some awful fate would befall him in a titty bar, just like Grandpa Earl.

Meanwhile, it turned out that the eyepatch given to Grandpa Earl came with an exorbitant bill that he refused to pay. He left the hospital with gauze taped to his head instead. It remained there for several days until it began to grow discolored and leak a yellowish fluid. Even worse, an awful odor accompanied the leakage, forcing Felicia to demand that he clean and replace it.

When it became evident that such a task proved too great for Uncle Earl, Felicia did it for him, holding his face over the sink of the tiny bathroom they all shared.

Eddie watched from the other side of the open doorway, fascinated.

Already, he'd formed some conflicting feelings about the vacant hole in his grandfather's head. He both wanted and *didn't* want to see it. Worse, he felt the strong urge to put his fingers inside of it the way he saw the doctor do when he scraped away the traces of ruined ocular matter.

"Hold still, old man!" his sister said as she tried to contain the old man's struggles.

"It hurts!" he cried.

"Well, I'm going to hurt too if your obstinance means I have to swing around a pole without a good night's sleep. The smell alone is keeping me awake. Besides, I'm nursing my own injury."

Her injury had resulted when the stripper pole came unbolted from the ceiling in the middle of a particularly acrobatic move, causing a nearly catastrophic fall at the feet of Curly Pomefroy, who'd found himself in the throes of infatuation since having Felicia's fingers in his mouth. Felicia fell off at the stage and into an agonized ball at his feet, and Curly simply stood there stunned, the dollar bill he intended to tuck into a crevice of her flesh still gripped in his hand. Fortunately, Felicia managed to shake off the injury and finish her routine without the pole, but she never got the dollar bill. Somehow, her fall managed to cure whatever spell Curly had fallen into, and the dollar went home with him. No doubt another sign of the Jessup Curse, thought Eddie when he heard the sordid account.

After cleaning Grandpa Earl, neither Felicia nor Eddie could find any gauze in the medicine cabinet. Fortunately, Felicia, the brains as well as beauty in the family, thought in advance of this problem and brought home a plastic eyepatch she secured from a pirate costume left at the titty bar after a Halloween event. Grandpa Earl grumbled, but he strapped on the eyepatch and then began putting on his shoes.

"Where you think you're going?" asked Felicia.

"With you," he said. "I need to show that son-of-a-whore Curly that I'm still the reigning champion of billiards."

"Oh, no sir," said Felicia. "You've been banned."

Overhearing this exchange and the string of profanity that followed it, Eddie knew that the curse had put another notch in its belt. Apparently, members of the Jessup family could no longer go where they pleased.

Felicia ran out the door soon after, leaving Grandpa Earl to face Eddie's quizzical stare. He clearly could not fathom what went through the boy's head at this moment, so he stared back with that plastic eyepatch before settling back in his recliner for a frustrating evening at home.

Eddie continued to gaze upon his grandfather in the recliner, even after the old man's wheezing breath turned into intermittent snoring as the hours wore on.

What did a curse look like? Eddie had to wonder if it had form and substance. All things consisted of matter. Did he not hear one of his teachers say so? Once, Felicia demonstrated her athleticism to him on the clothesline they kept in the backyard—fully clothed, of course. Nonetheless, the way Felicia's legs swirled in the air as she used her arms to hold herself aloft and twirl about the pole held him spellbound. The air itself suddenly seemed alive with designs and symbols, forms and patterns that lingered in the air before his eyes, slowly dissipating with the next hypnotic move. They looked so real and full of substance that he actually reached out to touch one, though that brought him too close, and Felicia's foot hit him the jaw. The impact knocked him unconscious momentarily and resulted in a broken tooth. Even worse, Felicia fell and sprained her ankle, causing her to miss a week's worth of dancing. Without her income, they had little to eat that week.

But when Eddie regained consciousness, he found himself with an ability to see intangible objects, and that should include something like a curse.

Which now, along with Grandpa Earl, he felt certain existed somewhere behind that pirate eyepatch.

If he could just reach in and grab it, he could pull it out and squeeze it to death. He could crush it with his bare hands, thereby making sure that it would never again plague the Jessup family. He could carry the wriggling form of the curse to the bathtub and plunge it into the sulfur-stinking water, keeping it there until it drowned. He thought of it as wormlike, pale and slippery, but corporeal nonetheless and capable of expiring in the painful way it deserved.

He just needed to get his hands on it.

He'd watched Grandpa Earl sleep many times. Plenty of nights he had nothing else to do. Over time, he'd learned that you could do just about anything around the old man while he slept, just so long as you didn't change the TV channel.

Still, Eddie stepped softly, approaching his grandfather as quietly as he could. Behind him, the flickering light of the television showed someone spinning a giant wheel, hoping to hit the jackpot on some game show. Eddie hoped to hit a jackpot, too. He intended to pull that curse out of the old man's eye socket by its tail. No doubt it liked the warm, cavernous space of raw, red flesh. It probably lay in there curled up in a little ball, snoozing in that sticky tissue, warm as a kitten. When Eddie got hold of it, it would extend its body in terror.

Instead of drowning it or crushing it, Eddie decided he would put it between his teeth and bite down on it, hard enough to break it into two halves. Juices would spurt from its slug-like body, but Eddie wouldn't care. He wanted to know what it tasted like, just like he wanted to know how the fungus-covered nail he peeled from his pinky toe tasted. He did that weeks ago, and although he suspected that the fungus would begin growing inside his esophagus as a result, he didn't care. He was glad he did it, just like biting the wriggling curse in half would make him feel good.

Sure, perhaps the curse would spread though his whole body later, but he truly needed to understand its texture, just as he wanted to discover the bitter chalkiness of that fungus.

With this aim in mind, he straddled Grandpa Earl, just like Felicia straddled her customers. The old man didn't stir as Eddie carefully lifted the plastic eyepatch from his socket.

The whole time, Eddie shivered, hardly able to contain his excitement at seeing what lay behind the eyepatch.

The eyelid itself curled downward at an odd angle, obscuring his view. Thus, Eddie carefully lifted it.

Eddie now understood why he'd heard so many complaints about doctors in his household. Doctors never did right by any of them, and he could see that this record didn't stop with Grandpa Earl's eye.

Everything under the eyelid looked red and sore. It reminded him of the scooped innards of a Halloween pumpkin, just without the orange stringy bits.

As he peered inside the gaping eyehole, he felt Earl shift under him. Eddie held his breath, dreading the old man awakening, for he wanted this moment to continue.

He relaxed when Earl adjusted his buttocks and continued to snore.

Eddie continued to study the chasm. Part of him hoped he could see all the way into the old man's brain. Fatty tissue lined the back of the socket, and Eddie noticed that it contained folds and striations where the curse might hide.

He looked for something to poke inside. He would do so delicately, careful to let his grandfather's slumber continue. However, he saw nothing in reach, not even a fork.

Thus, he determined that further exploration would require him to use fingers.

Carefully, with one hand still holding the remains of the eyelid, he probed the open area with an index finger.

His grandfather didn't awaken. He only snored louder, obviously enjoying a dream, perhaps one in which he finally subdued his sworn enemy, Curly Pomefroy. Maybe the spoils of his victory included a complimentary dance by one of the more attractive dancers at Squeaky's This fact would explain why he seemed untroubled by his grandson straddling him as the boy now inserted not one, but two fingers into the vacant eye socket, where Eddie thought for sure he felt something wiggling.

The curse.

Now, he would stop at nothing to extract it, to pull it free and squeeze it in his fist, feeling it burst within his grip, forcing out all the juices of misery it had fattened itself upon.

His fingertip touched something. A nub.

Fortunately, Eddie possessed nimble fingers. For example, before it expired, the family dog, Spike, suffered from a bout of worms. Each of the animal's agonizing defecations ended with worms hanging from its butthole. Eddie became quite adroit at grabbing these worms, despite the animal's resistance, and he always managed to pull them free from the dog's bowels.

Now, he willed his fingers to possess this same dexterous quality.

And they proved capable, managing to get a small grip around the nub.

So Eddie began to tug.

Gently at first.

Then he began to pull.

Then Earl awoke with a start.

"Hey, now," Grandpa Earl said, unsure of what to make of his grandson on top of him. He tried to shake the boy loose, but even in the bud of youth, Eddie's body still possessed a formidable quantity of muscle and mass he'd inherited from his dead father. He used his superior size to resist his grandfather's attempts to force him to dismount.

"Hey!" the old man said. "What do you think you're doing?"

But Eddie did not heed these protests. He had it, the thing that tried to hide away in his grandfather's head. He only pressed his fingers deeper. The old man's other eye opened wide in shock, unable to see what the boy was doing.

Eddie held it for sure, and he pulled and pulled. He felt it coming loose. His grandfather's objections degenerated into an incoherent wail of pain.

Finally, it came free.

Still seated on his grandfather, Eddie held it forth to see.

By God, it did look like a worm, if a small one. Not more than two inches long by Eddie's estimation. It didn't wiggle like a worm, however, and it seemed much too thin to possess a circulatory system. Less fettered by Eddie's weight, Grandpa Earl thrashed about in a struggle to form grammatical sentences. "I'm blind," he finally managed to say. "Completely blind!"

Eddie assumed he meant the left eye and felt tempted to remind the old man that everyone already knew this fact. Instead, something else troubled his memory—a vague recollection from biology class, where he always struggled to remain awake. Had he once heard the boring, monotone voice of his teacher say something about the optic nerve? He couldn't recall. And it didn't matter now.

"Don't you see, Grandpa?" he said to the old man, whose thrashings degenerated further into paroxysms of shock. "I've got it at last—the curse!

It won't trouble us again!"

And with that, he bit into the yellowish stalk of the thing. It proved fibrous in texture, tougher than one might guess, so Eddie clamped down with his jaw and dug in with his molars.

To finally break it, he needed to pull as well as bite. It stretched momentarily, not wanting to break in half. It was a stubborn curse. A curse that, once planted, resisted uprooting.

But Eddie did it, and as he ground down with his molars, he congratulated himself on saving the family. It tasted a bit like chicken gristle.

As he chewed, he stared into the wide remaining eye of his grandfather. He continued chewing until only small bits of it remained, and then he chewed those. He chewed everything that ailed him—his dead father and mother, his family's poverty and ignorance, their bad luck, his grandfather's misfortunes, his sister's exploitation. He chewed until those small bits became almost nothing, and then he swallowed, feeling fully satisfied.

The curse was now safe inside him, where it would dissolve in stomach acid, its remnants destined to be shat out and flushed into the sewer, where it could plague a rat or baby alligator.

His grandfather now only blubbered. A thick strand of drool formed on his lips. Eddie gazed into the old man's glazed eye, hoping to find approval staring back at him.

Instead, he saw his own reflection in the glassy pupil.

His own approval would have to do.

In the end, every Jessup had to take care of themselves.

And now they could to it without that goddamn curse.

Acknowledgments and Credits

These stories originally appeared in different publications, but one thing remains constant in all of them: the tremendous support system I enjoy in being part of the horror genre's writing community. I am especially grateful to Holly Rae Garcia, Matt Masucci, Lori Masucci, Owl Goingback, Elaine Pascale, Derik Cavignano, Joe Scipione, Cindy O'Quinn, Ruthann Jagge, Gaby Triana, Douglas Gwilym, Ken MacGregor, Jenn Lee, Bryan Dietrich, Mike Arnzen, Clint Smith, Joshua Rex, Christina Persaud, Josh Strnad, Eddie J. Morales, Michael Morgan, Stephanie E. Jensen, Daniel Braum, Lisa Lee Tone, and Josh Ginsberg. Thank you, each one of you, for being there for me!

To Lynne Hansen, thank you not only for your friendship, but thank you for applying your amazing talent in creating the cover art for this book. Additionally, I owe my heartfelt gratitude to the editors and publishers who accepted these stories in their original form helped make this book possible. A special thanks to John Baltisberger of Madness Heart Press and Dawn Shea of D&T Publishing for publishing my first and second collection of stories.

The biggest thank you of all goes to you for buying or borrowing this book. I hope you enjoyed these stories! If you'd like to know a little more about the genealogies of the individual stories within this book and where they first appeared, I've included that information here:

"Let's Cut Up Dad!" in *Trigger Warning: Speaking Ill*

"Sacrifices" in *Generation X-ed*

"Ladders" in *The Cellar Door #1: Woodland Terrors*

"The Layover" in *Dancing in the Dark: A Tribute to Anne Rice*

"Clotlice" in *Midnight Tales,* Spring 2022.

"Sounds to Make You Shiver" in *Haus: An Anthology of Haunted House Stories*

"The Widow's Tower" in *Monsters Monsters Monsters Monsters*

"The Revenge of Katrina Bloodspell" in *Dead Heat*

"The Stone Gate" in *Love Bites*

"The Baron of the Rails" in *34 Orchard*

"Papa's Night, or the Short Happy Life of Elena de Hoyas" in *American Cannibal*

"Gatortooth Sam" in *Monstorm: A Charity Anthology*

"Children of the Goat Man" in *The Darkened Doorstep*

"Wonce Was a Woman" in *Novus Monstrum*

"The Coat Closet" in *Literally Dead: Tales of Holiday Hauntings*

"What Finally Ended the Jessup Curse" in *Trigger Warning: Curses*

About the Author

Douglas Ford writes horror fiction while also chairing the Southwest Florida chapter of the Horror Writers Association. He has written two other collections of short fiction, APE IN THE RING & OTHER TALES OF THE MACABRE AND UNCANNY and THE INFECTION PARTY AND OTHER STORIES OF DIS-EASE. His novels and novellas include THE TRICK, THE BEASTS OF VISSARIA COUNTY, THE LAST SLAUGHTER, THE REATTACHMENT, and the award-winning LITTLE LUGOSI (A LOVE STORY).

You can connect with me on:

- https://douglasfordwrites.com
- https://www.facebook.com/profile.php?id=100064149938106